ONCE A YEAR

A story of love, heartbreak and
dangerous consequences

by Charlotte Rose

To Elli,

Thank you for test reading
once a year, I hope you
enjoy reading the finished
book.

love Charlotte

Dear Reader,

This book took me some years to finish because I wanted it to be perfect. But, eventually I realised it was never going to be perfect, because it isn't a perfect story. It's based on the truth. I hope to share my story with you and to be a hand to hold.

Love Charlotte Rose x

ONE

These were the last few precious minutes on my island. Total chaos.

I was sitting on a ferry packed with Greeks waving goodbye to their family and friends, some smiling, some crying, and some not really bothered, reading a book or simply munching on a few nuts.

The old man in the corner slowly raised his arm with a handful of seeds, popping them into his dry, crusty mouth, chewing about five times, before lowering to repeat the whole process all over again rather like a machine. He brushed the crumbs off his chalky checkered shirt onto the ferry floor.

There was a tall, slim, dark-haired lady, applying a coat of gloss to her plump lips to match her red Prada handbag and Gucci shoes. Don't ask me why she was on this ferry. I was asking myself the same thing.

There were the odd few children running about, their parents not paying attention or trying to control their wild animals. Two girls who looked like twins wore pink summer dresses with matching ribbons neatly tied around their hair. A suited worker blew his high-pitched whistle, waving his arms about trying to control the crowd beyond the boat's entrance.

Grace, my sister, was chatting to a crowd of people, using large hand gestures and facial expressions. You would think maybe to help them understand because they were Greek but no, she studied performing arts so it's very much a drama queen, fadazzel show whenever she's around.

To be quite honest, she's the oddest pumpkin I know but I'd be lost without her. She's always there when I need her. Even sometimes when I don't particularly want her opinion, I'll get it anyway.

People often think we're twins, although I don't think we look much alike. Plus, I am seventeen and she is nineteen. We are both tall at 5ft9. For girls anyway. I have very long, naturally straight, light brown hair which has zero ability to hold a curl for more than an hour. Grace has the same coloured but short hair. It's much thicker and will hold a curl all day long. I've got dark green eyes. Grace has light green. I have tanned skin. Grace has pale skin. Grace has beautiful curves and I'm a slender body shape, I guess. At one point I thought they were never going to grow unlike all the other girls my age. But I wear a bra now, so things are looking up.

Mum was sitting on one of the chairs in the shade tapping away on her keyboard, whilst talking into the phone wedged between her ear and shoulder. She went self-employed as a Pilates teacher and life coach and she's the worst workaholic I know! Sometimes I don't even feel like she's on this earth when I'm sitting right next to her. That's why whenever her phone rings (which is more often than the norm), our family disperses in all directions to avoid listening to the 'work voice talk' or we will all go insane. But if we can drag her away from it, she's the perfect mum. She encourages us to follow our dreams and supports everything we do. She made sure we took every opportunity possible - she has this quote, "No regrets", which I'm sure you'll hear more of.

And Dad's a typical dad, plus an extra dose of amazingness, constantly joking around. He is an oil paint artist. This would explain why he was next to me scribbling the view into a sketch pad.

This boat was about to rip me away from the one place I wanted to be, so it's safe to say I was praying for the boat to break down. There was nothing I wanted more than to stay here. No, it wasn't because of the stereotypical, gooey reason that my sexy summer love was waiting for me. Well, it might have been if he hadn't already gone from the island himself. It was this place, where not one fluffy white cloud floated in the sky and a beautiful bright blue spread from Poros Town to where it met the sea in the distance. A luminous sun shone above the mountain tops, its rays engulfing the picturesque surroundings.

On the ferry, the Greek flag waved softly in the breeze, casting dreamy shadows on a blue floor. So, that was my surroundings and compared to grey Essex with its persistent rain and clouds, this was a slightly more tempting location.

It was 2017 and I was going home from the same holiday I had every year and never got bored of. Mum and Dad got married here - a place where I could forget all my worries, pretend reality didn't exist and that I wasn't Delphine Rose Ward, but Delphine Kyprios (you will understand the reasoning behind the second name later).

This place was my paradise. I found myself enchanted by the mesmerising views of an open sky full of shining stars and the moon reflecting on the sea at night. We always stayed with the Collins family from Scotland. We met them one year on holiday. Grace being her confident and outgoing self brought us together and now we were all very good friends. There's Nina and Mike, and their children, Will who's my age and Lucy who's eleven.

I would miss the Greeks saying Kaliméra and Kaliníhta each time we passed them, a gentle smile on their faces. I would miss the air smelling like heaven - a humid, sweet, sea salt smell with hints of fresh jasmine and home-cooked Greek food.

The sound of waves lapping upon the shore and the ski boats driving up and down the ski course with the faint whistle from Bob the boat driver and main instructor of Passage, the water ski place. Bob moved to Greece to live and work here.

And at night, I would miss the crickets singing and Greek music playing in the distant bars and restaurants. It had always seemed like nothing could go wrong here, until now.

This holiday went a little differently from those of previous years. A few years ago, in 2014, I met a boy. Wow! hold up, she met a boy. Here we go! His name is Nikos Kyprios. Yes, he is Greek, so he has a gorgeous tan and a heart-melting accent.

The first time I saw him, he had just finished water skiing and very well, if I might add. I ski too but nowhere near as well as him. When he got out of the sea, he did a film star flick with his hair. You would think they were shooting for a shampoo advert, in fact, I was half waiting for him to announce, 'Because you're worth it'. He also had some funky multicoloured shorts. He walked passed me where I was sunbathing; well I say walk, it was more of a stroll, a cool chilled one, and he put his ski in the Passage garage.

He gave me a glance and a quick smile. My stomach flipped over five hundred times. This was all new to me as I had never been interested in boys or girls, just to clarify. I mean, of course I have crushed over the odd film star, but they were normally thirty times my age like Johnny Depp or Leonardo DiCaprio. But anyway, in the real world, boys... ehh. But this boy - this gorgeously sculpted masterpiece of a boy had me feeling things I didn't know were there.

Before I had a second to run and jump into the sea to cool off and calm these unfamiliar butterflies flittering in my stomach, he had strolled back and sat on a chair near my sunbed. That was the exact moment when I landed in a situation destined to fail and break me, but at that point I didn't know. I looked up at him, looking at me.

Did I shave my legs? Underarms. Don't lift your arms. Oh. What about my bikini line? I curled my nails under my palms to hide my chipped pink nails. Having Mr. Perfect sitting next to me made me overanalyse how imperfect I was.

After a self-evaluation that felt like it went on for hours, and the poor attempt of my brain telling my mouth to respond to his dreamy voice, I eventually started functioning like a normal human being. Nikos and I got talking and he made me laugh so much! He spoke English amazingly well for someone of our age and it was all from teaching himself. Seeing that all I could remember from compulsory French class was bonjour, he was outstripping me on every level. We spoke for hours and swam in the sea together. Walking home that day felt odd. I realised how happy I was feeling from spending time with him.

Every morning I would race through breakfast, slap on some sun cream, curl my eyelashes, brush my hair through and head to the beach to see him. When I was around him, I had a whole new level of energy and a bounce in my step and a smile which refused to leave my face.

One morning we decided to go into town together. He stood waiting for me at the bottom of the steps of my apartment holding a deep pink flower. I walked down smiling and he gave me the flower, grinning back at me. A perfect romantic moment until Mum came passed holding her heart.

"This is what life is about, sometimes it's the little things that make all the difference." *Life quotes. Ugh.* My face screwed up in embarrassment. "Have fun," she called, walking off.

Nikos smirked, and I shook my head. We jumped into the water taxi, Nikos offering me his hand as I stepped on. The boat driver watched, smiling at us. As we approached town, Nikos pointed to the mountains where the outline looked like a naked woman lying down. I had never noticed this before, but it was beautiful. Once we got to town, we walked along the port and stopped at the biggest ice cream shop on the island. I had a lemon sorbet and he had a cookies and cream. We took our ice creams up to the top of town to the clock tower. Now let me tell you, there were too many steps to count and too many rays to bear and way too much self-conscious sweating going on. The problem is, when guys sweat it's somehow socially acceptable and maybe even somewhat attractive but girls - that's a different story.

Once we eventually got to the top, it was stunning. I could see all the people in the town going about their business, drinking frappés, laughing and chatting. There were families going passed on their bikes - sorry, I mean bike without the 's' - yes,

8

they somehow manage to load a family of four or five onto one bike here. Bonkers! We were sitting on a rock where I was repeating in my mind, 'please don't touch me and feel my sweaty skin, please don't touch me, please don't touch me.' The only thing that did touch me was his ice cream on my nose! I opened my mouth in shock, then tried to get him back unsuccessfully as he held my wrist and licked my ice cream! *How very dare he.*

"You have a very cute nose," he said, chuckling.

"Is that why it deserved ice cream plonked on it?" I asked, laughing. We chatted for ages up there before tackling the steps back down. After strolling through the shops, we walked all the way back to our bay.

Later that afternoon, I was sunbathing on the beach with my eyes open, hoping my sunglasses were dark enough to hide me watching him. He walked onto the platform - sorry - *strolled* onto the platform, carrying his ski and giving me a quick smile as he passed. His two little minions were following him like puppy dogs. One tubby boy and one extremely skinny boy always followed Nikos, two steps behind him on either side, like he was a celebrity. They attended to his every need as though they were always trying to impress him. From observing them, I think they both wanted to be exactly like Nikos. A tweak in their appearance each day showed their efforts - coloured shorts, hairstyles, interactions with Bob and quick smiles at me. They were clones. Obviously, neither of them mastered the Adonis persona that Nikos so effortlessly had.

The rest of the holiday consisted of ice cream dates, crab-catching competitions and many, many giggles. Before I left that year, he gave me his number.

Back in England my body fluttered for a few seconds when his name popped up on my screen. We chatted for a couple of months over texts, which ran up a spectacular phone bill for my parents. At the time, I wasn't aware we were about to lose touch and I would no longer hear from him. When this happened, I didn't quite understand the feelings I had. All I knew was that every day felt empty and dull without him.

After a year of boring English life and anticipating seeing him again, before I knew it, it was August 2015 and I was back in the sea with Grace. Grace came swimming up to me.

"Is that boy over there Nikos? You know, that one you liked a while back?" A city of cocoons burst in my belly, releasing hundreds of butterflies flapping around inside me. I think I went under water and screamed with excitement having a mini fit. I casually swam over to him, where he sat on the same chair as last time. I propped my elbows up on the side of the platform.

"Hello stranger," I said, softly smiling at him. He looked down at me and his eyes lit up. To be honest, I didn't recognise him at first as he was taller and no longer had flicky Bieber hair, and instead, it was shaved into a slick style. He had also ditched the funky shorts and gone for a simple plain pair. His face had matured and seemed more defined with sharper features around his jaw and eyes.

Now I had realised it was him, I remembered seeing Mum speaking to this person a little while ago! *About what*? Then I clocked it. Of course - it would have been about the phone bill. It transpired later that he'd offered to pay for this. Cute, right?

"Is this the beautiful Delphine I've been dreaming of since she left?" he grinned, walking towards me.

I giggled, splashing him with water.

This holiday had taken a sudden upturn and we slotted together like pieces of a jigsaw. It was the same as the previous year when we spent hours by each other's side. He taught me some Greek words, which was hilarious for him as obviously, I was rubbish at pronouncing them, but he was patient and I eventually got the hang of it. He would call me Omorfi (pretty girl) and I would call him Omorfos (handsome boy). How cliché!

One morning, I came down to the beach and he was waiting with a life jacket. I walked up to him nervously and he had a cheeky smile on his face. He handed me the life jacket and gestured to Bob's boat. I tilted my head, worried about what dangerous sport I was about to embark on. But no matter what, if he was by my side, I was up for anything.

We sat on the boat as Bob sped off out round the island. I bit my lip anxiously and Nikos placed his hand on top of mine. His touch made me melt into the seat as the boat slowed down by a pontoon. Bob jumped up fiddling with ropes and harnesses. Harnesses? What on earth were we about to do? Eventually, I was strapped in beside Nikos, my hand in his. The boat's engine started and took the slack out of the rope. Before I knew it, my feet had left the platform and I was floating above the glistening sea.

It was the most magical thing I had ever done, and my body was tingling with excitement. After a while, I glanced at Nikos, realising his eyes hadn't diverted away from me.. His gentle smile remained on his face till the very end, where we were very inelegantly dumped into the sea, both of us laughing and half choking on the water.

As we got back to Passage, Lucy was jumping up and down on the platform.

"You were flying! I saw you flying!" she screeched with excitement, clapping her hands.

Mum was also on the platform, her face glowing with joy. Nikos looked all proud of himself, stretched out on a sunbed, when his mum came marching onto the platform on a mission. She was loaded with sun cream galore ready to smother Nikos. His eyes were still closed when her cold, white creamed hands stuck to his stomach, rubbing in the cream. He jumped in confusion as his eyes flew open. I bit my lip trying not to giggle, hiding a smirk behind my shades. He glanced over and shook his head in embarrassment. I had to jump into the sea so I could laugh under water. He moaned as she painted him white. As he was always boasting about how he doesn't have to wear sun cream and I was always telling him he should, this was priceless. As soon as his mum finished and sped off in her car, he ran and jumped into the sea, bombing.

"Don't need sun cream aye?" I said. I laughed as he grabbed me under water and tickled me until I took it back.

One evening, he asked to take me to watch a movie at the

rooftop cinema. It was beautiful up there. There were loads of cushions and candles lit around them. We picked two bean bags and settled there. Off to the right, the town lights reflected off the sea. The movie started, and of course, he had picked a scary one. Low-key scary though.

"Don't worry. I'll hold your hand if you get scared," he said, winking at me.

"Oh, how very kind of you."

Surprisingly, he didn't try the classic yawn and arm over the shoulder move. I discovered that I was very good at not getting scared, but Nikos on the other hand, was flinching every second. At the climax, he almost jumped out of his seat. I placed my hand on his and giggled.

"Don't worry. I'll hold your hand if you're scared," I said, mimicking him from earlier. It was eight when the movie finished, and we decided to walk back to our bay. At some point on this walk we thought it a good idea to go skinny dipping. Well, I say skinny dipping, but I was still in my jean shorts and bra and him in his pants. I could have taken my jean shorts off, but I decided against that remembering I had my massive Hello Kitty knickers on that Mum got when I was about twelve that still fit me. We bobbed around for a while until I felt a sliver around my leg. I jumped, squealing a little.

"Something just touched my leg!"

"It touched me too!" He was panicking but started laughing as I freaked out. "I'm joking; I'm joking." I squinted at him.

"Very funny, but something did actually touch me."

"Ah, there it is again," he said, swimming away quickly.

"That's not funny," I said, splashing him.

"No, I'm serious this time," he said. I raised my eyebrows at him, then something blobbed in front of me below the water's surface. My eyes reluctantly looked down. There, I kid you not, was a jellyfish the size of my head! My body tensed up and a shiver ran down my spine. I swallowed hard, preparing myself to freak out as I spotted one - no - two more of them.

"Je, je, jellyfish!!!" I screamed, splashing about back to shore.

I looked back in the water confused as to why Nikos wasn't rushing out too. Well he wasn't panicking, in fact, he was standing and holding a jellyfish in his hands!

"What are you doing? You're going to get stung," I screeched.

"No, I'm not. These ones don't sting," he said.

"What are you? Some kind of jellyfish expert?"

"No, I just live by the sea and I am very smart." He smiled whilst pretending to push a pair of glasses up his nose to look intelligent. He placed the jellyfish back in the water and strode out.

"Pfft," I said, rolling my eyes at his ego.

We grew closer that year, and on my birthday, we spent the most beautiful day together. I woke up in the morning to a fresh orange juice and croissant on the balcony with a little note that read, 'To my beautiful Delphine, today I will take you on an adventure xox.' I leant over the balcony, following the sound of a motorbike horn. There he was on a red bike, his hands gripping the handles, his unbuttoned shirt revealing a small drop of sweat rolling down his abs. I think I could have died on the spot right there and then. I ran down after slipping on a bikini and a dress over the top. I was slightly worried that my mother would come out any second and plonk two helmets on our heads, so I jumped on the back of his bike, wrapping my arms around his waist. We sped off around the island, my hair dancing in the wind. Throughout the day he showed me all the most stunning spots on the island and the views were dreamy. We went for a meal in a little taverna where he gave me a little red gift bag with a delicate pink bracelet inside it. He held my hand and gently slipped the bracelet on, adjusting the charms. It had four little dangly gems, one Greek eye, one butterfly, one little silver girl and one pink crown. I wore it every day for years.

When he left that year, I went into a pathetic phase, didn't eat much and everything I did reminded me of him. Walking passed the garage in the morning, sunbathing by the chair he always sat on, playing with the ball we played with, and in almost everything else I did that I could link him to, I did.

Back in England, I would sit on my windowsill, staring at the stars, remembering the times with him and counting down the days until I would see his perfect, chiseled face again. At the time, this seemed to be as many days as stars in the sky. Thinking back on that cringes me out so much. I'm one of those people that will tell you to snap out of it if you're hopelessly in love. I guess I don't believe in true love anymore.

2016 holiday - I didn't see him which really sucked.

Then in 2017, we met again.

TWO

B ut before we go into that, we better jump back into reality and tackle the first year of college. Luckily, my two best friends from school, Kirstein and Brad, were going to the same college. Kirstein (pronounce the 'I' more, k-ear-sten, she likes the Danish roots to be recognized) and I have been friends since forever. We all met in the 'golden' group. Yeah - I had some difficulties with spelling and reading. A little dys-lexic but didn't make a big thing of it. Obviously, my parents had their concerns as I wasn't achieving what most people of my age could, although I was the youngest in the year, being a summer baby, if that counts as an excuse. I got on with it and turned out to be one of the best achieving pupils in my class.

Then moving onto Year Eleven, I studied like crazy, day and night. Dad had to bring trays of food up to my room as I refused to take a break. My walls were covered with revision notes and posters. Seriously, when exams came up, it looked like my school had been sick all over my walls. But my grades improved so worry over.

It was my first day at college and I was so nervous. I didn't know anyone in my class and thought I may end up eating my lunch in the toilets... joking. But I was worried about finding the classes and making friends.

After figuring out the train journey, asking an old lady where the college was and finally finding it, I approached my new home for the next two years. It looked quite impressive from the outside, colourful and different to ordinary colleges. As I entered, it was rather odd because it was so quiet and there was so much open space. I walked to the reception desk in the middle of this open space and my footsteps echoed off the walls. The lady at the desk peered over her glasses but continued tapping at her keyboard.

"Um, hello, I'm er, late I think, I'm new. I don't really know where I'm going," I said, stuttering.

Wow Dee - that was a great first impression sentence you managed to throw together there. I shook my head. The lady reached to a phone beside her, placing it between her ear and shoulder, still tapping away.

"Hello George, how are you today? Uh, huh, maybe a drink later, that would be nice."

My face crumpled up, confused. Was she ringing her date and totally ignoring my existence or was this normal? She carried on as I fiddled with my fingers uncomfortably.

"You know I'd love to chat, but could you ask Jolene to come down from the office before the stampede. I've got a newbie. You too, thanks," she said, popping the phone down and smiling at me. I forced a convincing smile back.

"Stampede?" I asked, slightly alarmed.

She nodded towards some doors behind me where a lady appeared. I guessed this was Jolene. Her footsteps clonked along the floor as did mine until they were lost in a muffled noise that grew louder. Then from behind her merged hundreds of students all at once. She was quite literally engulfed by the crowd.

"Stampede," I whispered to myself, understanding.

After a second of panic, thinking I was going to be swallowed by the crowd, Jolene emerged in front of me. She bubbled with personality as her five hundred words flew at me all at once. I was late due to not enrolling in time as I was in Greece, as you know. But Jolene sorted my induction and paperwork and then led me to join my class. Jolene was still speaking at one hundred miles per hour and it wasn't until I focused on the door numbers that I realised every corridor, corner and class door was an exact replica of the one before. I thought I had been walking up and down the same corridor, but I had been through about five. Before I had a chance to panic about never being able to find my way back out of the college, Jolene stopped talking and opened a class door. She waved me in, then introduced me to a bunch of eyes staring at me.

"This is Delphine everyone. She is also in our class, just a little late due to topping up the tan I guess. Don't be too envious everyone - right, pop yourself there dear."

I gave an awkward smile and settled down opposite two harsh looking girls - the two same girls I saw at the station sniggering at a shy girl. The tall freckly, husky-voiced one peered at me.

"Looks like we've got a Little Miss Barbie here. Got any brains or just beauty?" I was already confused as to whether that was a compliment or an insult.

"All these new people are right babies. I bet you've never smoked, have ya? And never had one drop of alcohol in ya life. Definitely never been drunk," the blonde girl next to her said in the most exaggerated Essex accent ever. Yes, we had entered chav city.

Whilst looking at them, my mind had a quick switch, a lightbulb moment of, why do you always take the back seat and let spiteful girls like them sit up front? One thing that gets my blood boiling is bullies. I had always been an observer except one time in secondary school when I shut down Kirstein's lifelong bullies. Since then, no one had spoken one bad word to Kirstein. I took in a sharp breath ready to spit some harsh words back but slowly let the breath back out, remembering it was my first day and I was better than that. I laughed a little, raised my eyebrows, looked them up and down and walked off to another table, thinking them pathetic. *What, just because I started a tiny bit later than everyone else, they think I'm some sort of alien? Let them undermine me all they wish to entertain themselves. Doesn't bother me.*

"Oh yeah, run away." They sniggered to each other. I sighed

and shot them a look, squinting my eyes.

"I haven't ever smoked and I'm proud of it. Smoking isn't something to boast about, but by all means, carry on, blacken your lungs so they're just as dark as the fake tan all over your face," I said, smiling sarcastically. Some of the quiet-looking girls gasped or giggled, going red when the mean girls shot them a look. I smiled and shook my head thinking it funny how this very situation is like all the movies. They didn't say anything back, instead their faces crumpled up in confusion that the new girl spoke up.

"Girls please. Chelsey - I thought we had an agreement for this year," Jolene snapped. The blonde girl squinted her eyes but bit her tongue. At the end of the lesson, I was held back by Jolene, even though I was the victim.

"Delphine, that really wasn't a good first impression," she said, sighing.

"Miss, I," I began, not quite able to call a teacher by their first name yet. I thought I would just be honest. "Someone clearly had to say something. I bet you... you've had complaints about them girls before. Well they need to know their place and that not everyone is weak and going to be scared of them. It was simply defence." I spoke quickly, and started to get distressed, thinking about Kirstein when she was bullied.

"Yes, I know but that isn't your job. Look Delphine. Between me and you, I don't favour them any more than you do, but that's how life is. We have to put up with difficult people. Next time just ignore them - they want a reaction." I could have carried on, but I agreed and left. The blonde girl Chelsey was waiting outside as I came out the classroom. She stared at me, and took a breath in, stepping towards me, like she wanted to say something, but nothing came out. I had stopped waiting for her to do so, but nothing.

"Don't worry, you can say whatever you're attempting to say when your sidekick is back with you." I smiled at her and walked on as she went red. I decided to follow the crowd, but I kept going around in circles, so I thought the lift would be a good idea to use as I couldn't find any stairs. Bad idea. I ended up cramped between ten tall, overly pungent, aftershave-drenched guys.

"Make room for the little lady," one of the guys yelled, shoving another guy. I'm not little but among them I felt it. One guy near the buttons smiled at me between the others.

"Floor?" he said.

"What?" I replied. I know. I'm an idiot.

"What floor do you want?" He laughed.

"Oh um, I don't really know, just down," I stuttered.

"Right, you're new I'm guessing. We don't have many models like you. You will be wanting the second floor. That's where the canteen is," he said, smiling.

"Right," I nodded. We filed out the lift.

"Feel free to sit with us," the guy said from above me.

"Oh, thanks, but I'm meeting someone, well, if I can find them that is," I said. He nodded, smiling, and caught up with the other guys.

I spotted Kirstein sitting at one of the tables with a folder in front of her. She had already been here for a week, so she knew where she was going. I flung myself down onto the chair opposite her. She looked up from the folder and slid a mocha towards me.

"How's the first day going?" she said, already knowing the answer. I shook my head.

"You know what, I have no idea. I'm already so confused even though I don't even have one sheet of paper compared to your massive folder there. Already drowning."

"Oh, you will have your own tree load of paper in no time, don't you worry about that." Whilst we were discussing our strange first impressions of the college and I was explaining about the mean girls, the confusing corridors and the guys in the lift, two girls that I recognised from my class came over to us. They warned me about all the other girls, telling me the gossip and what's what, telling me that I had opened a door of girl war with Chelsey, the college bitch by the sounds of it. I thanked them for the heads up. Once they left, Kirstein glared at me in disappointment.

"So much for a low profile, drama free day, aye?"

"Well, what can I say? It's not like I chose any of them situations to occur. The drama chooses me, I'm sure." We both laughed.

"Oh, that's him," I whispered, spotting the guy from the lift on the opposite table.

"WHO, WHERE?" Kirstein looked around wildly.

"Stop, stop, oh, what are you doing? Okay calmly... the tall dark one in the group of guys your six o'clock," I clarified. Her eyes flickered from nine to three o'clock as she figured out the clock reference.

"Behind you Kirstein." I sighed, disappointed by her lack of understanding of spy talk.

"Well you could have just said that in the first place." She turned and stared directly at him and after about five seconds swung her head around pretending to look at anything other than him. Oh god, I whispered to myself. As he smiled at her, I hid my face behind my mocha cup. She turned back.

"Oh, the sexy one?" she asked, raising her eyebrow and smirking.

"Yeah, the sexy one that clearly knows we were just talking about him due to your crappy discreetness. What is wrong with you?" I snapped. She giggled, holding her hands up. Break was over way too quickly and Kirstein showed me the way to my next class.

Momentarily, back in class, I was daydreaming about Nikos, gazing out of the window, not paying attention at all. Having to mumble some totally off topic guess when the teacher surprised me with a question

"Delphine, what's your opinion on the matter?" My heart rate increased dramatically, as I felt my cheeks flush a tomato red. I swallowed hard and looked around desperately for a hint as to what on earth they were talking about, let alone what lesson I was in. But everyone's faces looked glum as their hands either fiddled with some torn up piece of paper from their scruffy textbooks or tapped constantly on the table. Except Morgan who eagerly waggled his arm in the air, almost popping it out of the socket, desperately bursting to shout out the answer. Almost as much as the buttons on his top bursting to pop open around his stomach. No, as you can probably tell, Morgan was not my favourite person. Unfortunately, he was in almost all my classes and always seemed to be sat right next to me! I had only been in this college for a day and I already remembered his name, which was either really good or really bad. It was bad.

At least I had something meaningful to daydream about to distract me from my irritation. My teacher walked over to my desk, peering down over her glasses. I slid my hand over my doodles of hearts in my textbook, delicately surrounding 'Nikos' and my name.

"Try page forty-seven," she said, raising an eyebrow. I smiled, flipping the pages as she walked over to the board, her nattering fading as I went back to my daydream date. Although I thought a great deal about him, I didn't really talk to him much on the phone and it could take him up to a week to read a simple *hello* and another week to text back *hi* or *sorry, I'm busy*, which was a bit of a stab in the heart but I ignored it. I didn't want to be annoying so I let the conversation rate drop to a minimum, to basically non-existent until we would meet in person again.

Before I knew it, the day was over. Other than the initial making of enemies and bad first impressions for the teacher, it was fine. Also, this was disregarding the five hundred sheets of paperwork, essays and homework.

That evening flew by as I was trying to file all the pieces of paper and organise everything. I also stalked the girls in my class to find something to use against them when they decided to try and regain their baddest girls in the class reputation. The redhead girl's profile was only full of pictures of her smoking or looking like a right pleb. Scrolling through Chelsey's Facebook page, I saw that her brother passed away about five years ago. I didn't know how to feel, of course. I felt sorry for her but then again, there is no excuse to channel your anger and pain onto other people. I shut the laptop, allowing the screen light to peel off the walls, and curled up in bed.

I woke up to my same morning routine. It went a little like this. Walking to the station. Waiting for the train. Hopelessly daydreaming about Nikos more than I should. Imagining his comforting touch - the way he would put his arm around me, and I would melt. And his eyes! Oh, his eyes. Now that was a dangerous thing to look into. I avoided looking into his eyes as much as possible but when I did, I never wanted to leave his side. I wanted to capture and hold all the happy moments with him.

"Excuse me love, I think you will find this is the only train that stops at this platform, so I'm sure this is your ride and you're going to miss it." And so it was - my train was right in front of me. "She's away with the fairies." Well, I'm a bit old for fairies but if a beautifully sculpted Greek boy counts, I'll agree.

Approaching the college, Chelsey was outside the gates, sat on some boy's lap, her legs wrapped around him and her lips glued to his face. I gagged at the sight of them, his hands on her waist. It unsettled my stomach. Her eyes broke away from him for a second, catching a glimpse of me. The boy leaned round her, his eyes analysing me. I was through the college doors before either of them could do anything. The college was going through a whole refurbishment programme with certain blocks being sectioned off, knocked down and rebuilt, whilst our timetable got screwed dramatically with changed classrooms. In one way, it was good as it gave an excuse for missing half a lesson, if you 'couldn't find it' or 'didn't know the room changed so thought class was cancelled.' But after a while, teachers sussed students out and we were all warned. Plus, they were much more attentive, making sure that everyone was fully informed about classroom changes.

In my first class, compulsory and pointless Mentoring, I had this painfully irritating teacher, Terry Bull. No, I'm not kidding. - His name was Terry Bull - 'terrible' - and it was just about right.

A very fitting name. I didn't even particularly want to do mentoring or enjoy it so when Terry was in a bad mood because of the drilling, I couldn't deal. He liked to pick on people and today was my lucky day. Mentoring was all about 'life'. If I didn't get enough of these talks from Mum, I had to sit through them in college.

"What do you want to do as a career Delphine?" Terry asked.

"I really don't know," I admitted.

"Okay, well what are your interests?" he pushed. I nibbled on my pencil.

"Um, I like travelling. I want to do something in that field I guess." He looked disappointed.

"You have good grades Delphine. You would smash university; you are worth more than a travelling job." I rolled my eyes. Was this a talk about what I wanted or what was expected of me? I didn't want to be someone who went to school, then college, then uni, and then work and then died. How utterly boring. To make this class better, this kid next to me… remember Morgan? Yeah, well, he was taking the piss because I spelt something wrong, so surprise surprise, he started digging at me.

"Can you spell this Delphine? Go on, give it a go, sound it out. Can you spell that? I bet you can't." Prick. I was on my period, so I was emotional already without having Morgan in my ear and a stressed teacher. If it was another time, I would have stabbed my pencil through his hand to teach him a lesson. But at That Time of the Month, you know how it is. Something in Terry's heart spurred him to ask what was going on. Morgan being the little goody fat face he is, went bright red and looked at me, begging with his eyes for me not to say. I'm not a snitch but telling on him seemed like a good idea just to see his face well up.

"Morgan's taking the piss because I'm dyslexic," I said, staring straight at Morgan. Then, I'm not even joking, Terry sighed and made a full-on joke about dyslexia in front of the whole class. People sniggered or looked shocked, probably in disbelief that a teacher had done that. I was angry because I was stupid enough to not even understand the joke.

One plus to your teacher being a prick...it gives you an excuse to leave. I decided to leave the classroom before destroying it.

"SOME FLIPPING TEACHER YOU ARE!" I slammed the door behind me, and got a bit carried away, still yelling whilst storming down the corridor. "I hope your wife gets workmen in to drill right through your crappy teaching skills..."

I walked right into a man holding a load of stone from the building site. He dropped it, turning around to shout at me.

"Really little gir..." he turned, halting mid-sentence, staring at me. His face was familiar. He had a sharp jaw line, dark skin and piercing blue eyes. Oh. Lift guy! The guy who knew I was talking about him when stupid Kirstein was a terrible spy. *Ah god.*

"Delphine?"

"Well this is embarrassing. Hi, um, how do you know my name?" I choked out, scratching my head. Before he could reply, I realised I should probably apologise for being a clumsy oaf. "Um, sorry about the..." I nodded towards the stone on the floor. He laughed a little, showing his dimples.

"Aha, that's okay." He bent down, gathering up the slabs of stone. I stood there, biting my lip in embarrassment, brushing some dust of my skirt.

"Were you about to call me a little girl?" I said, remembering.

"Was that you yelling?" he said, squinting a little in the direction I came from.

"No," I said quickly. He raised his eyebrows at me. I sighed. "Okay, it might have been. But I had good reason to."

"I bet." He smiled.

We figured I had half a lesson of time to kill and he had done most of his work for the day, so we sat in one of the old blocks. It was taped off as it was due to be knocked down, but we climbed in and chatted for half an hour.

"So, I'm confused. Are you a student or are you with the refurbishment people?" I asked.

"Both. I'm a student but I'm doing work experience with the refurb team," he explained.

"Oh, well, in that case, seeing as I have to stay here for two years, could you build me a personal place where I can escape every now and then?" I joked.

"Depends."

"On?"

"If I am invited or not?" he said.

"Mm, depends," I repeated.

"On?" he asked.

"If I like you or not." He pulled out a sheet of paper from his back pocket, handing it to me.

"What's this?" I asked, confused. Unfolding it, I saw a picture of me holding a certificate. It was a Student of the Week picture. I got that because I agreed to ignore those two bitches in my class after many bickers with them. Obviously, it didn't say 'for ignoring the two bitches.' Jolene said she was very proud and put 'for mature behaviour and excellent classwork'. I know what you're thinking... this is college, not Year Five. And believe me, I had the exact same thought.

"Oh my god. That's so embarrassing. Why do you even have that?" I said, as he giggled.

"How can you be the Student of the Week and a little rebel now?"

"Mm, enough of the little please." As I went to explain, the bell rang for Lesson Two. I slid off the table.

"I gutta go, I would stay but I don't actually mind Child Development class so, I'll see ya around? Oh, and there ain't any posters of you being Student of the Week so...probably something we should have covered already but, what's your name?"

"Oh yeah, I'm Carl, and try not to break anything on the way," he joked. I laughed and rolled my eyes, walking out.

Child Development was the only lesson Kirstein and I had together, as the class linked her course and my course. She stuck to my side, whispering over the teacher as soon as I got to class. Although we spent almost every hour of every day together, we always had at least one hundred things to talk about each time we saw each other.

"I cannot stand that Morgan kid! Is he in any of your classes?" I asked Kirstein.

"Yeah, he's in my English class, he sits at the front and answers all the questions, in that respect, I'm quite thankful he's there really. But I haven't really spoken to him," she explained.

"Oh, you really don't want to. He's an arrogant pig. He wouldn't stop going on about how I can't spell. I could have killed him," I said.

"Oh, no he didn't! Don't worry girl - I got you. Next time I see him..." She made a little joking growling noise before our teacher shot a look at us. We both bit our lips, looking down at our worksheets. Once she looked back at her computer, we started again.

"Also, walking into college this morning, Chelsey and her little gang were eyeballing me and I'm sure she was sat on Kane's lap - that guy from our school," I told her. But before she could reply, we got split up for talking. Kirstein was sat next to this girl who wouldn't stop coughing without even covering her mouth. I was wetting myself with laughter as Kirstein's face screwed up at her arm that had been germed.

"Delphine! Do you need to take a minute outside?" the teacher warned.

"Nah, but I think Amanda needs a drink," I said, trying not to laugh. Amanda looked up embarrassed and scurried out to the water fountain as our teacher nodded at her.

"And some hand sanitiser?" Kirstein was still rubbing her arm.

"Girls, please!" the teacher warned for the last time. After class, we met Brad for lunch in the canteen, but we stopped dead when we saw who he was sitting with.

"Oh my god, Brad is with the sexy lift guy," Kirstein said, shocked. We looked at each other, then back at them.

"Well this should be fun," Kirstein said, smiling walking towards them. I grabbed her arm and pulled her back

"What are you doing? We can't sit with them," She grabbed my arm and pulled me towards them. When Carl looked up, I shoved her off and smiled. Brad looked up.

"Ah, here they are. This is Dee and Kirstein. Guys, this is Carl." We all paused.

"No way, you're the best friends of Brad, the lost beauty and the not so secretive spy." He laughed and Brad looked confused. I cringed and sighed.

"Okay, thank you, well I know where I'm going now, kinda. And Kirstein here, well she meant to do that," I said, trying to sound convincing.

"Oh really?" he asked. I paused for a second.

"No, who am I kidding?" I admitted, sitting down opposite them.

"Yeah, it was exactly what it looked like. We were checking you out," Kirstein said, so blatantly. I quickly butted in.

"Um, no, she was checking you out. I was just sitting there, more interested in my mocha if I remember correctly." Carl laughed.

"Yeah, you'd already done the checking out bit in the lift earlier right?" he said cheekily.

"Um okay. Hold up everyone, sorry to interrupt. I'm lost - can someone explain what's going on here?" Brad asked, looking baffled. We all laughed and spent lunch explaining.

After college, Kirstein, Brad and I went to my favourite tea shop called Pink Cups. Brad settled a tray down on the table with a pot of tea and a custard slice for me, a chai latte and cupcake for Kirstein and an espresso and cookie for himself. Kirstein held her cupcake towards me to scoop the icing off as she didn't like it. As I did so, we both watched Brad repetitively tap his fingers on the table.

"What's wrong with you?" Kirstein said, taking back her icing free cupcake. Brad looked up and his face crumpled. I raised my eyebrows.

"Okay, spit it out," I said.

"It's not me, it's you actually Dee," he said, sipping his espresso.

"What about me?" I questioned.

"Don't tell me you've fallen for her too, because there's a queue, so join the back of the line please," Kirstein interrupted. I giggled, shoving her.

"Not quite. Basically, all the guys on my course are talking about you," he said.

"Surprise, surprise, she is a popular topic," Kirstein said, through crumbs of her cupcake.

"Explain?" I said.

"I'm not sure if you want me to." Brad pretty much squirmed in his seat.

"Explain," Kirstein repeated more forcefully.

"Oh, come on Brad, I can take it. I'm a grown girl."

"Okay, they're saying you're like, untouchable. They're betting on which one of them is gunna be able to sleep with you, except Kane who just seemed to want to know information about you." I rolled my eyes at the assumptions. They're the same as secondary school guys. I was known as CHB - 'cold hearted bitch' - mostly as a joke from friends. I was known as this because of rejecting guys, from being uninterested, not listening or refusing any kind of help. I was Little Miss Independent who didn't let anyone in. The superior label followed me everywhere. I'm not. I'm just mature and happen to have a good posture. I do a lot of things in life - experiences, holidays. That doesn't make me superior but hay ho.

"Wait hang on, you haven't even spoken to any guys at college yet, it's been just short of a week," Kirstein said.

"Oh, but all superior snobs get noticed before they have even opened their mouth, as we all very well know, right?" I said, sarcastically shaking my head in my hands. Kirstein rubbed my back. Kirstein and Brad kept discussing it, which made me so angry because they were talking about me like I was some object. I cut them off. "Look, it doesn't even matter, none of them are gunna sleep with me, and I really don't care what they think about me so forget it." They both sighed.

"Anyway, I can't believe you're the fit girl that Carl was talking about and I didn't even realise, oh, and explain to me this walking out of class thing?" Brad said, lightening the mood.

"Wait, Carl said I was fit?" I said.

"Wait, you walked out of class?" Kirstein said.

"Wait, I think we all need to get each other up to date here," Brad said. So, we spent the next hour explaining everything going on.

That evening, for the short period that Mum wasn't in the office working but walking up the stairs to change, she acknowledged my existence.

"How's school darling?" She smiled as we passed on the stairs. I stopped, confused by this communication and walked back up the steps, leaning on the banister as she got changed.

"It's college and it isn't going great to be honest."

"Yeah," she nodded, checking her phone on the side.

"Yeah? That's not a logical response to what I just said," I said, huffing because I noticed she wasn't actually listening.

"For god sake Mum, don't ask me something if you're not bothered about the answer." Then Dad butted in from the bottom of the stairs.

"What's this arguing about?" he called, a paint brush in one hand and a pallet in the other.

"It's not an argument, an argument is between two people, and clearly it's just me here. I could say, I got beat up and Mum would probably respond with, that's nice dear." I watched Mum type a text out. Getting no response, I sighed and walked down the stairs.

"She's just busy, tell me what's up Barbie," Dad said, walking me into his studio. He was working on a painting of Poros called 'Poros at Night'. It was beautiful, but he stared at it unhappy and kept tweaking it.

"It's just college, it isn't what I expected I guess," I explained.

"Why not?" Dad asked.

"Well, I thought I would make friends in my classes straight away and they wouldn't all be douchebags, and I thought that teachers would actually teach but they are all useless." Dad's face crumpled, but I wasn't sure if it was from my story or his painting. "You're missing a glow of orange just below the clock tower," I pointed out, remembering that there is a rock that the tower lit up orange. Dad's eyes brightened and he waved his paint brush in the air.

"That's it, what would I do without you, my little chicken?" He danced, hugging me. I smiled because at least we had solved one of our problems with this conversation.

The next day when walking into college, I felt so paranoid, like every guy's eyes were examining my body, undressing me in their heads. Every step I took further into college, I felt another pair of eyes glue to me. I walked quicker and quicker until I found the closest toilet. I shoved the toilet doors open and leaned back on the locked door, breathing heavily. As I came out, Carl came out of the boys' toilets at the same time.

"Are you following me?" he asked.

"I could ask you the same thing," I said, walking towards class.

"Well, you are a tempting thing to follow," he said. I stopped and looked at him.

"Thing?" I snapped.

"Oh no, not thing, I mean, you're not a thing you're..."

"Whatever." I went to open the door of my class, annoyed. He reached over and held my hand on the handle.

"Wait, look, I'm sorry, I didn't mean to offend you. I wasn't trying to..."

"To what? To get one step ahead of all the other guys that are trying to sleep with me to win a bet, huh?"

"Wow, that's what you think of me? Ouch, no, actually, Brad and I are the only ones that stuck up for you. Why do you think I wasn't with my group the other day?" He nodded, letting go of my hand and walked off. I took a sharp breath in to apologise, then let it out in a sigh.

I was a little late for Child Development. We had a lady who came in to talk to us about sexual diseases. She was small and blonde with lots of tattoos and piercings. She handed around disgusting images. After twenty minutes of her speaking, I started feeling sick. The images of our insides and... that in your vagina was way too much. This wasn't a little 'ew that's disgusting' kind of thing. I thought I was going to faint.

Her words started vibrating off the walls and a sudden rush of hotness made me sweat all over. My head and neck tightened as if I was having an allergic reaction. I tried to look normal slipping off my jacket, but my legs felt jellylike and sick started stabbing at my throat. I ran over to my teacher in the corner asking if I could be excused. She looked at me and told me to go to the first aid room.

I rushed out, walking down the corridor to get to an open door with fresh air ASAP. It was odd being in an empty corridor as you hardly ever saw that. Our college took way too many students compared to the size of the corridors. We had traffic jams where corridors crossed, and teachers had rotas to act as the traffic lights. But even though this corridor was empty, it felt the most claustrophobic it ever had, the walls shrinking into me.

I felt so faint that my vision started fuzzing and the next thing I knew, I was lying in the middle of the corridor.

I woke up in the first aid room on the bed, and images started flashing back. A figure running towards me. Carl picking me up. Being carried. Being laid down on the bed. The nurse leaning over me.

I sat up feeling fine but dazed. I walked towards the office where the nurse was and poked my head through.

"Um, hi," I mumbled.

"Are you okay? You should be lying down," she said, peering over her glasses as she scurried over to me.

"Um, no, I mean yes, I'm fine, I, I don't need the bed. I'm good thanks." She put her hand on my forehead to check my temperature.

"Right well, you fainted so you need to fill out some forms. Do you know what happened?" she asked.

"No, not really but I'm okay now. I'll fill out the forms, and can I go back to class? Wait, what's the time?" She walked me back to the first aid room, handing me a half filled in sheet with my name on it.

"It's the end of the day love, classes are over, just fill out that sheet, I rang your parents," she said, smiling calmly. I was so confused. How could I have slept through half of Lesson Four, lunch and Lesson Five. What if someone saw me sleeping? People come in the first aid room all the time, mainly as an excuse to get out of lesson.

Once in secondary school when I was in Year Seven, I had a bad headache so sat in the chair and there was a Year Eleven girl lying on the bed exactly like I was here. I just watched her. Someone might have watched me. I had no idea. The nurse watched me begin to panic.

"It's okay dear, you probably were just exhausted, maybe hadn't eaten enough. Don't worry just yet." I wasn't worried. I was just thinking about how Mum would fuss back home, friends would ask, rumours would spread. Ugh.

I walked out of the college gates when Carl came jogging over from his car.

"Delphine are you okay, what happened?"

"Yeah I think so, and I don't really know."

. "Well can I give you a lift home?"

"No thanks, I can catch the train. Oh, and I'm sorry about earlier. I'm just paranoid about it."

"Nah, it's okay, don't worry about it. Go get some rest."

I managed the journey home and as soon as I stepped through the door, Mum was cradling me like a baby. Although it should be the other way around, her face was squished on my chest because she is tiny.

"Oh baby, what happened?" she fussed, rubbing my head and examining my body for any signs of injury.

"Mum please, nothing happened," I said, trying to pull away.

"Dee, you fainted and slept for a couple of hours, that's not nothing. We're going to the doctors."

"Oh no, that's not necessary," I said. But as you can tell, it was necessary according to Mum and she was not backing down. I went to bed to try and forget the happenings of today. Mum came in and kissed my forehead, and that was the first time she looked at me like she didn't understand me.

THREE

On Thursday morning, Mum woke me up by letting the blinding light shoot through the window into my eyes.

"Come on, you have an appointment in forty-five minutes," she said, pulling my covers off. She handed me a cup of tea.

"Mum! Please can we try a gentler waking up, or maybe I could set my own alarm. You know your mood is determined by how you wake up and this isn't a good start," I said.

"You talk a lot more than Grace does when woken up." I rolled my eyes as she had ignored what I just said. I was forced to go to the doctors.

"Mum, I really don't understand why I have to be escorted here. I am capable." I let out a major huff.

"Mm, and who's to know if you actually go on your own? Plus, you don't understand Doctor um…however you pronounce his name." She shook her head. I raised my eyebrows.

"And you do?" I really didn't like our doctor, and I guessed it didn't help that I couldn't understand him. I sat in the chair as he flashed a light in my eye, took my blood pressure and asked me to explain what I thought happened. I had no idea, so I wasn't very cooperative, which annoyed Mum.

"Come on dear. What do you remember? Anything? Did you faint? Maybe inhale any fumes from that worksite at school?"

"Mum please, I'm seventeen, not seven, and I'm in college, not school. I don't know what happened, okay? We were in class talking about something that just made me feel ill and that's it." The doctor said something else, but I didn't quite manage to pick the accent off the words and unscramble the sentence structures, so it resulted in every child's response, to look at the mum in confusion.

The doctor watched me intensively.

"Have you noticed any changes in Delphine?" he asked, turning to Mum.

"Changes regarding...?" Mum looked as muddled as I was with that question's point.

"Attitudes, social life, eating habits?" He read this off a poster half stuck on the wall, the Blu Tack stretching as it clung on to the poster's corner. I studied it as Mum searched for a reply. In bold letters, it said, Spot the Signs Early. Spot the signs for what?

"Well she..." I shot Mum a look, like *hello, I'm still here*, annoyed by how she was about to make a judgment on how I've changed when she doesn't have the time of day to notice anything. She smiled nervously, rewording her sentence and acknowledging I was in the room.

"You don't go out as much as other girls your age - do you darling? And you skip meals sometimes." I raised my eyebrows, taken back. Um... maybe because she didn't have time to go shopping for food as she must send one last email, ring a client or teach a class. "And you seem a little..." She searched for a word. The doctor stopped nibbling his pen and peered up from his notebook at me.

"Distant, withdrawn?"

"Yes, distant," Mum agreed. I was so confused. Everything that was wrong with Mum, she had reflected as something wrong with me.

"Right, there's nothing wrong with me, I fainted because the topic in class was disgusting, simple as. My social life is fine, thank you, and I don't purposely skip meals." Mum's face screwed up.

"Ever since Greece and Niko..."

"Okay, okay, we are not going there. Mum! Really?" My

voice scratched a little high.

The doctor observed me and twisted round to his computer, editing my file, ticking boxes and typing notes. He reached over me to the printer, taking the sheet of paper and scribbling his signature. He handed it to me.

"I would like you to go for a blood test to see if there's any abnormalities, and I would also like to refer you to see one of our counsellors." My mouth dropped.

"Counsellors, seriously?"

"Yes, you have signs of..." He was interrupted by the Blu Tack clinging to the Spot the Signs Early poster, which was perfectly timed to release and float to the floor between the three of us.

"Depression and anxiety," he said. And there it was. In small red print at the bottom.

"Okay, let's just set this straight. I am not depressed or have anxiety or anything like that. I just fainted, that's all. There's nothing wrong with me, so I'll have the blood test, but I don't think a counsellor is necessary. I'm not mentally unstable and no offence but I doubt you can make any judgment otherwise. Plus, I really don't want to have mental health issues all over my NHS records for the rest of my life."

"Denial is one of the most common factors," he said. I was fuming and about to blow, when Mum shot up and thanked the doctor, leading me out.

That doctor had twisted everything I said and now Mum was concerned for my mental health and thought I was a rude teenager. We went straight to the hospital for the blood test. I had a million things to rant about, shout about and explain, but I didn't have the energy to climb over this new possibility that I was mentally unstable.

We had to wait two hours in the waiting room with a wingeing boy who wouldn't stop moaning about his big toe hurting. The mum was sweating through her tight pink vest top, flapping a sheet of paper in her face, making her fringe fly up and down and up and down. Two hours after having to deal with people chewing gum and Mum pushing me to try counselling, it was time to go in.

The nurse was gentle and reassuring. The needle wasn't too bad but when the blood began to get sucked out of my arm and flood into the tube, I felt like I was going to throw up. My eyes went a little fuzzy when she pushed a plaster onto the tender spot. I felt exhausted after that day and passed out as soon as I got home.

On Friday morning, we went back to see the doctor to discuss the results. Apparently, this took priority over college, but I didn't really mind avoiding Chelsey and little immature boys. The doctor concluded that I had had a panic attack and fainted after. He said people have panic attacks for many different reasons. As my blood sugar was a little low, he addressed the eating habits again, where Mum changed her story a little, saying she always made sure I had a very well-balanced diet. He also gave me ways of identifying the panic attacks and stopping them, like counting to ten and taking deep breaths. He said if it happens again, to go back as I may need some medication. I sat there not really listening whilst Mum flapped about asking too many questions.

"So, Delphine, if you feel dizzy, hot, confused, out of breath, or have any other symptoms you experienced before fainting, what will you do?" the doctor said, his eyes reading off the now securely stuck poster. Stuck but wonky.

"I shall count to ten and I will then miraculously defeat the oh so serious panic attacks." Mum shot me a look. The doctor took a deep breath in, possibly because of the difficult patient I was being.

"Let's practise that technique, shall we, so that you can feel more in control." He began to count, expecting me to join in. I squinted my eyes a little thinking how utterly stupid this exercise was. I can count to ten 'slowly and steadily' without practice, thank you very much. The doctor noticed his efforts to encourage me were failing.

"Okay, just remember, breathe and don't panic," he said, stopping his count at six. It was ironic that his attempt to help my panic attacks was to advise me not to panic. I nodded.

"Okay. I got it, thank you." And I walked out.

I went to college for the rest of the afternoon. Rumours had spread, as I imagined they would, and it was hella fun trying to ignore it all. It's funny how many people you don't know speak to you when you're the main attention of gossip. Rumour one - I was kidnapped by one of the workmen. Rumour two - I went into a coma. Rumour three - I fainted (closest one to the truth). Rumour four (best one yet) - I jumped off the English block stairs down to the corridor floor because I didn't want to read in front of the class. You know, if we got all these rumour makers' and gossip lovers' minds together, they could pass their creative writing exams with flying colours.

As I guessed, I had missed coursework being handed out, so I needed to sort that. I decided to do that rather than go to lesson as they probably weren't doing anything in class anyway.

"Girl, are you okay? I've seen you walk passed my class about five times with more pieces of paper each time," Kirstein said, appearing from around the corner.

"Oh yeah, well actually no, I'm really not okay. I've had a crappy few days, but I have to sort all this coursework out before I can think about that," I said, propping the folders up on my hip.

"Right, three-thirty is Mocha o'clock, and you better be there because my counselling skills are not offered often, okay?" I laughed thinking it ironic she had said the word, counselling.

"I'll be there," I said. We parted and I headed towards the library. I edited and printed two pieces of coursework and handed them in right before three-thirty before going down to meet Kirstein. She wasn't there yet so I ordered two mochas and sat down.

"You're three minutes late," I said as she sat down opposite me.

"And thirty-two seconds. If you're going to call me out, do it properly," she said, looking at her watch.

"So, what's going on?" she asked, sipping her mocha. I took a deep breath in.

"Well, I fainted as I guess you have heard and from there, everything has gone wrong. I was forced to the doctors and after arguing with him about being depressed, which I am not by the way, and having a blood test, he decided that I have panic attacks and must count to ten when I feel like it's happening. Oh, and to top it off he wants me to start counselling! And I'm sure Mum will force me to go," I said, rambling on. Then Kirstein started counting to ten.

"I'm sorry, I think I'm going to have a panic attack with all that information," she said, breathing deeply. I hit her with my folder across the table. We both laughed a little.

"Well Dee, I guess it isn't all bad, maybe this counselling thing will be good to talk to someone."

"Do you think I need to speak to someone?" I asked her, seriousness seeping onto my face.

"I think you are a little different lately, feistier and you don't care about getting in trouble in college and that." She wriggled uncomfortably in her seat.

"It's not that I don't care about getting in trouble - it's that I do care when something is wrong, so I do something about it. Why haven't you said that before?" I asked.

"Well, because I didn't realise it was that serious." She shrugged.

"It isn't that serious, everyone is just being dramatic," I said. I let out a frustrated huff. After our chat, I had one dull lesson before going to meet Brad and Kirstein at the station.

When I was on my way out, a group of guys were close behind me. I could hear them talking too loudly but I tried to ignore it.

"I'd one hundred percent smack that."

"Please, you'd never get that, fifty quid if you do mate." They all sniggered.

"Dunno mate, feel like it's been everywhere, might catch something."

"Be worth it." I stopped walking and breathed angrily. I turned around to face them all, and they stopped in their tracks, all half-smiling evil smirks.

"First of all, we are not objects. Secondly, none of you could get anything even with a prostitute. Oh and talk about me again, I will make sure every girl knows how crap you are in bed and how unfortunately small it is compared to the size of your ego, because after all I'm obviously a slut that has been 'everywhere' and obviously they're going to believe me. I can be very convincing." They all stared blankly at me. One of them stepped forward opening his mouth, so I held my hand up towards his lips making an uh sound to make him suck his breath back in. I squinted my eyes, turned around and walked out the college doors.

"Cor, she can tell me what to do anytime," one of them muttered.

Brad came jogging up behind me to meet Kirstein at the station.

"What was that?" he asked.

"Nothing," I said.

"You know you're going to make it worse, Dee, if you keep snapping at people like you did with Carl the other day," he said. I stopped walking, looking at him.

"What? Oh sorry. Next time I'll let them carry on, shall I? I won't stick up for myself," I said.

"That's not what I'm saying. I'm just saying that there is a different way to go about it," he said. He was calm as he carried on walking.

"It's exactly what you're saying. Look Brad, your way of dealing with it isn't going to help, tell a teacher, great idea - that's going to solve it." He looked around, cautious of observers noting my tone. I noticed and laughed. "Brad, if you're embarrassed to be seen with me... seriously you don't have to stay," I said, offended.

"Dee! I'm not, I'm just…"

"No, it's fine. I'm getting the early train. Wait for Kirstein. She isn't so much of a liability and reputation destroyer." Before he could respond, I jumped on the train. He kicked a bin on the platform as the train pulled away.

Later that evening, my phone was buzzing on my bedside table as Kirstein and Brad inundated me with texts and calls, but I ignored them. Sleep felt like the better option instead. In the morning, I went for a jog and when I got back, Dad was waiting for me in the car. He had obviously been sent by Mum to make me go to my first counselling thing. I stopped when I saw the car and sighed. Dad made a half-sorry smile and lifted his hand off the wheel gesturing, 'Better do as we are meant to.' I pulled my headphones out my ears, sighed and flopped into the car. He promised to take me to Pink Cup after. That temptation and the happy endorphins flying around inside me from exercise convinced me to go. It wasn't too far from the college. It was a small red house hidden behind a small jungle of trees. It had a few flowerpots with every coloured flower possible outside a large, arched, brown door.

Before I reached out to knock, the door flung open to reveal a small, middle-aged lady with crazy red hair and bright red glasses that made her eyes look massive. Her smile was bigger than any smile I'd seen and clearly rehearsed for first-time clients. I stepped back a little, feeling like I had met the wolf in Little Red Riding Hood and could be gobbled up any second.

"You must be Delphine!" Her high-pitched voice pierced through my ears. I stared at her open arms. Was that a gesture to hug her or simply a welcome gesture? "It's nice to meet you, I'm June." Of course. When a parent doesn't know what to call their kid, they go for a month.

"Come in, come in," she said, waving me in and holding her cold-looking hand out to shake. After ignoring her hand, I walked into her house.

She was wearing about five bright colours in this one outfit, which annoyed me. You should only wear three colours maximum in any one outfit and at least have some colour coordination. Her house had the same issue. There was no theme at all - it was like rainbow-infused lightning had struck her house. However, everything was neat and tidy which made it slightly more bearable. She led me into a back room that had sofas and odd-looking therapy objects.

"Delphine, it means dolphin in Greek. It's a very interesting name you have," she said, smiling at me. She had looked that up on Google before I came. I didn't respond – instead, I stared back at her, wondering if I was meant to be impressed and wondering if I should reply with the meaning of June, a summer month when a lot of people fall in love on holiday and then ache for the rest of the year.

But I decided against that. This first meeting was going along the lines of 'I'm your friend and I'm going to be sickly sweet nice so that you open up to me', and from then on, I decided I would be the most difficult I could be to get rid of her. What made it worse? She chewed. Ex-smoker - apparently it helps. Well it definitely helped aggravate me.

Later that evening, Dad decided he was going to treat us to a family meal as his Poros at Night painting sold. Grace and I ended up wearing almost identical outfits without planning to.

"Right, are we all ready?" Dad asked. We all looked at Mum, tapping away at her keyboard in the office.

"Oh, why don't you have some father-daughter bonding," Mum said.

"Mum, really?" Grace said, letting out one big huff.

"I just have a lot to do," Mum said.

"Mum, if you don't come out of that office and spend some time with us, I will have a panic attack and die!" I shouted. She then stopped typing and poked her head out the door.

"Will you carry on going counselling?" she said.

"Wow, why can't we blackmail Grace instead? Yes, I will go to stupid counselling, just please be a mum for one night."

Eventually we all made it to a restaurant, a small Italian with nice music and deep purple décor. As we waited for our table, I straightened a picture on the wall and Grace watched me intensely.

"What are you doing?" she asked.

"Straightening the picture."

"Yeah but why?" She looked confused.

"Because Grace - it's irritating." I felt like Grace looked at me like I was an alien always about to freak out.

For half of the meal, Mum was actually present in conversation, but that's only because it was about how her work was going. For the other half of the meal she was in her own work world zone. After a while, Dad went into his dad jokes which do somehow always make Grace and I giggle, and Mum roll her eyes while secretly wanting to laugh.

"Oh, I love this, it feels just like it does when we are in Greece," Mum said. Grace looked at Mum probably thinking, she's the one who prevents it being like this all the time. Mum looked at Dad for some backup. Dad looked at me most likely thinking, is that going to make her panic mentioning Greece? So, it was an interesting family date.

The weekend flew by and soon enough I was heading back to college.

Today on the train journey I agreed with myself that I would try to keep a low profile and have a calm day. Until, of course, I hit an obstacle: the old 'let's read out loud class it will be super fun and good bonding.' *No, I don't think so.* I would not read out loud in college. That girl who spoke to Kirstein and I on my first day was reading and she said she was done reading, and the teacher asked why, as she hadn't read much. That went on for a while, so I stepped in.

"She doesn't want to read any more, so can we just move on?" My teacher then went on a rant about boosting our functional skills and confidence.

"I understand that, but she doesn't want to read any more," I said, impatient.

"Okay then Delphine, as you are so vocal this lesson, would you kindly read?"

"No thank you, I would prefer not to." As you can probably guess, this started a disagreement, but I won't go into it. All you need to know is I got sent to the 'cool off' room, which is full of pretty butterflies and calming things to do in there like colouring. After being in there for ten minutes, Carl walked in red-faced and sat opposite me and my blank butterfly. I stared at him and he stared at me. I scribbled, 'Sorry again I still feel bad', in my butterfly and slid it over to him. His angry face softened. He wrote on the back and gave it back to me. It said: 'It's okay, you're not the first person to deny checking me out, I'm happy you've come to terms with it.' I giggled out loud and a teacher shot me a look. I got up and walked towards the door.

"Excuse me, where are you going?" the teacher called from the corner over his laptop.

"I'm sorry, but I can't sit here and colour in butterflies. I come to college to learn and if I'm not allowed to go to class for defending a student who was scared of reading in front of people, then I don't see the point in today. I would rather cool off at the gym which is much more effective." Then I walked out. I know, I know - it went from a low-profile day to the cool-off room, to walking out of college but come on, God was not on my side today.

Carl came running out a few seconds after me.

"That was the best speech I've ever heard, so inspiring, I just had to follow."

"Why were you in there anyway?" I asked.

"Ah, it's nothing," he said, shrugging.

"Okay Mr. Secretive." We walked to the station and split at different platforms.

I caught the train home ready to go to the gym, but Mum was waiting for me at the door as I walked up the drive. She had a disappointed look on her face, and I gathered she must have had an email or call about my little episode.

"Look Mum, I was just defending a girl, sticking up for her like Dad always tells us to do. Maybe I went about it the wrong way, but I can't stand it whe...." I rambled on, pulling off my coat and throwing my bag down as my massive folder of paper spilled out onto the floor. I was interrupted by Mum as I leant over to pick it all up.

"Delphine, Delphine, slow down, I don't know what you're going on about."

"Oh, I thought... you looked... and you're out of your office, so thought I did something wrong?" I said, stuttering.

"By the sounds of it you have, which you can discuss with June later." I made an 'ugh' noise from the word June.

"Let me finish. So, June rang. Said you missed your session on Sunday and the one before that was uneventful, shall we say?" She raised her eyebrows waiting for an explanation.

"Firstly, I didn't know I had one on Sunday, I thought I only had one a week. But I don't like how she digs into my personal life and paints problems that are not there," I said, getting angry.

"She said she will move it to today as you missed it. She is your counsellor Delphine. You're meant to talk about your personal life - that's the whole point. She's a professional and if you just opened up maybe we could solve these problems."

"Oh, I'm sorry, I thought she was my 'friend', but you say she's just my counsellor, well, I feel so hurt I've lost a friend," I said sarcastically. Mum's patience ended.

"No, you pushed all your friends away, remember? Now you're going to start attending all sessions and work on these issues and that's not up for discussion." Her first comment felt like a stab in my heart.

"Yeah thanks Mum, don't worry. Pass your daughter's issues onto a professional as you don't have time for me. Maybe if you spoke to me I would be able to stop bottling things up but obviously it's too late for that. You call yourself a life coach, yet you have absolutely no idea about your own disastrous daughter's life."

Mum now also looked like she had been stabbed in the heart. Obviously, none of it was her fault, but blaming her seemed like the easiest option at the time.

Going to June's was the last thing on my list of priorities. I rang Kirstein instead and we went to the gym. After sweating and talking out emotions, we went to Pink Cup for cake. Yes - cake after gym. Perfect sense. I bought Nikos's favourite cake, coffee and walnut. I hated how so many things reminded me of him. I guess I made it worse by never taking off the bracelet he gave me which then made people ask about it.

Brad walked into the café as I was nibbling on a walnut. I looked at Kirstein, understanding the situation

"Really?" I said, huffing.. Brad sat down opposite me, and I stared at him.

"Before you make some smart comment about me not wanting to be seen with you in public, shut up," he said assertively. I gasped, raising my eyebrows.

"I don't care about that, I do care about you and I'm trying to look out for you," he said. I half smiled. "The reason I was like that was because the guys wouldn't shut up about it all day. They don't like me because I'm your friend, anyway, Carl ended up in the cool-off room for a week because Kane was being a prick to you and well, Carl's bigger than him and yeah."

"Oh, Brad I'm so sorry, I, I didn't realise. Wait, Carl was in there because of me?" I said. I let out a big sigh.

"Don't apologise, it's not your fault, and being your friend is worth whatever crap they can throw at me, even if you are a sassy pants," he said, hugging me and ruffling my hair.

"Okayyy, now we are all friends - can we go get a stronger drink than tea?" Kirstein piped up.

"Yes, but first Brad, who's Kane? Is he like the main guy of their group?" I asked.

"Kane Knight?" Brad said. Together, Kirstein and I repeated the name in unison. Kane went to our school - he was one of those extremely annoying populars who always called me Phiene rather than my real name.

"He's your enemy's boyfriend," Brad said.

"Chelsey?" Kirstein asked. We both nodded.

"That makes sense. Okay, now we can definitely have a stronger drink," I said.

We went back to Kirstein's and decided to make a night of it. We raided the alcohol cupboard and chatted for hours. We all flopped down, and I shared the corner sofa with Brad, his chest making a surprisingly comfy headrest. We were all drifting off to sleep when Brad started muttering.

"Dee, who hurt you?" I rolled over to face him, confused. "Don't try to deny it, you fear love and attachment, so what happened?"

"If this is because I rejected the guy at the station the other day, it really isn't that deep," I said, giggling and avoiding the question. He huffed and stared at me, waiting.

"You're my best friend but I feel like there is a massive part of you I don't know."

"Ugh, okay," I said, wriggling onto my belly and propping myself up on my elbows.

"His name's Nikos and he's from Greece and he broke my heart, that's all," I said, trying to spit it out quickly. Clearly, I still had alcohol in my system as usually I would tell him to do one. He read my face and hugged my head, allowing that to be enough explanation.

"I'm gunna hunt him down and eat his heart," Kirstein said, mumbling through a pillow. We both laughed.

In the morning, as we hung over our cups of coffee, our bed hair made us look like wild lions. We all travelled into college together and separated at the gate.

FOUR

Luckily, the rumours had died down by November. I carried on meeting Carl in mentoring classes, or in the first aid room when he decided to almost break his toe on-site. Kirstein and Brad complained as they needed my attendance to get extra cookies free at Snack Shack because the guy likes tall brunettes apparently. To Mum's disappointment, I had missed many of the counselling sessions. They were the most tedious and irritating things I had ever been to, college coming in at a close second.

This week in college, my year was having a focus week on teen health, meaning normal lessons were off - hallelujah. Instead, we had workshops and presentations in the main hall. I already did two days of it in the wrong group. We got put into groups and I got split from Kirstein and Brad which was typical. But no teachers seemed to notice if after the register in the mornings I sneaked into their group. It was a third of the year, so I blended in.

"I can't believe you haven't been caught yet," Kirstein said, huffing and puffing as we were doing a lesson on the evolution of exercise. We had now got to the year when step classes were the next big thing. As the instructor announced we were going into Zumba, Kirstein looked like she was about to collapse at the thought of it.

This week Kirstein and I had changed from mochas to cloudy lemon water due to the constant thirst. Carl sat our drinks down on the table and we all drank half the bottle without breathing before saying thank you.

"So, how's this teen health thing going?" he said, laughing at us all.

"I have decided it's actually a discreet form of punishment," Kirstein said, still out of breath from Zumba.

"Or it's telling us we shouldn't visit Pink Cups as often," Brad said, laughing. I gasped at the mere thought of no longer going to Pink Cups.

"I don't even eat the icing, yet Miss Strong Stamina over here eats a custard slice AND my icing and still slays!" Kirstein complained, looking at me. I giggled.

"Well, we're going there after college but we're skipping the food."

"Would you like to be taken to the most wonderful tea shop there is, Carl?" I said.

"Sure, I'll drive us."

"I don't know if I should admit this, but I actually really liked the Zumba," Brad said. Kirstein and I smiled at him.

"Oh, please be my Dance Fit class partner" I said, thinking how fun that would be.

"Um absolutely not, that was a one-off thing. Plus, you would show me up big time. I've seen you come out that class and the amount of sweat on you shows that after the warm-up that would be me done," Brad said.. I huffed, crossing my arms.

"You know what, I think we need to lock Dee in the gym to get her muscles to tire as much as everyone else's so we're equal, because no one can keep up," Kirstein complained, slamming her lemon water on the table.

"I think I can help with that," Carl said. We all looked at him. "Thursday, come to the new trampoline place with me?" he said, looking at me.

I looked at Brad and Kirstein waiting for them to reply but they were just looking at me.

"Oh, just me?" I said, realising.

"Yeah, it will be a fun date."

"It's not a date" I said, too quickly. Kirstein and Brad laughed and sighed.

"Okay, it will be easy competition," Carl said.

"Easy?" I said.

"Yeah, my brother worked at the old centre, and I was there all the time. I'll thrash you on the courses," he said cockily. I laughed.

"Pff, well it's gunna be an embarrassing day for you then," I said, just as big-headed.

Kirstein was glad to know the afternoon was just presentations. But presentations with a room of teenagers that desperately needed a shower is not the best. When we were dismissed for the day, Jolene called me to the side. *Oh, crap.* I was busted.

"Delphine, I heard that you are a qualified Pilates teacher?" she asked.

"Um, yes I am." I was curious as to where this conversation was going. I took a Pilates course when Mum needed more teachers. I taught an odd class here and there for her still.

"I was wondering if you would be up for teaching a class for this week's workshops?" she asked, smiling.

"No chance. Do you realise how much abuse I will get from these students?" I said, raising an eyebrow, knowing she had already thought about this.

"It will be an optional class at the end of the week to see the outcome of the student's opinion towards exercise," she said.. I thought about it.

"Well I doubt anyone will come but sure, if you want me to," I said, not really knowing why.

I rejoined Brad and Kirstein as we walked out of college and Carl drove us to Pink Cups. We all sat down with our usual drink order, minus the cakes. This fitness week was impacting us!

"So, I guess we won't be seeing you tomorrow or Friday?" Brad said, looking at me.

"Huh? Why not."

"Isn't that what Jolene was talking to you about?" Kirstein said.

"In trouble, again?" Carl added jokingly. I fake laughed at him.

"Funny, no I wasn't in trouble actually. She asked me to teach a Pilates class at the end of the day on Friday."

"And you said no, right?" Kirstein said, on edge.

"Originally but then I said yes," I said, smiling.

"What were you thinking? That's almost social suicide. You know how the class will be, they won't take you seriously," Kirstein said, panicking.

"Not to mention Chelsey," Brad said. I flapped my hands about.

"Okay, both of you, calm down, it's not compulsory so Chelsey won't come. There will probably only be like two people, being you two."

"Oh no, are you going to force me?" Kirstein complained like I had told her to run a marathon but smiled to show that of course she would come.

"I bet Chelsey will come and no doubt she will do something," Brad said, not convinced yet.

"Look if she does, it's my class and if she thinks she's going to get one up on me in my own class, she can think again."

"Right, Carl is coming, because I am not going to be the only guy doing Pilates, and I am not wearing tights," Brad said. Kirstein and I laughed.

"Tights are compulsory," Kirstein joked.

"I don't know if you will be allowed in because it's our year thing," I said to Carl.

"It wouldn't stop you," Carl said, sipping his drink. Then in unison Kirstein and Brad both agreed.

"True." I rolled my eyes at them and they all laughed.

#

On Thursday morning, our year was called to the main hall after registers were taken. We were watching a performance on eating disorders. Before the performance began, Jolene stood at the front talking into a mic.

"I have to say that I'm very proud of how you've all got involved this week. Due to you all doing so well, we are making Friday a half day." She was interrupted by some cheers and clapping. "Workshops will finish at twelve noon but there will be an extra Pilates class. It isn't compulsory but if you would like to join it's going to be taught by Delphine who is a qualified teacher," she said, searching for me in the crowd, smiling as she spotted me. Lots of heads turned to me and then to Chelsey as her hand shot up quickly. Brad sighed and shook his head, waiting for the drama, and Kirstein gave her evils. Jolene looked at Chelsey and hesitated before allowing her to ask her question. Chelsey had a smirk on her face as she lowered her hand.

"I'm sorry, I was just wondering how a dyslexic person can manage to become a qualified teacher," she asked all innocently, prolonging the word dyslexic. I closed my eyes and sighed as loads of people gasped. Kirstein jumped up from her seat and started climbing over people towards Chelsey, yelling.

"Oh, you're a right bitch! And I think someone needs to teach you..." She was interrupted as Brad jumped up, holding her back and sitting her back down next to him. My eyes widened in shock as I watched Kirstein's outburst. It was secondary school reversed except no one held me back that time. Chelsey was still smiling. Then Jolene snapped out of her gobsmacked face.

"Chelsey, that is not an appropriate question." Chelsey stood up feeding off the attention and my embarrassment. She was about to say more but I stood up.

"You know what, it's fine, I'll answer your question," I said, breaking my stare from her, then climbing over everyone down to the front. Brad caught my hand along the way.

"Stop," he said, quietly, and with a serious look in his eye. But I pulled my hand away, taking Jolene's place.

"Hit me," I said, nodding at Chelsey.

"Gladly, dyslexic people can't pass level three qualifications."

"Well that's funny because this one did. You see, in Pilates people don't jump up and down and change places like letters do for me, if you don't know that's what dyslexia is."

"Oh, that really sucks, well if you ever need help there's this website dealingwithdyslexia.org but I don't know if you will manage to get onto it. Maybe get your sidekick to type it for you." Before I had time to think, my hand dropped the mic and my legs started marching towards her. I don't know what I was thinking. My hands were clenched, and my body was on fire. I wanted to fling every burst of energy I had directly at her face. Before I could, I was stopped by two guys metres away from her.

"Were you going to hit me? You know that's assault. The best way to deal with criminal dyslexics is to give them a long sentence, and you wouldn't want that now, would you?" She couldn't stop herself laughing at that one. Her friend sniggered. The whole hall was stunned and in shock. I was about to scream and kick until I could get at her, but my head quickly switched to panic. I felt it happening, or maybe it had already been happening without me realising because one, two, three, and I was out. Black. Kirstein and Brad were both around my bed in the first aid room when I woke up. I looked at them confused.

"Please tell me I managed to hit her at least." They looked at each other.

"Nope, but she is going to the cool off room for the whole of next week," Kirstein said.

"Everyone saw me panic and faint, right?" I asked.

"Yeah, the whole year, one second you were firing like a broken machine then the next second, boom, you shut down," Kirstein said dramatically with massive hand gestures. I cringed. Brad hit her and then looked at me disappointed.

"Why did you do that?" he asked. I rolled my eyes.

"We are not having this conversation now," I said, out of energy.

"You make it worse," Brad carried on.

"Shut up Brad, she gets it." Kirstein hit him back. Jolene then came into the first aid room and pulled up a chair between the two of them.

"Delphine, I am sorry that happened, I think maybe you were right. It was a bad idea. I spoke to your Head of Year and he is okay with you taking tomorrow off," she said, sighing and looking guilty.

"What no, I'm teaching the class." Kirstein smiled and nodded, liking my fight. Jolene ensured I was okay and left. Brad looked even more confused.

"Dee are you serious? You can't. When you fainted, Chelsey said she would see you at Pilates," he pleaded.

"Not teaching the class was never an option," I said, ending the conversation.

"Carl's waiting for you outside for your date, shall I tell him you're not feeling up to it?" Kirstein asked.

"It's not a date, and absolutely not. I've gotta woop his ass on the courses," I said confidently, trying to convince myself I could actually beat him. I strutted out to his car in a self-assured manner. He smiled, watched me get in all poised, started the engine and pulled away.

"So, are you a sore loser?" he asked after a while.

"That's something you're never going to find out, are you?" I replied.

"If it's to you, probably yes, but I won't lose," he said.

"Why specifically me?" I asked.

"Well because you're a girl, and it's you," he answered. I instantly got defensive.

"Excuse me? Because I'm a girl? For that, you are going to lose," I said, slightly aggravated. I made it my mission to beat him on everything we did today for the women of the world. As we got to the front desk, I made sure I opened the door to enter just to avoid stereotypes.

"After you," I smiled sarcastically, gesturing for him to go in.

"Why thank you." He smiled back. We got up to the front desk and he chatted to the staff he knew.

"Two hour passes please, I've got socks, but she will need small, I'm guessing size five," he said, looking down at my feet, then at me. I nodded. "Ah, I'm too good," he said, proud of the guess.

"Apart from the facts that the majority of the women population have size five feet on average," I said smartly. He rolled his eyes but giggled and the girl serving us put a pair of socks on the desk.

"Okay, that's twenty for the tickets and two pounds fifty for the socks please," she said, looking at Carl. Typical. I quickly pulled out twelve pounds fifty and reached over Carl's handful of money. I popped it into the girl's hand, grabbed my socks and started walking into the main hall.

"Dee, I've got this," he called, trying to give me my money back.

"It's not a date," I called back, going through some doors and sitting down on a bench to change into the socks. We both chucked our bags into the locker.

"Will you let me pay the pound for the locker or do you want to give me fifty pence?" he asked, mostly seriously because I was quite feisty now due to his undermining of women.

"I shall allow it," I said, turning my head and strutting towards the trampolines. He followed me and grabbed my hand as we jumped to the long trampolines. I did a couple of cartwheels to set the mark. He watched smiling.

"But can she flip?" he asked, jumping super high and flipping in the air, landing perfectly on his feet. I bit my lip, doubting whether I would be able to do it, weighing up if proving a point was worth breaking my neck. He watched my brain tick and giggled.

"Here look, out of all people I know Delphine Rose is one woman who can definitely do this, right start jumping," he said confidently. I smiled at the word 'woman' and started jumping.

"Higher," he said, "okay now when you are ready, tuck your knees up to your chest and fling yourself backwards and open back out." I repeated what he said and went to do it twice but couldn't.

"Ahh I can't," I screeched, attempting it again.

"Yes, you can, I will count you in, just go for it, three, two, one, go," he shouted, and I tucked up tight and flung myself back. I uncurled upside down, looking at the room backwards.

"Feet, feet, feet" Carl called, biting his finger. Here came the broken neck... I kept turning until I landed on my butt, although I wasn't going to lose so I did a swivel hip move I learnt from when I used to go to trampolining club. He started clapping.

"Very impressive, you brought that back, we are equal," he said, smiling.

"Okay, what's next?" I said, eager to win with flying colours.

"Let's shoot some hoops," he said, walking towards a basketball hoop.

"Oh no, I play netball, I would win way too quickly at that, let's do this," I said, pulling him into a dodgeball court where a new game was about to start. Of course, we went to opposite teams. A man counted down from three and blew his whistle and everyone ran forward to the balls in the middle. Carl and I ran for the same ball and held it at the same time. We looked at each other as our teammates both targeted us.

"I'll take you out at the end," I whispered, as we abandoned the ball. I dived dodging one ball and he ducked missing one too. We played for about ten minutes, both of us taking people out like flies. On his team, there were two big, muscly guys who were super aggressive. They hurled balls at all the girls on my team, taking out the 'weak ones' first, I guessed. I was the last girl left so they both lobbed balls at me forcefully.

I squinted at them after dodging four balls and then grabbed two balls. I stared them out before hurling one ball at the biggest guy who jumped but was too slow. It hit him right in the stomach, winding him and making him fall back. The other one watched and panicked slightly. I smiled and threw the ball up in the air as it flew back down. I met his eye and whacked the ball using a volleyball technique. It hit him in the side, and he went off the pitch in a huff.

I was now the last one left on my team, as was Carl on his.

We smiled at each other whilst grabbing some balls. I threw one but he dodged it well. I threw my second straight after and he dodged that too. He raised his eyebrows realising I had no balls left. He tossed and caught them, teasing me, then I found one catapulting towards me, so I did a saddle jump. Then he threw another as I was landing. I shot my hands out quick and caught the ball centimetres from my chest. I smiled, surprised I caught it, then threw the ball in the air, sprinting and leaping on Carl excitedly.

"I can't believe you caught that," he said, holding me.

"Me neither!" I said with a big grin on my face. "I mean, um of course I caught it, of course I won," I said, getting off him. He laughed and walked us towards the obstacle courses. My eyes lit up as I saw the courses: it was a vision of greatness – people racing, balancing, jumping, hanging and all sorts.

"Okay, this, I will definitely win at because it involves strength and skill," Carl said, half scared and half ready for my response. I hit him on the arms.

"Strength and skill are my middle names," I said confidently. We both put on the protective gloves.

"Let's start with the little course first because I don't want you to be too far behind," he said, winking at me.

"Oh, shut up Carl," I said, rolling my eyes, moving forward in the line. We got to the front and the numbers on the screen counted down from three. We both ran across the beam, Carl almost falling. We climbed up the net and over the top down a pole. He took the lead but only because he's heavy, so gravity worked in his favour. I did the monkey bars and threw myself onto the platform. There were four big balls you had to jump across. Carl fell off the first and was climbing back up the platform. We both started jumping. I wobbled a lot but regained my balance, jumping again. Our feet hit the end platform at the same moment and we both squinted at each other, laughing.

"Not too far behind, was I?" I teased.

"Just a little, so I jumped off so you could catch up," he said, walking to the next course.

"Oh really?" I said, following. On the second course, there was a big wall to climb, then a big foam shape pit you had to run through. Carl threw a few pillows at me and I threw them back at him. He got out and swung from some ropes, leading us onto the third course where you had to sprint to the trampolines and jump along them to the big beam. On the beam, you met in the middle, and had to knock each other off with big foam clubs. We picked them up.

"Oh, this isn't fair. I can't hit you," he said. I walked towards him at a pace.

"Why, because I'm a girl?" I challenged him with a sharp look.

"Well, yeah," he said, shrugging. I raised my club and whacked him on the side, sending him flying. He lay on the floor looking up at me, a bit dazed.

"The only girl around here is you," I said, smiling and walking off the beam. He ran up behind me and picked me up.

"Hey... put me down," I said, hitting his back. He carried me to the ball pit and lobbed me in like a doll. I laughed whilst throwing balls at him, and he floor tackled me till we were both out of breath. The bell went for our hour being up and we made our way to the exit. On the way home, we went to a drive-through and grabbed a Coke as we were both thirsty.

"So, you have a class to plan for tomorrow then?" he asked, sipping his Coke.

"Oh yeah, I'm nervous about Chelsey coming though."

"Ah don't be, she's got nothing on you," he said, starting the car.

"Well, she had something on me today, she told the whole year I'm dyslexic, I went crazy, so did Kirstein, then I missed the rest because I blacked out."

"What, you fainted again today?" he asked.

"Yeah."

"Why didn't you tell me before I made you jump around," he asked, looking guilty.

"Fainting doesn't affect my ability to beat you in a trampoline park Carl," I said, smiling.

"Of course not, I don't think anything would stop you." He laughed. "As for Chelsey, that was bang out of order, tell me if she plays up in the class, she shouldn't even be allowed to go," he said.

"I can handle it," I said.

"Of course you can." He smiled again as I got out the car.

"I really enjoyed our date," he called out the window as I walked towards my house. I looked around thinking my neighbours could hear.

"It wasn't a date!" I shouted, walking into the house.

That evening I planned a Pilates class. Mum walked passed and caught a glimpse of my lesson plan. As it had exercises on, she was interested.

"What's this?" she asked, holding the paper.

"I'm teaching a Pilates class at college tomorrow for Teen Health Week," I said.

"Oh, that's wonderful, proud of you poppet," she said, hugging me before going back into the office. A weird interaction there but I'll take it. The college obviously hadn't called her about my episode.

On Friday, I was a little nervous as well as paranoid that everyone now knew I was dyslexic, had panic attacks and fainted all the time. May as well have told them I'm broken-hearted too whilst we were at it. In break time, we sat with Carl. He asked about yesterday as his year all now knew too. We explained everything to get him up to date, and he agreed with Brad that teaching was risky. But he also agreed with Kirstein that I shouldn't back down.

I left my last presentation twenty minutes early to get ready in the main hall. Jolene had boxes and boxes of mats at the door. I looked at her as though she was mad. I wasn't going to need anywhere near that number of mats. I picked up four mats, smiling at her. I rolled mine out at the front and rolled three out in front of me for Brad, Kirstein and Carl. I set up the music and played it in the background. I sat down cross-legged on my mat waiting, looking over my lesson plan. The door opened and Kirstein and Brad came in and sat down, followed by Carl shortly after.

"Excuse me, where are your tights?" I said, laughing. They smiled at me. Then the door opened again. I swallowed hard waiting for the bitch to walk in, but it was the two shy girls from my class followed by five of their friends. I smiled and welcomed them, surprised as they rolled out their mats. Then one by one students started filing in, each of them making an effort to smile at me before settling down. Carl watched my eyes flicker between them all in shock. I almost wanted to cry happy tears as forty, fifty, sixty students' eyes blinked at me kindly. By the time it hit ten past twelve when I was due to start, I had at least one hundred students in the main hall. Well, one hundred and one if you include the vile girl that walked in last. Chelsey stopped as she saw how many people had turned up and she went slightly pink with frustration. Then she smiled and rolled out a mat in between Brad and Kirstein like there was enough room. I ignored her.

"Hi everyone, I'm sorry I don't have a mike, I really didn't expect to see you all here but thank you so much for coming." One of the tech students jumped up and handed me a mike from the side, fiddling with some wires at the back. I thanked him.

"Okay, so does anyone have any injuries I should know about, just raise your hand and I will come chat to you. We are going to do a mobilisation into the main mat phase and then a mindful relaxation." Bing. The lightbulb goes off for Chelsey.

"We're going to be taught mindfulness by somebody who has to go to counselling because she is mentally unstable?" she said, glaring at me. Jolene sighed from the corner, ready to intervene.

"Please roll your mat up and leave my class," I said calmly. She laughed.

"You can't send me out, you're just a kid."

"In here I'm your teacher and qualified exercise professional and I take that very seriously. If I feel that you are making other people in my class uncomfortable, interrupting their class or putting yourself at risk, I can't have you in here, so please leave," I said honestly. She looked at Jolene to see if I had this authority, and I wasn't sure I had, but Jolene nodded towards the door and even opened it for her. Chelsey went bright red and started strutting out.

"Your mat please," Jolene said, backing me up. Chelsey turned in a huff, snatched the mat and marched out. As she left everyone smiled at me. Carl started clapping and the rest of the room followed. I glowed feeling like I had an army of kind-hearted people on my side. As the clapping faded I spoke back into my mike.

"Sorry about that everyone, shall we continue?"

The class flowed beautifully, and I enjoyed having all these bodies to correct - a slight tweak of a limb in a move to make them perfect. I observed the class following my every word and felt so proud. When the class ended I had a queue of people thanking me and asking if I would teach again. I was so happy. Once everyone had left, Carl, Brad and Kirstein bombarded me with a group hug. We decided that weekend we would all go for a meal to celebrate.

Carl picked me up first on Saturday evening. I jumped into the car, still bubbling from Friday's class.

"Hello superstar," Carl said. He gave me the warmest smile.

"Not quite a superstar," I said, giggling.

"Are to me, you smashed Friday's class and handled everything perfectly," he said, starting the car.

"Oh, you mean compared to the day before when I flipped out, nearly broke her bones, then fainted?" I laughed and half cried at the same time.

"Yeah it was a slight improvement, maybe it's when you're in professional teacher mode, because I was ready to catch wild Dee when she freaked out, but she wasn't there," he said. We drove and listened to the music. When we reached Brad's house, Carl beeped the horn.

"You really are amazing Dee," Carl said, still smiling at me. I looked at him confused.

"What has got into you?" I asked, half cringing.

"Nothing, I just think that you're not even eighteen yet and you're already a qualified teacher. You stand up for what you think is right and don't take any crap from anyone."

"Well that's one way to look at it, or you can focus on me being a mentally unstable girl who gets into trouble a lot, has no career path and has a mum that doesn't know she's alive half the time." I sighed, thinking how people who watch me probably think I have a perfect life but if they really knew me, they would realise it wasn't as perfect as it seems.

"Ah don't focus on that, you know what you need to do, you need to figure out why you started having panic attacks and tackle the problem from there." I smiled, trying to form a polite sentence.

"Thanks Carl, I know you're trying to help but I need time with friends to feel normal and have a break from counselling," I said. He held his hands up off the wheel and said he would shut up. Brad got in the car and Kirstein came strolling from around the corner, hopping in too.

We drove to a restaurant called Rhianna's, owned by Kirstein's aunty who made the most divine food. Kirstein ordered prosecco for us non-drivers and sparkling elderflower for Carl - very manly. She made a toast to 'never giving up - no matter what stands in your way.' After a clink of glasses and a few more bubbles, we eventually went home, and I chilled for the rest of the evening and Sunday.

Waking up for college on Monday morning, I felt refreshed and happy knowing that Chelsey was in the cool-off room for the week, although by the time I had got to Lesson Two, I already felt like it was the end of the day. We were studying Romeo and Juliet and I actually paid attention. It was a new approach to distract me from thinking about him. However, when you're forced to watch clips of star-crossed lovers, it doesn't exactly help. As I was having this mini war in my head fighting off Nikos thoughts, Carl walked in asking if he could do something with the wires, promising that he would be quiet.

All the girls giggled and whispered to each other about a cute guy being in the room. I rolled my eyes thinking, of course this is happening. He kept looking over smiling, which a couple of girls saw, opening their mouths in shock or jealousy - I don't know which. I turned around pretending he was smiling at someone behind me. Once the girls stopped staring, I darted a 'stop it or I'll kill you' look at Carl. He squeezed through the tables towards the back where I was sitting.

The teacher rolled her eyes, annoyed by his distraction to all the girls as well as the trail of dusty stone he was leaving on her carpet. He wanted to get to the wire that happened to be right behind my chair. I tried to concentrate on copying the text from the board into my book, but Carl banged on my chair.

"Oh sorry," he said, smiling. I turned around.

"Are you serious? I don't need any more girl gossip, and if you keep prompting it maybe your toe will get broken this time." He held his hands up in a surrendering sign, then the teacher called over.

"Excuse me, could that be done after my class?" Carl stood up holding a wire, wiggling it in front of her.

"Don't worry Miss, all done, thank you." He winked one last time back at me and walked out. I widened my eyes and breathed out deeply trying to ignore all the stares.

I had a free period next which I didn't like because Kirstein and Brad were both in class. I would normally find their classes and distract them from the window until I got caught and sent away. So, if I had extra work, I would do it in the library or I would wander around. Today I had achieved distracting Kirstein, but she giggled and got me caught. As the teacher finished telling off Kirstein, I stood at the window mouthing, "Sorry".

Later, I was minding my own business trying to relax in the sun outside of college when I was rudely interrupted by big-headed popular prick and boyfriend of enemy, Kane Knight.

"Hey Phiene," he said, lying down in front of me, resting

his head on his hand. I looked up at him and then back down. "What's this then, a calming technique?" he said, smiling slightly lop-sided. I screwed up my eyebrows confused.

"What?" I gave up ignoring him.

"A calming technique for your mental issues." *Mental issues...* I breathed deeply.

"My mental state is fine, thank you." I stood up, walking towards the closest college block. He jumped up to follow me.

"Na ahh, no need to lie to me Phiene, I've seen you go to the counselling place." He smirked like he had revealed the highest of secrets.

"What are you, some sort of stalker? And my name's Delphine." His eyes crawled up and down my body.

"Calm down, I don't want you to get yourself into a muddle up there," he said, tapping my head.

"Leave me alone," I said, shoving his hand away. Before he had a moment to reply, Carl shot out from nowhere.

"I suggest you leave her alone," he said calmly with a dangerous stare. Kane's eyes flickered between us. He wouldn't take on Carl again as quite frankly, Carl made Kane's muscles look like nothing.

"Alright mate, sure, I'll back off of your underaged girl, but I'd be careful, she's tempting but she's psycho in the head." Carl stomped a foot towards him and clenched his fists. Kane was quick to start jogging away, laughing.

"Gee, thanks Carl, you have just accomplished making me the headline of gossip. Again."

"What? What did you want me to do? Let him carry on?"

"I expect you to stop treating me like a kid. I can handle things myself."

"Clearly." He raised his eyebrows.

"What did he mean underaged girl?" I asked confused.

"Oh, because I'm twenty-five and they think me and you, we, are like, a thing," he said.

"You're twenty-five?" I screeched. He jumped.

"Yup." Noticing I had hundreds of questions, we walked

back into the college to the canteen.

Little to my surprise, by the looks Carl and I were getting, Kane had told almost half the college about my 'poor head' and pedo 'boyfriend'. Perfect. Although everyone had been told this gossip, I felt like there was a mini war going on. Half the year were on my side. I could feel their good energy, and still got smiles from all the people that came to my Pilates class. So, I didn't leave college that day feeling completely defeated like normal.

After college on Tuesday, I saw June. I told her about the Pilates class and how half the year supported me against Chelsey. She said I did very well handling it in the class but I had to tell her about the assembly before too.

"You were doing so well, you hadn't had any panic attacks," she said.

"I know but I wasn't even panicking, it wasn't panic I was feeling, it was anger. I was so angry with her and then I just passed out before I knew it." I was annoyed at my incompetent brain for abandoning me when I most needed it. We talked about the things that could trigger the panic attacks. My conclusion from the conversation was; if humans had emotions that went from a scale of one to ten, I couldn't pass two or I would probably pass out. If I get angry, excited, nervous or I overthink I need to box up my emotions, yet I thought I was meant to express them.

#

The rest of the week went by in a blur as I was too excited for Friday night. It was my old school reunion prom. Instead of a leaving prom, we had this. The thing all the girls had been preparing for and dreaming about for three years. Kirstein and I had been waiting for this evening for what felt like an eternity, and it had finally arrived. We met at mine to start getting ready, sitting on my bed cross-legged as we painted our nails. Whilst singing extremely loudly along to 'My Bitch's Fave Songs' playlist, Grace came in and started doing my hair in soft curls. She did my makeup with gentle pink, sparkly eyes and long, full lashes. Then we both slipped into our dresses. I had the most beautiful dream dress ever! It was a pastel pink strapless ball gown, full of beaded flowers and sequins on the bodice and a couple falling down the netting of the skirt. Brad turned up suited and booted and stopped instantly when he saw us.

"My god, I'm the luckiest guy alive, you both look beautiful." His eyes sparkled.

"Why thank you, you don't look bad yourself Mr.," I said, smiling. After taking hundreds of pictures, we called a large cab big enough for my dress to fit in.

As we arrived, we walked down the red carpet and were greeted with a drink, and had our photos taken by a photographer. It was odd seeing all the faces we used to see every day who were now all on different paths in life. We had dinner and moved on to awards and a speech from our former headteacher. He was a lovely man, very jolly and involved with his students unlike our last headteacher who burrowed away in her office and hibernated.

"And this award goes to a lovely, committed, determined girl, who had one hundred percent attendance throughout her five years at the school." I knew that was me. All my friends knew too - they were all smirking and nudging me under the table. I went up and collected my award, a little shyly but happily showing off my gorgeous dress. Kane was smiling at me oddly from the corner and I thought he may have put a trip wire out or something.

After prom, we had the after party. I walked there with Kirstein and Brad and he brought Carl as his plus one. The walk was quite long and a bit odd as we were all dressed up. I had a pale pink and black laced, detailed short dress on. My hair was down, and my makeup was on point if I may add. I could tell we were close when I heard booming music coming from down the street. We arrived at this gigantic house (and by the way, when I say gigantic I mean like, the toilet was big enough alone to have the party in). All the girls were waiting for us outside, looking wonderful and ready to party!

The back garden was decorated with fairy lights and there was a section with blaring music and flashing lights. I chatted and danced with the girls. It was strange dancing with the big group as if we still saw each other every day. And tomorrow I would go back to having two friends again. After a while, Kirstein pulled out a whole bottle of vodka from her purse! Very unexpected, but I wasn't complaining. We had a couple of drinks and I started to realise that I was drunk for the first time ever. The feeling was kind of good at the time – letting go and having a laugh. I was standing with the girls talking, as we all needed a bit of a rest from dancing. We had all gone to the toilet together and as we all walked back to the dance floor, Kane dragged me away from my group.

"Um excuse me?" I said, pulling my hand away from him.

"Sorry, I just want to talk to you," he said, leaning against a wall close to me.

"Well I don't want to talk to you, so goodbye," I said, thinking there was nothing he could say that I would have the slightest interest in.

"Look, Delphine don't walk away, just hear me out." He stepped forward, going to touch my arm but stopping as I backed away. As he said my real name and not Phiene, I was intrigued, so I raised my eyebrow, waiting for the explanation.

"Okay, so I know I'm with Chelsey, but the truth is, I like you." I laughed in shock. "I know, I've been a prick to you because you were basically my girl's enemy, but she is just jealous of you and I don't blame her."

"Okayyy, just stop talking a second. Look, thanks, I think, but also, I really don't care," I said, being truthful. Then I walked off, leaving him to punch a wall.

I felt a bit dizzy so went to a wall and stood there. As I was leaning there, I felt Carl's hand on my shoulder.

"Delphine, you're drunk, let me take you home," he said, shouting over the music. I turned around to stare up at both of him, squinting to try and see straight. Brad came over and he pulled me away and out the front, claiming he needed to go buy more drink. I knew the shops were all closed at one in the morning but didn't mind going for a walk. My head was spinning with the drink and music. Brad was dancing down the street, then he turned.

"Carl is coming." And yes, there he was, strolling behind us.

"Oh, that's just great," I muttered, knowing I wasn't fully in control and my normal witty self.

"I noticed you two hanging out a lot in college. In lesson time as well Mrs... is he going to replace me?" I watched Carl approaching before snatching and downing Brad's drink.

"I didn't invite him, you did," I said.

"No, he's your plus one," Brad said, stuttering. He looked confused. Carl had nearly reached us. I marched up to him.

"Whose plus one are you?" I questioned. His eyes flickered between Brad and I.

"Um both of you." His voice went all high-pitched as he realised he had been sussed out. I raised my eyebrows at him.

"I just wanted to be here to look out for you." He stroked my arm.

"OI OI, perfect picture moment," shouted Brad, flashing his phone at us. I squinted and put my hand in front of my face.

"Don't hide that pretty face," Carl mumbled. I was annoyed that he was acting like this was normal.

"I thought I made it clear about looking out for me." Before he had a chance to respond, I shoved him off and stormed back to the party.

I was so annoyed. What, just because I'm a girl I needed looking out for? Back at the party, I searched through the crowd for Kirstein but a tiny luminous orange dress clinging to a slightly too big figure blocked my view. Of course, Chelsey was Kane's plus one. She stood in front of me, her mind obviously ready to spit out a line she had been rewriting in her head for too long.

She opened her mouth, ready for the opening line.

"Ah ah." I held my hand up.

"Give it a rest Chelsey, I'm not in the mood for your naive performance." I dodged round her.

"Why, did your boyfriend Carl just bang your ability to maintain your oh so superior reputation?" she spat. There was a crowd around us now, waiting for a fight. Carl stepped forward from the crowd towards Chelsey, but I pushed him back warning him to stop trying to protect me again! I sighed and shook my head, turning back to her and I contemplated whether to do what I was about to do. I stared at her proud face blankly.

"You know what Chelsey, I should feel sorry for you, but I don't, I feel sorry for your dead brother, all he has to look down on is what a horrible person his big sister became. Or maybe he's lucky that he didn't have to live with you." I said it softly, not spitefully. Her neck looked as though it tightened, and her eyes glazed over. Everyone around us were silent, in shock. I didn't break my stare, until she disappeared running and shoving through the crowd of people. Brad was in the crowd supporting Kirstein. He didn't move or talk - he just watched me.

I ran up to Kirstein realising how drunk she was, taking her from Brad as she started throwing up. I held her hair back for her and she looked up, giving me the vodka bottle and noticing I was troubled. She pointed behind me. As I turned Kane was standing close. He didn't say anything. He got closer and reached up to my face. His lips got way too close to mine before my reactors kicked in and pushed him off. I turned back to Kirstein to find Chelsey running at me like a lion through the crowd of people. I started breathing quickly as she shoved everyone out the way. I started backing up, not ready to be in a physical girl fight. As she got a metre away from me, Carl's arm shot out and wrapped around her waist, as her hand flung forward, centimetres from my face. She started kicking and screaming as Carl started dragging her back.

"You bitch, you, absolute bitch, ahhhhh!"

I stood still in shock, everyone staring at me. Brad steered me away, counting to ten on repeat, like if he shoved numbers into my brain it would wedge the panic button from going off.

In the morning, I woke up with my head banging and one text from Brad.

Brad - Good morning sleepy head, I gave your coat and bag to your mum, yes you forgot both those things. I got you to go home in a taxi last night, which took a lot of effort btw. Carl had a fight with Kane after he kissed you, look at you making all this drama. Anyway, you got all the guys fighting, a girl of many talents. Just checking you're okay.

And a text from Carl.

Carl - Hi. I am so sorry about last night. I should trust you're okay on your own. It's just your first big party and that ...it scared me. I know you're gunna have a go about the fight, I'm 25 and Kane is 17, I know it was wrong, but he was disrespecting you.

One from Kirstein.

Kirstein - Last night was soooo good!! But I can't believe we took that, wait, did we take it?

And one from I can only guess was Chelsey.

Unknown number - YOI FRUCJING BITCHH!

I'm not the best at texting, in fact, I'm very blunt apparently. I didn't reply to anyone except Kirstein, because what was she talking about? What did we take?

Dee - My house now!
Kirstein - Yes ma'am.

Ten minutes later, Kirstein was lying beside me on my bed, us both looking like death.

"Please explain that text," I said nervously.

"What, about the MDA?" she asked. My eyes sliced towards her, waiting for her to say it again. "About the MDA last night?" I jolted up far too fast as my brain bounced around in my head a bit and my tummy turned over.

"The what?" I said, hoping she had got that wrong.

"MDA, you know, the drug," she said, like it was nothing. I shoved my hand over her mouth and her eyes went into confusion.

"MDA?" I repeated, trying to allow it to compute. "We took MDA?" I said in shock.

"Well I don't actually remember, that's why I asked," she said, still calm.

"Kirstein, you know MDA is a class A drug right?" I whispered in a panic.

"What? Oh my god. You should probably take them out your bag then," Kirstein said, a little worried.

"WHAT!" I started breathing heavy and my eyes started flickering about. I grabbed my phone and started reading Brad's text. "Brad gave my bag to my mum last night!" I wanted to faint.

"Okay, calm down, she wouldn't have gone through your bag - just go and get it." I stood up and walked down the stairs, my eyes searching the lounge frantically. I couldn't see it anywhere. I walked up to the door of Mum's office and took a deep breath, trying to look calm and normal instead of guilty, worried and panicked all at once. The palm of my hand was shaking and sweating as I gripped the door handle. I opened the door as normally as I could. Letting the handle go, my steamy criminal finger sweat marks faded from the metal. I walked up to Mum after spotting my bag on her desk. She hadn't turned around, captivated by work – that was normal. If she had looked in my bag she would be clawing down my throat by now, right?

I got beside her and reached for the bag as my fingers met with it. I let out a little sigh of relief. Then Mum's hand whipped away from the keyboard and jumped onto mine on the bag. *Shit,*

shit, shit. I'm going to jail for seven years, and I'm making my own mum make the hard decision of handing me in. She looked away from the screen and her eyes shot through me, searching. For the drug chemicals left in me.

"Good morning, darling," she said softly. I tilted my head waiting for the bite, thinking, that's a weird approach to this conversation - maybe she felt bad. I mean, darling is only used when she wanted something or was about to offend me. "Did you enjoy your night?" she asked.

Is that a trick question? What do I say? I didn't know whether to break down, apologise and beg her to pretend she never saw the pills or to carry on pretending I didn't know she knew, before she told me what she knew.

"Oh babe, you look a bit pale, I was going to ask you to make me a coffee but go back to sleep if you need to," she said, looking back at the screen and tapping again.

"Coffee?" I squeaked.

"Yeah, but don't worry, I'll get your dad to make me one," she said.

"Oh no, I'll make it, of course I'll make it, that's not a problem." I blurted this out so relieved that this was about coffee. She looked at me confused. I mean, I was acting very odd and needed to stop talking, so I quickly went and made her a coffee. With the bag, of course. I took the coffee in to her then ran back up the stairs to Kirstein. I flopped onto the bed, sweating like I was a secret agent who had just completed a world-saving mission.

"Phew, you got it," Kirstein said, looking at the bag.

"I don't want to open it," I said, holding it away from me like it was diseased. Kirstein snatched it, not waiting a second and ripped it open, examined the inside, then quickly shut it again. I searched her face for confirmation, but she gave nothing away, so I grabbed the bag and looked myself.

Two little white pills!

My eyes were glued to them. I breathed in and screamed a little, breathing out.

"There's two, so we didn't take them, that's good, right?" Kirstein said, looking at me for some reassurance. "One, two, three, four, five, six, seven, eight, nine, ten, one, two, three..."

"Stop counting. You're making me panic more," I said, flustered.

"I'm not counting for you bitch, I'm counting for myself," she said. I looked at her confused, then laughed. Even though this was not a time to be laughing, I laughed! Then she laughed and we were both laughing. We both should have been crying, but we were laughing, until my door flung open.

"Why are you two so alive after a night out? I wish my hangovers were like that," Grace said, popping her head around the door. We both jumped, looking at her

"Kirstein was sick," I blurted out, trying to think of anything we could be laughing about from last night.

"That's funny?" Grace asked, looking at us like we were aliens.

"Over Chelsey," I added.

"Yeah, I gave her what she deserved," Kirstein said, both of us now fake laughing in fear. Grace nodded slowly and backed out again. We looked at each other and cringed.

"Okay, what are we going to do?" I whispered.

"Chuck them in the bin!"

"No, I'm not leaving them in my house!"

"Um, sell them!" she said.

"Kirstein, are you stupid? That would be worse than taking them!" I said, trying to keep my voice to a whisper and not a shriek.

"Oh, bury them!" she said. I stopped, thought about it, and nodded.

"Okay we will bury them... somewhere where there aren't any cameras... at the Glen." We both got up, not wasting any time.

"Take your sanitiser," Kirstein said, grabbing it from the side and handing it to me.

"Your detective skills are getting better," I said, proud for a moment, poking it into my pocket. "Get them." I nodded to the bag.

"Why me?" she asked, scared. I shot her a look and she grabbed the bag.

"No, not the bag. Don't you think carrying around a sparkly bag in our hoodies is a tad obvious," I said. She opened the bag and held it open towards me. I huffed and grabbed the pills, dropping them into my pocket.

"Where are you going? Don't you want breakfast?" Grace said as we got to the front door.

"Nah, we're just going for a walk. I don't feel like eating," I said.

"Welcome to the world of hangovers, although I admire your abilities to get up off the bed girls," she said, and carried on munching on her honey-smothered toast. On our quick walk to the park, I felt like I had a bomb in the middle of a busy shopping centre, even though there was no one around. We picked a spot right at the back of the park in the trees and dug a hole with our feet. I dropped the pills in the hole. We heard someone behind us.

"What are you doing?" Brad's voice boomed from the trees. We both jumped and turned around quickly to face him and Carl. We stood close together, hiding the hole and trying to casually kick soil over the pills. We both said nothing for a while, an excuse not coming to us.

"Um, just taking a walk," Kirstein said, not very convincingly.

"In the trees?" Carl said.

"Hmm, I know both of you well enough to know neither of you would be out of bed unless something was going on," Brad said, examining us. We both looked at each other.

"Dee wanted to smoke," Kirstein blurted out.

"What!?" I said, looking at her, not wanting to go along with that excuse.

"Right, well, that's not a shock," Brad said, looking at me.

"Excuse me?" I said sternly. Carl walked towards us and

pulled me and Kirstein apart. We reluctantly budged. Kirstein tried to pull Carl away, but Brad grabbed her hand. I watched. That's all I could do. Carl bent down, fiddling in the soil. He picked up one of the pills and started tossing it up and down.

"Are these the pills from last night?" he asked.

"Wait, you know about them?" I said, confused.

"Yeah, Kane gave you them. And I told you to get rid of them straight away," Brad said. Carl looked down in the soil.

"Where's the other two?" he asked.

"Other two?" Kirstein said. She held her belly like she was going to faint. Carl came up to me and grabbed my face, looking at my pupils.

"Did you take them?" he said firmly.

"I don't remember, I don't even remember getting them," I said, confused.

"That's probably a yes then," he said, releasing his hand from my face.

"Oh, you idiots! I should have known from how you were last night," Brad shouted, pulling his hair back.

"Idiots? You're the idiot for giving my bag to my mum! She could have found out!" I shouted back at him.

"That's what I get for looking after you?" Brad said, staring at me.

"We're not children," I said, gritting my teeth.

"You were last night, and don't even try to argue because you don't remember. You just pulled Kirstein into your bad decisions," Brad said. I growled and started marching towards him, but Carl grabbed me and held me back.

"Don't you dare! I didn't make her do anything," I screamed, trying to break out of Carl's clutch.

"Like she would have taken it if you didn't?" Brad yelled back.

"Oh my god. Brad, what are you trying to say?"

"That you're a train wreck, that you're making stupid choices all the time and pulling Kirstein down with you, look at you, you're a mess!" He didn't hold back. I looked at him, anger pulsating through me.

"Both of you, shut up. Look, no one else knows. It's happened, and we can't change it so let's all pretend it didn't happen and move on," Kirstein said, letting out a big huff.

"Until she does it again," Brad muttered under his breath. I propelled forward, towards him again. Carl's grip tightened.

"Okay that's enough Brad. Let's leave it," Carl said, trying to make the peace.

I stormed home angry and went back to bed, trying to get over the fact that I had taken a class A drug - that my best friend basically just told me I was an utter mess. Trying to forget that Kane knew – how many people would he tell? All whilst trying to ignore the feeling of death I was experiencing.

FIVE

This wonderful hangover didn't feel like it was leaving any time soon. I lay on my bed, staring at the ceiling and trying to forget the far too many dreadful events that had occurred over the last few hours. It was enough to make me never want to leave this bed again. Maybe if I stayed here forever, nothing bad would happen. Trouble couldn't reach me here, surely. I found my mind drifting to Love Bay, a beach Nikos and I walked to every evening. If I could be anywhere right now, it would be there. If only.

We would sit on a little old wooden bench which overlooked the sea, the horizon connecting to the sky in the distance. In the middle of the sea was the island where Mum and Dad got married. We would look at the stars and moonlight reflecting off the water and listen to the waves gently brushing passed the rocks, or to faint music in the distance. Each night we talked and talked, intrigued by each other, wanting to know everything.

Until one night, he didn't talk much. I asked him what was wrong, and he said, "Nothing." He tried to act as though nothing was bothering him. For about an hour, we sat in silence, my sarong over us. I was focusing on the glistening sea when he came out with it.

"I'm in love." I think my heart dropped into my stomach when he said it. I couldn't say anything back. I didn't know what to say but he carried on. "I can't stop thinking about her, she's...

everything." He spoke softly, and I could feel his pain in his words.

How do you become everything? "I just don't think she will feel the same and I don't want to lose her." Although it felt like I was being crushed into the sand below our feet and my tears would join the many drops in the sea in front of me, I didn't want to see him unhappy. I breathed in deeply and put my feelings aside.

"Tell me about her and why you think she's so impossible." He didn't speak for a long time.

"She's beautiful, she's so effortlessly beautiful and I get lost in her smile. She's funny and kind and there's nothing I can fault about her," he said, lost in a daydream. Why couldn't I be this perfect?

"Is she with someone else?" I asked, trying to figure out the problem because anyone would want to be with Nikos, I was sure.

"No," he said.

"Then, what's the problem?" I asked. He brought his voice down to a soft whisper.

"What if I told you, it was you?"

My heart thumped heavily in my chest, my muscles all seemed to weaken and tense up at the same time, and my head felt dizzy and compressed. My mouth was unable to function, and my breathing was all over the place. I stared at the sea, then at him, then back at the sea again. I swallowed hard, feeling as though I had swallowed something as big as the boat in front of us. His big brown eyes were fixed on me now. My mouth really couldn't function. I mean, loads of words were dashing round my head, but none of them seemed right.

"Me?" I said, my voice a mere squeak.

"Delphine, I have had feelings for you since the day I met you. They only get stronger every time I see you, but I was afraid of saying anything in case I lost you." If he had told me that on the day we met, the day we met when I was totally obsessed with him like a silly fan girl, I would have literally died on the spot! And he felt the same way about me as I did him.

After composing myself, I explained to him how I felt back then. I was (and still am) so confused as to why I didn't say I love him more than anything and that every time I saw him, I fell in love all over again. That I loved the way he talked and looked and the way he made me feel and made me smile effortlessly, that I had spent more time thinking about him than anyone before, that he's basically engulfed my every thought. That he was the only person I wasn't afraid to let in. Yet instead of announcing any of those things, I looked at all the negatives. He lived in Greece, I could never hug him or be comforted when I was sad, and he would be so far away.

In five days, I would be on a plane back to England. I explained that I had never let anyone in before and that I was afraid of what love is and to be so attached to and reliant on someone. All I had ever done before was push people away. If they got too close, I shut people out, keeping myself to myself. What the hell was I doing? The one thing I thought would make me complete, I was pushing away.

He held my hand and looked me in the eye.

"Delphine, I will never push you into doing something you don't want to do, but I have to tell you the way I feel about you, I want you and everything about you. You're perfect to me. And to lose you would kill me." I couldn't say anything. He walked me home. "Please don't push me away like you've done with everyone else, I couldn't bear that, just think about it, goodnight Omorfi." And thought about it, I did - all night long staring at the ceiling, wondering if I dreamed it.

The next morning, I swam and swam and swam until I found a little cave where I sat in the sea fiddling with pebbles. My thoughts raced along the surface of the sea, shooting up the horizon and bouncing back off the sun. I cried in confusion. Eventually I swam back, finding Nikos standing on the shore, peering out eagerly. He looked relieved when he spotted me and swam out towards me. He insisted on us talking. We got back to shore and agreed on meeting that night.

All I remember from that night was this…

"We can make it work. We can at least try. I can skype you whenever you need me or when I need to see that beautiful smile. I can visit you. I have enough savings to come to England from working on the boats, shall we try?" His smooth voice flowed through me. I smiled and nodded.

Under the moonlight and shining stars by the sea, our bodies were entwined. There was a tingling energy that flowed through my body. I had never felt so comfortable and safe in someone's arms. His hand cupped the back of my head and his fingers stroked my hair. Our faces were close, and our breathing was in sync. His breath was warm on my skin and sweet in my mouth. His lips hovered above mine as I breathed in the comforting warmth from him, then his lips gently pressed against mine. It felt like smooth syrup. His mouth curled into a smile and his eyes blinked slowly.

"There's something about you Delphine. You're everything." That was my first kiss (followed by many more) with the sweetest boy I knew. Perfect. Romantic. Amazing.

On my birthday, I went for a meal in town with my family, the Collins family and Nikos. In the taverna, he held my hand under the table, gently stroking my skin. My body was glowing. I had all the people I love around me and someone I thought to be so perfect wanted me as much as I wanted him. A smile didn't leave my face for the whole evening.

Everybody went for cocktails after. Three cocktails later, I was singing and dancing with Lucy and the bar staff. Nikos watched me, smiling, and then whispered in the bar manager's ear. The music changed to a slow beautiful track. Everyone stopped dancing and went back to their seats. Nikos walked towards me. I looked around and realised that all eyes were on us. I stood alone on the same spot watching him, watching me. He got close enough so that I could feel the warmth of his breath. I took a sharp magical breath in as his hand slipped around my waist and mine linked behind his head. Everything around us slowed right down. The only thing alive in the room was the two of us. We gently swayed, our eyes closed. He lifted my hand and swung me around, my dress floating up and I smiled as everyone clapped. He pulled me back close, so his lips were to my ear.

"Let me call you mine, Delphine." The music got louder, and my heartbeat pulsed. I looked him in the eye. It's all I wanted. I wanted to be his, and him to be mine.

"Okay," I whispered, quietly smiling. And he kissed me. Everyone was watching and I totally forgot about them until people started clapping. I pulled away, going red and tucking my hair behind my ears, giggling. He bowed and raised his arms to start clapping too.

"Drinks on the house for the lovely lady's birthday," the manager called, raising glasses in the air. When it got late enough, Mum came and hugged me gently and whispered in my ear.

"Happy Birthday angel. I'll leave the door unlocked, no regrets." She smiled and gave me a little wink. It was like Mum's approval and permission to allow the night to go where it goes. Nikos and I decided to walk back as they all got a taxi. We walked all the way back to Love Bay where we stopped by the sea paddling. He handed me a pink ring box. Inside was a beautifully delicate infinity sign on a silver necklace. It was in a ring box because he insisted on it being my favourite colour. He took it out of the box, and I lifted my hair, turning my back so he could put it on me.

A wonderfully romantic summer romance.

That's all, nothing more. From the moment I left, I waited, waited for a text, a call, something, anything from him. But there was nothing. He didn't text me, like he said he would. Maybe because I never officially said I would be with him or maybe because he didn't know what he wanted. I know I didn't know what I wanted. I spent days questioning why he didn't contact me. After everything he said. What I didn't know was that I would struggle so much this year knowing I played a small part in putting a wall up against the one thing I wanted.

In summer, my heart was full and happy, and I came home to find myself being ignored again, broken and stuck in a loop.

SIX

I made this Sunday's counselling session without being forced. June's eyes were soft and patient, letting me talk.

"To be a cold-hearted bitch I would need not to feel and of course, I feel, maybe more now than ever. I hate to think that all my thoughts, actions and even dreams are all controlled by him. I'm sure I could write a whole book of all the dreams I have dreamt of him. I wake up in the mornings having been held in his arms all night long, to wake up and find he's not there. Yes, I definitely feel. He's so far away and he has no clue how much he's engulfing me. When I find myself smiling, thinking of him, I only hurt more, realising he's so impossible. I mean, the nickname has reasoning behind it, not because I enjoy shutting people out. Truthfully, I'm just scared - scared of relationships, of being classed as someone else's. I fear being hurt. I break down thinking of the emptiness I feel without him. So yes, whenever someone gets close, I do push them away unintentionally. I never explain to people why, because I hardly know how to explain it to myself. I tell myself I don't need anyone, that being uninvolved with other people is so much easier. But of course, there are times when you wish you had someone there." The words tumbled out of my mouth like a fizzy drink had been shook violently, building up a huge pressure inside the bottle before being opened. I spoke dramatically fast and couldn't believe June kept up. I couldn't quite believe I just told her, but it felt good.

On Monday morning, I eventually gave up trying to forget him. My intention was not to talk to him unless he made the effort. But I couldn't help myself. Thinking of him was driving me crazy, and I had to know if he even acknowledged me when I wasn't physically there. After having this thought, I sprang out of bed and marched down to the kitchen to grab a bowl of cereal. Then I sat contemplating over my cereal bowl whether to hit send on a text I had already retyped too many times for him. My thumb hovered over the send button, and I closed my eyes and… it was gone.

Delphine - howdy, how's the new school?

HOWDY? HOWDY? WHAT WAS THAT DEE? I didn't type howdy. I typed 'howu' forgetting the space and auto-type changed it to howdy! Oh, kill me now. I face-planted the table and stressed about life for another five minutes before deciding to put the 'howdy' behind me and just roll with it. Other than that, the text was kind of casual, right? Like he just popped into my head out of the blue.

I spent the day in college explaining to Kirstein my embarrassment and cringing. I was in class checking my phone every ten seconds to see if he had replied. But the group chat with Carl, Kirstein and Brad kept buzzing.

Kirstein - what if someone finds out about the pills?
Carl - Don't worry about it, I'm sure no one remembers that night.
Brad - I'm sure they do, and who's the best person to know that they did it, oh that's right, Dee's enemy's boyfriend!
Carl - why would he say anything when he's the one that was providing them, he would get into deeper shit than anyone.
Kirstein - guys you are not reassuring me!
Dee - All of you shut up, we talk about this in person, not over the phone!
Kirstein - that's a good point! Oh, now there's evidence on my

phone too! Kill me now.

Brad - stick with Dee, that will happen soon enough.

Carl - Bit harsh mate.

Dee - typing...

"Phone now," my teacher said, holding out his hand. He had already told me three times so this seemed reasonable. I tried to type that my phone had been taken off me, but my teacher snatched it away before I could hit send. I prayed that he wouldn't look down at the screen because I didn't know if our conversation sounded like we were talking about drugs. But when he stopped midway back to the board, looking down at the phone, my tensed body pulsed with fear. He turned and looked up at me.

"We will talk about this after class," he said calmly. I panicked. *What part of the chat was on the screen? What part?* I was in trouble and might get my friends in trouble and I couldn't see if Nikos had replied. The lesson dragged but eventually the bell went, and the class filed out. I stayed sitting, waiting for the lecture.

The classroom door closed after the last student. I looked at my teacher and he sat looking at me. There was silence for about two minutes. I felt very uncomfortable and looked around the room, avoiding eye contact.

"Okay, what exactly are we doing here?" I asked, pointing between me and him. He sighed, got off his chair and started walking up and down across the front of the room, biting his pencil. My eyes followed him as if watching a hypnotising shiny object swing in front of my face. Another two minutes passed, and I grew impatience.

"I'm super confused at your handling of this situation," I said, baffled. He ignored me like I wasn't in the room. I stood up in a huff ready to march out, then he stopped walking and faced me. He stared directly at me.

"Sit back down." I rolled my eyes.

"Well he speaks, that's a start," I said, sitting back down. He started walking again, saying nothing. My eyes widened in frustration. "Are you playing with me right now?" I asked, irritated. His direction changed and he sat on the desk right in front of me.

"I'm showing you what it is like to be a frustrated teacher due to a student ignoring your requests. I asked you to put your phone away three times Delphine."

"Thank you for the demonstration. I understand your frustration fully, and you can't go through my phone."

"I don't like your sarcastic tone Delphine and I need the names of the other people in that chat."

"Well, you can't have them," I said bluntly, knowing there was no chance I was going to drop the others in it.

"You don't have a choice."

"I think you'll find I do, you can't force me." His face went red.

"I'm going to have to take that chat to your Head of Year." I exhaled deeply. He picked up the phone and walked out of the room, so I quickly followed.

He walked straight to Albert's office. I'm surprised I hadn't been here before actually; he knew of me though. I was either going to be storming out raging or calmly leaving. Albert looked up as we entered, and his eyes settled on me.

"Delphine was on her phone throughout my class and has come to show you a group chat she has with other students in this college," my teacher said. I squinted at him, relieved there was no comment regarding the conversation topic. He couldn't have noticed.

"Actually, I haven't because on my behalf that would be a silly thing to do. I'm not prepared to show my phone to you, I think that is an inappropriate request," I said, aggravated.

"Thank you, I'll handle it from here," Albert said softly, smiling at my teacher. My teacher glanced at me as he walked out. My blood boiled as I sat down on the chair opposite Albert. I decided I would talk first.

"I'm sorry about going on my phone. Truth is, I wouldn't normally. I just had something I was nervous about and wanted to check but I would prefer not to discuss it. It really isn't anything serious."

"Okay, well if it is something like that then maybe talk to your teacher before and just ask to have your phone beside you. I'm not going to ask to see it. You're right. I have no authority to do that, but I will ask that you are sensible in future classes," he said. I was surprised at this very nice and calm adult conversation. My body relaxed and I smiled at him.

"Thank you for being so understanding," I said, still slightly stunned.

"Sometimes it is what's needed," he said, handing me my phone and nodding to the door. The phone was dead which was perfect!

As I walked out, I thought about what he said: Sometimes it is what is needed. If all people handled things calmly, trying to be understanding rather than being defensive and angry straight away, everything would be so much easier. I wasn't one to talk because as soon as I'm in that situation, the switch flicks and my brain roars, ready to pounce. But maybe if I tried to be calm, I wouldn't have panic attacks. But then again, it's very easy to say that – harder to do.

Whilst I was in these deep thoughts, Brad came out from a corner and grabbed my shoulders, making me jump. I turned around, hitting him on the arm which had zero effect as he just laughed.

"Away with the fairies, are we?" he asked, surprised by how much I jumped.

"No, I was just thinking about Albert and how calm he was unlike all the other teachers."

"Albert?" Brad asked.

"Yes, Albert," I replied.

"As in Albert our Head of Year Albert?"

"Yes, Brad, that's the one."

"I'm guessing you didn't see him for any good reason seeing how shocked you are at him being calm, what did you do?"

"What is that supposed to mean?"

"I'm just asking what you did that was bad enough to be sent to the Head of Year."

"I didn't do anything that bad, in fact you were doing it too, I just had my phone out on the group chat," I said.

"Oh great, and now we are all in the shit," he said, sounding disappointed with me.

"What? No, we're not. Obviously, I didn't tell him who was in the chat. I'm not that stupid. The only reason I went to see Albert was because I refused to tell him, so you should be thanking me actually!" I carried on ranting as Kirstein approached us on our walk to the station.

"Wow, I feel some heat in this conversation, lucky it's raining," she joked. Carl's car pulled up beside us on the road.

"Want a lift? Judging from your conversation I could hear down the hallway, I don't think the train is the best place to carry it on." I raised my eyebrows with all the sass I had and got in the front seat, peeling my wet hair off my face.

"Brad's acting like a sensible dad again." I squinted at him through the mirror.

"You almost got us all caught," he shouted.

"But I didn't!" I shouted back. "Plus, it's not a big fricking deal."

"It's MDA Delphine, it is a big deal! See this is your problem, nothing is a big deal to you anymore, you don't care."

"No Brad, you know what my problem is? It's that my best friend is always disapproving of me, and only ever tells me what I do wrong!"

"Wow, guys, calm down, how did you nearly get us caught?" Kirstein asked.

"They took my phone, which by the way, if you didn't all talk about it on the chat, it wouldn't have been a problem, but he didn't even see anyway."

Carl took a sharp turn with the car down a road and drove quickly, pinning us all back to our seat. He stopped the car with a jolt.

"All of you get out," he ordered.

"What?" Kirstein said, looking out the window at a dark

street.

"You all need to sort yourselves out. You're meant to be best friends and you're down each other's throats all the time."

"What? So, deserting us on a dark street in the middle of nowhere is magically going to help, is it?" I said with attitude, getting out the car.

"No Miss Sassy, we're going paintballing so you can shoot the rest of your anger at each other," he said, locking the car and walking to the entrance of a dark building.

"Is it me or does it feel like he's about to murder us in there?" Kirstein said.

"You're a very paranoid person Kirstein. It's an old centre but I used to work here and it's the same inside, come on." Carl unlocked the door with these old-looking keys.

"How old are you again?" Kirstein said, having the same thought as me about what year those keys were made. He laughed and opened the door, some dust falling onto our heads as we walked in, making us all cough.

Carl hit the lights and they flickered before lighting up the reception room which was surprisingly colourful.

"So, have you guys been before?" Carl asked, grabbing some suits and guns. We all shook our heads. "That's surprising, you're all the type of people that should have been." He fiddled about with the guns.

"What type?" Kirstein said.

"Wacky, "he said. We all raised our eyebrows at him. He explained the rules as we got suited up and he showed us how to use the guns.

"Okay soldiers, I think you're ready for the field," Carl said, pointing to the big door in the corner.

"Are you not coming in?" I asked.

"Mm, I'll give you all a little head start, then the big guns will come in." He winked. Pfft. We all sighed.

We entered the dimly lit room, and all separated to find a place to start. I crouched down behind a wall with netting on it, hugging my gun to my chest. The room echoed with a voice coming out of the speakers, counting down from three, then a bright red light flashed. I poked my head around the corner and saw Kirstein creeping along the side of the room. I aimed my gun at her and was about to shoot when Brad jumped in front of me, his pointing right towards me. I jumped up screaming and ran away from him as he chased me. I ran behind another wall and around a corner, coming back out the other side and losing him. I spotted him searching for me as I peered around, and I aimed at his back. I shot and he jolted forward yelping. He spun around, took a shot and I leaned back like I was doing the limbo before losing balance, the shot skimming my stomach, then hitting the wall. I got back up and shot again but missed as he jumped out of the way and ran up a ledge and along the top of a wall. He jumped down and landed in front of Kirstein, pointing his gun at her. She panicked and pressed the trigger as many times as she could, spinning around in a circle screaming. It was like she wanted to decorate the room with rainbow colours. Brad and I both watched her in confusion. Once she stopped as her gun ran out of bullets, Brad smiled and re-aimed his gun at her. I looked at the back of his head and thought about his comments, all his comments lately that were driving me insane, always telling me I was bad for Kirstein. Well, I wasn't. I sprinted towards Kirstein from the side and leapt up, launching myself in front of her. Brad's bullet hit my chest midair and I fell onto the floor. I grabbed my chest as Kirstein flopped down beside me.

"You took a bullet for me," she said, smiling.

"Mm hmm, and if you don't shoot my gun at Brad right now, it wouldn't have been worth it," I said, shoving the gun in her hand. I got up and ran to the side, leaving her with the gun. She picked it up and aimed at Brad, shooting like a film star on her knees and hitting Brad in the leg. Brad bent down holding his leg and ran off down an alley bit. Kirstein ran towards me and flopped down on her belly next to me.

"What are we looking at?" she said, watching my eyes fixed to top of the door that we could just about see from the ledge we were on.

"Carl," I said, concentrating on the top of the door. It creaked open, letting a little bit of light in.

"Okay, he's in here," I said, whispering.

"What's the plan?" she asked. I bit my lip, thinking.

"I'll be the distraction. You have to shoot them, and calmly, no wild freaking out stuff," I said, staring at her.

"Okay, I'll follow you keeping cover," she said, smiling and all excited. I nodded and did some army sign language to get in the zone. I heard two gunshots and a yelp from Brad. I followed the sounds on the top platform, keeping low. Scanning below, I spotted Brad on the floor holding his shoulder. I searched around him and saw Carl, so I looked back at Kirstein and she nodded with her gun, already following him. I jumped up and ran along the top wall in Carl's eyeline, his gunshot twice missing me and Kirstein's gunshot hitting him in the butt.

"Yes," I said, giggling and running back out of sight.

I watched him look at his butt then turn quickly and face Kirstein. I ran and jumped down, landing behind him and snatching a gun from his side belt. I skidded onto the floor, rolled on my belly and shot at him. Kirstein ran up beside me and aimed her gun at him too. He stood in a dilemma until Brad came up beside him and aimed his gun at me. Kirstein aimed hers at Brad and Carl aimed his at Kirstein. We were all at gunpoint. Kirstein's hand was shaking. Mine and Brad's eyes were locked on each other. Carl ran and I hit the trigger but missed. He grabbed Kirstein and pointed the gun at her. Brad's gun moved onto Carl and so did mine. Brad and I stood next to each other, protective over Kirstein who thrusted her hips back and fell, leaving Carl's front vulnerable. We both shot Carl and Kirstein swivelled around, shooting him too. Carl was taken out. Then Brad unexpectedly shot Kirstein twice, leaving us two the only ones still in. I turned to him in shock.

"You killed Kirstein after we just saved her," I said.

"I'm copying you, you saved her in school and you're killing her in college," he said. I aimed my gun at his head which wasn't allowed.

"Shut up," I said.

"Why, because you know I'm right?"

"Go on Dee, pull the trigger," he said, opening his arms. I looked at him, confused. "You never hesitate to take a bite. What are you doing?" he said.

"I never want to, you just push me," I said.

"No, I don't, I talk to you openly, then you snap at me," he said.

"No, I don't!" I shouted.

"You just did it," he said, raising his eyebrows. I shot the gun quickly at his leg to shut him up. He looked up at me and everything he said ran through my head like a tsunami, his voice echoing off the walls in my brain. "You're a train wreck, stupid choices, you idiot!" I shot again at his chest and he fell. I ran up to him and held him and his chest, looking down at him. I apologised through my eyes and he smiled through his, then Carl came in clapping, switching the lights on.

"That was great, I've never seen such an entertaining game," he said, smiling. We all left at peace with each other. Who would have known? If you and your friends are falling out, just go shoot some guns at each other - it really helps to bond. Carl dropped me off last. He was flattering me by complimenting my skills in the game. I got out of the car feeling happy.

"Thank you," I said softly, turning back to him.

"You're welcome."

We got through the whole week without bickering once. No arguments, and no Chelsey. It was the beginning of Christmas break and I felt good. I had made friends with my Head of Year. Sort of. I was on good terms with my friends. There was still the possibility of Nikos acknowledging me, as he still hadn't opened my Snap. Everything was going well.

After seeing June on Sunday, I had a notification from him. A burst of nerves jumped about in my belly. I was half expecting a, 'read at something O'clock' and no reply. I got an eight second reply with no caption, just a selfie. My eyes were glued to the screen as the quick eight seconds passed and I studied his face. Although having no words was slightly annoying, it was enough. There was contact after two months of nothing. I contemplated asking if he forgot to add the text, but I didn't. At least I had crossed his mind.

That evening, I sat in the garden despite it being chilly, drinking hot chocolate, whilst wrapped up in a blanket like a caterpillar. Sometimes I like being outside even when it's cold. Outside was quiet and calming with the fresh air.

I could see glowing yellow lights from each house through the fog and figures walking back and forth through each window - some cooking, some watching TV, some drinking and some laughing. All these people with different lives, facing their own little problems, enjoying their own little pleasures. There was a girl that looked about my age with long, dusty, blonde hair sitting at her windowsill. She did this most evenings, looking at the sky. Sometimes I watched her wondering what her story was, and if anyone had looked at me, the girl in the garden, and wondered what my story was.

Mum came out into the garden - my daydream faded into the fog. She sat down beside me, rubbing her hands together and looked at me like I was a mad little sushi roll in my blanket.

"It's a bit early to be waiting for Santa, isn't it? What do you want for Christmas poppet?" she asked. I smiled at the Santa comment wondering if she thought I still believed in him (PS. If you do, he is definitely real, just ignore me). I thought about it.

"One thing, I want one thing and nothing more."

"What's that? Sounds expensive." I swallowed.

"Nikos." I sighed and found myself falling into her lap. It was strange as I never spoke about it openly because it made me feel weak and stupid. She stroked my head softly but said nothing. We eventually went in with frozen fingers and got cosy in bed.

I woke up in the morning to Grace singing, "It's Decoration Day," almost as excitedly as Ana from Frozen is on Coronation Day. Before I had a chance to finish my breakfast, I was being beckoned to help.

"Dee, can you help me get these boxes down from the loft?"

Grace called down the stairs. I slurped up the rest of my milk and ran up.

"Coming!" I shouted. We grabbed sacks of decorations from the loft and my back felt like it was broken in several places after. As you can tell, Christmas decorating is taken very seriously in my household. With all family members present and correct in the front garden in our puffy coats, we looked like a group of marshmallows. Grace was sticking odd bits and bobs up whilst the rest of us were struggling with the Christmas lights. I climbed up on the roof with Dad like always, whilst Mum stood a few metres back on the ground instructing us. My fingers were frozen like icicles and numb when fiddling with the lights. Chief Marshmallow Mum was shouting orders and as I leant forward, I reached a little too far, slipping and starting to slide down the roof. Dad shouted, immediately moving forward to thrust his hand out.

"Dee!" But I was already slipping further. Grace ran from underneath towards Mum because she is the best sister ever and observing rather than catching me is more in her skillset.

"Ohhhhh my goddd eeekkk," I screamed, as my body slipped off the edge. My hands grabbed the gutter. My fingers ached with pain as I desperately clung onto the rooftop and were sore from being scratched on the way down. Whilst all the marshmallows below me panicked, I heard Brad's voice.

"Oh my god. Dee?!" I heard footsteps running towards me. My cheeks were squished by my coat and I couldn't breathe through it.

"One, two, three, four, five, six, seven, nine, shit, I missed eight. Oh my god, I can't hold on anymore!" And that is when I fell to my death breaking my spine.

I'm totally joking. Carl caught me.

I lay in his arms in shock and we stared at each other. Of course, he was the knight in shining armour. The guy that's meant to be my friend but has surprisingly cute dimples that are definitely not attractive in any way.

Dad came running around from the back garden with a ladder. He saw us and put the ladder down. He came over and hugged Carl, squashing me in the middle.

"Umm, guys, this is nice and all, but would you mind separating and allowing me to touch the ground," I said, pushing Dad off. Mum, Grace and Brad still stood in the same position, frozen. Mum blinked a couple of times like she was trying to erase the past few moments.

"Hot chocolate Bradley?" Mum asked, already walking inside.

"And the hero," Dad said, patting Carl on the back. Carl smirked.

"Oh, don't boost his ego." I rolled my eyes, giggling. Brad and I smiled at each other, shaking our heads.

After we all drank our hot chocolate and I complained that if Brad and Carl hadn't turned up, I would have been dead due to my family's incompetence, I went to show the boys out so that we could carry on decorating.

"Oh, don't kick them out Dee, we could use some muscles for the tree," Mum said.

"Oh god Mum! Stop with the ego-boosting. My muscles are bigger than both of theirs put together," I said. Soon after I was tackled to the floor by Brad and Carl. I got them out and shut the door and Grace almost knocked me over with the speed she approached me.

"Whooo is that?" she asked, her eyes glued to the boys as they walked away. I scrunched my face in confusion.

"What, Brad?" She shoved my arm, laughing.

"No not Brad, Brad's fit arse friend?"

"Right, you do remember you have a boyfriend, right?" I raised my eyebrows, giggling.

"Yeah, but you don't," she said, smiling back at me.

"What, no, we're not. No." I pointed at her, emphasising my no. She giggled, singing Carl's name.

Grace and I decorated the Christmas tree and to no surprise, like every year before, Mum adjusted a couple of bits before taking it all off to redo it in her perfectionist way. We both moaned, but I secretly let out a sigh of relief that she made it look neat and tidy.

Angel (the cat, not the one on the tree) often liked to run around in the boxes and bags while we did all this, and occasionally climbed up the Christmas tree, knocking it over.

"Oh Angel!" Mum fussed over him as he leapt at the tree, making it wobble. Once all was done, we packed away all the boxes, had a lovely lamb dinner, then watched Elf the movie while nibbling on some chocolates, which mum enjoys way too much every year.

#

I woke up on Christmas morning smiling, enthusiastically trying to hold on to the young Christmas spirit. I stretched out, then climbed over a moaning Grace, checking if it had snowed which yippee, it had. I hopped out of bed and ran down the stairs to see if 'Santa' had visited. After doing those two most important things, I ran back up the stairs, bursting into Mum and Dad's room, jumping on them to get them up.

"Come on, it's Christmas!" I shouted, running into Grace's room, pulling her duvet off. They all followed me down the stairs half asleep. The Mariah Carey went straight on which sprung Grace into action. We danced around the lounge singing (croaking) some Christmas songs. The music faded into Michael Bublé (God of Music heaven) and we sat down to open our stockings as Mum and Dad sat on the sofa watching. Grace and I normally have the same things in there but mine's normally pink and hers blue or purple. So, when we pick out the same shapes, I have to put my best unwrapping skills to the test, but I always lose and she opens hers and gasps, giving it away. You could tell we have grown up as this year our stockings went from chocolates, teddies and stickers to makeup, phone cases and jewellery. Oh, and not forgetting the nectarines that are always poked in the bottom.

"Thank you, Santa," I said. We both giggled.

"Oh, he does know what you like, doesn't he girls?" Mum said, looking at the gifts, smiling.

"And we know what he likes," Dad said, looking at the cookies we left out for 'Santa' which happen to be Dad's favourite. Mum clapped her hands.

"Right, everybody to their places. There's lots to do. Grace, finish wrapping your grandparents presents, Dad, tidy up a bit, Delphine, in the kitchen with me." Dad moaned at his job. Mum looked at him before he could complain. "You would probably add baked beans to the Christmas dinner and make the wrapping itself look like an art exhibition, which we don't have time for, off you go." It's true. Dad is a very... experimental cook, shall we say, and a unique wrapper of presents.

I grabbed the speaker bringing Michael Bublé into the kitchen with us. We put on our aprons and started chopping, peeling, boiling and baking. I was happily peeling carrots singing along to the music when Mum came out with the most random of sentences.

"So, when do you think you will get a boyfriend?" she asked. I paused, looking up from my carrot to her.

"What?" I said, confused as to why this was a conversation we were going to have on Christmas morning.

"I was just wondering. You're nearly eighteen and well, when you get to eighteen you have all these hormones and want to do things." Her words were elongated on hormones and things.

"Wow, okay slow down Mum, it's Christmas! Santa is listening and you're talking about things!"

"Well it just crossed my mind, you're not on any kind of contraception or anything." I cringed, looking down at my carrot. She laughed. "Okay, okay, I'm sorry, I just want you to know you can talk to me if you, you know, want to talk about that kind of stuff," she said, waving her parsnips around. I put my carrot on her parsnip, pushing it back down onto the chopping board.

"Yes, thank you Mum." I could talk to her? Was that because

she didn't have time to be a grandmother let alone a mother, or was this that chat mums are meant to give you?

I left Mum to do the final bits as Grace and I decorated the Christmas cake. It was Mum's scrummy fruit cake recipe, wrapped in marzipan and frosted over with thick royal icing to look like snow. I whipped up some green icing and piped it around an ice-cream cone upside down to make a Christmas tree, decorating it with some ball-balls. Grace made some presents out of marzipan and sprinkled on some silver and gold stars. Then we plaited green and red strands of roll out icing, laying it around the base of the cake. Just as we finished, the doorbell went.

"I've got it," Dad called with a duster in his hand, picking the manliest of jobs. I gave Nanna and Grandad both a kiss before they settled in the chairs in the corner.

"Was there strong wind last night? Or are you lot just terrible at Christmas lights?" Grandad asked curiously. We all laughed nervously.

"Well Grandad that's a very good question," I said, smiling.

"Definitely the wind I think," Dad coughed. We all laughed, and Grace told the story, and as you can guess she told it very dramatically. I think Nanna broke out in sweats from the drama.

"Oh goodness me, this Carl must have been a strong boy," Nanna said. I opened my mouth, offended.

"Oh yes, he is," Grace smiled, teasing me.

After Dad's Christmas jokes every five minutes, we all sat down for Christmas dinner. My taste buds danced about in my mouth throughout the whole meal.

"Thank you, that was delicious," Nanna said, wiping her mouth with a napkin.

"You're very welcome, right, present time," Mum said cheerfully. Of course, like every person on Christmas Day I got a pair of socks. What's with that? Why does everyone get socks? Grace was opening her Christmas card from me and inside was two tickets to a spa and stay in two days' time.

"Oh, my goodness, you're taking me to a spa!" she said, all excited, examining the tickets.

"Yes, well actually no, you're taking me because I can't drive but I'm paying." She gave me a big hug and way too many kisses. By the time everyone had opened their presents, our lounge looked like a sea of multicoloured Christmas droppings.

After a while, Nanna and Grandad got sleepy and headed home. My family also retired one by one up to bed. I lay in the middle of the lounge in the quiet left-over Christmas surroundings with all the lights off except the Christmas lights. My tired eyes blurred out the dark lounge and focused on the lights on the garland above the fireplace. As they made the baubles glow, it almost looked like Poros at night and he popped into my head.

Delphine<3 hi. Do you have five minutes?

He read that but didn't reply so I carried on.

Delphine<3 so I just wanted to ask you where I stand, even if that's nowhere, could you at least let me know because it kinda sucks constantly wondering?

He read that too. The little blue dot was on the Snapchat screen meaning he was on the chat right now reading my messages. It went about two minutes and he hadn't started typing, only watching.

Delphine<3 really? You're just going to sit there looking at the screen, but you can't manage to press a couple of buttons?
Okay.
I don't think you get how much it's hurting. Could you please say something?
Was everything you told me a lie?
Nikos please…

Then the blue dot disappeared. I lay on the floor with a

blank mind until it started talking at five thousand miles per hour. My heavy legs took me up to bed, where I counted to ten, and I counted till my mind finally switched off.

I had a session with June in the morning. I got myself up and dressed and walked there. There was still a thin layer of snow left on the pavements. Raindrops fell, melting away the white snow, fading like my hope of hearing from Nikos. By the time I got to June's, my grey hoodie was soaked through. June flapped about as she opened the door and plonked me by the fire, offering me leftover Christmas cake. I nibbled on some of the cake.

We were making progress in our sessions. We did these creative art expression activities. These sessions were helping me open up and tell her my issues and feelings without actually telling her. I wrote poems, drew pictures or wrote lyrics songs. It took me a while to participate because I was being stubborn and couldn't help but feel like a five-year-old in therapy. One day, I found myself drawing a picture that told so many stories and handing it to her felt like a communication to say, 'actually I think this is a good idea, I'll give it a go.' I just needed time to figure that out. June still couldn't quite figure out all the issues, but she decided it was healthier for me to express and her to not understand than for me to bottle it up. I told her about how I felt different to everyone my age due to being so afraid of relationships.

I wrote another poem called Blind Pain. June picked this one apart better.

"You fear love or getting close to people, why?" I sat staring back at her. "If it is getting hurt that you are afraid of then maybe that's not a bad thing." I looked at her confused. "Let me explain, a heart that is hurt, is a heart that has been loved." She smiled gently. Although she was referring to me, I couldn't help looking straight through her at her own pain. She lived on her own. She had a picture on her fireplace, of her, a man and a boy – I guessed her husband and son. But there was no trace of them living here and she had never spoken about them.

"Was your heart hurt?" I whispered. For the first time her

counsellor training looked like it didn't cover the response to that question. She halted. She hadn't rehearsed for this.

"Yes," she said, back putting on a brave mask. I nodded slowly then glanced at the fireplace picture, as did she. "I lost my son to cancer when he was seven," she said, blinking slowly. "And as for my husband, he didn't cope well. I lost him to alcohol. I don't know where he is now."

Her face didn't crack, and her eyes didn't water. It was as if she was talking about someone else's life. Her cat came brushing up around my legs and I thought about how her cat was her closest thing. I cleared my throat, pushing back tears and tried to plunge the wedge out of my throat.

"So, you don't have to fear it," she said, smiling. I sat up confused.

"I don't have to fear it?" I laughed in misunderstanding. "You, you lost everything that made you happy, and you're telling me I don't have to fear that?" She sighed.

"But the important part is I had that happiness; I have…"

"No but you don't have, it's gone, what you're saying is that all happy things are meant to hurt you in the end?" I said quickly.

"Not all, but some will, and you focus on what you had, not what is gone." I shook my head in confusion.

"What and try replace it with things you pretend make you happy but never actually will? You put on a happy mask even though you probably ache at night?" I spoke without filtering. Her professional persona didn't break.

"It's a healthy pain. Mine made me who I am today. I wouldn't be a counsellor if I didn't experience what I did." I studied her face for any sign of doubt in what she was saying but saw nothing.

"So, losing your son was a good thing? Because you became a counsellor out of it? I'm sorry, I just don't understand your logic and I think that you bottle up your emotions just as much as all your clients, but you just won't admit that to yourself," I spoke rapidly. She spoke calmly.

"It might be hard to understand that concept right now. You're still young. All I'm saying is if you push away opportunities and people because you fear being hurt, then all you are going to do is live with regret rather than the pain of losing something," she said.

"You know what you're right, you're so right. My current situation is so pathetic. I'm so 'young', too young to understand, in fact I'm just depressed and blaming him for my mind's incompetence to function normally. I shouldn't be able to waste your time when you have people who actually need you because someone close to them has died and they're not just weak like me?" She flinched at the word died, then repositioned herself in her chair. She nodded and closed her red book signalling I was getting too emotional in a way that wasn't releasing my emotions but bringing new ones. As I walked home, I wondered if she would break down and cry cuddling her cat or if she would not give it a second thought.

When I got back, I lay in bed scrolling though social media when I saw a picture of him. My muscles all tensed as I quickly scrolled passed it. *Don't look, don't look.* But of course, I looked, and I looked and looked until tears pricked my eyes and a storm of anger circled around my chest. Her red lips hovered gently on his cheek. His other cheek had a red stain on it. My hand gripped tighter round the phone until my case cracked and pierced through my skin. I gasped, dropping the phone onto the bed. I don't know who she was to him. I don't know what he thought of her. But I spent an hour searching for her profiles trying to find out.

In the morning, Grace and I drove to the spa in Hastings called Bannatyne. We spent the car journey rocking out. Her car is tiny, but her speakers are massive, so we look very innocent but sound very wild. Once, Mum got into the car and when Grace started the engine, Mum almost had a heart attack from the volume. As we arrived, we drove through some tall gold gates and down a gravelled path with perfectly cut, bright green hedges. The building was beautiful.

"Oh god, you didn't tell me it was this fancy, I think I need to do a quick change in the car," Grace said, looking down at her tracksuit bottoms. I laughed, about to say we don't have time for a quick change but Grace, out of all people, always had time for a quick change due to her many quick changes backstage.

"You look fine!" I reassured her. We got our matching little suitcases out of the back and rolled them up to the reception desk. I sorted out all the official stuff, then we went to find our room. We walked through the hotel in awe of the stunning décor.

"Here it is," I said, popping the key card into door 7K to reveal a large room fit for queens. Grace smiled and started exploring straight away. Delicate gold painted leaves were across white walls, and silky purple curtains perfectly pinned back to show the elegant gardens through the window. The bathroom shined like in all the adverts and I imagined a little Mr. Muscle prancing around in his gold suit. As I slipped off my shoes, my toes wriggled and were hugged by the soft carpet. I sat on the bed and was jumped on by Grace.

"Thank you, thank you, thank you," she said, squishing me.

"You're welcome, you're welcome, you're welcome. But hurry up - we have afternoon tea and some spa treatments to get to," I said, going to get changed.

"You booked spa treatments too! Oh, you are in my good books today." She squealed with happiness.

"Hey, I'm always in your good books!" I slipped on a bikini and a fluffy robe over the top. Once she was finally ready, we made our way to the spa. I felt like a 1950's girl going for afternoon tea in a fancy, cosy and posh hotel. The spa smelled like lavender and roses and the music was so calm and peaceful. Just outside on the balcony, there were little tables laid with delicate china afternoon tea sets We were greeted by a lady in a floral dress who took our names and sat us by the water fountain. Our eyes danced about the plates as we decided where to begin. The sandwiches were soft and light like little clouds. The scones and petite colourful cakes were baked to perfection. As we finished, we went to the outdoor jacuzzies and were handed a glass of champagne. I was allowed it with Grace's 'adult' supervision. We slipped out of our robes and placed them on the side. We were wearing identical bathing suits in different colours, mine white with yellow flowers budding around my body, hers white with red flowers. As we got into the jacuzzi, my body tingled with goosebumps as it adjusted to the warm bubbles twirling around me. I clinked glasses with Grace.

"To bubbles in our belly and bubbles on our body," I said, giggling and hiccupping.

"That is probably the oddest toast I will ever hear," Grace said, smiling. The soft breeze felt nice on my face and skimmed across the top on the water.

"So, what are your New Year's resolutions?" Grace asked me. I thought about it.

"Hmm, well honestly, to not text Nikos. He doesn't bother with me, so why should I? I mean, obviously I want to talk to him, but I guess I'm just wasting my time and holding on to false hope," I said in realisation.

"I did always tell you Dee. Don't get me wrong, when you're together he treats you like a princess but when you're not there, he doesn't treat you right at all and probably moves on to the next girl till you come back again," she said. Grace let out a major sigh of frustration.

"Time to let go until eight months' time. Oh my god! That sounds like forever, but it's been four months already so it's okay. The worst of it's over, right?" I said.

"Time to let go all together if you ask me, eventually you will, but you have to do it in your own time," she said, and she knew what she was talking about as she went through something similar.

"And then you will find a Jake and be as happy as happy can be," she said, smiling.

"Maybe not Jake, he's a bit too British for me. I need a little spice in my life." I giggled as Grace splashed me.

"What about your New Year's resolutions?" I asked, intrigued. She swallowed and bit her lip. I knew her too well for her to hide that she was about to tell me something bad.

"To tell you something I've been meaning to tell you," she said nervously. "I went for an interview, and yesterday I found out I got the job," she said into her champagne glass.

"Well that's brilliant, why didn't you tell me? I can't bear to think how long you took to decide on an interview outfit without my help," I said, laughing. She laughed too.

"It did take me a while. It was when you fainted in college for the first time and that weekend you were so busy with doctors or hospitals or something, I didn't want to get in the way."

"You wouldn't have, a distraction probably would have been nice. So, what is it?" I asked.

"Well..."

"I'm going to be a chalet host for a ski company in France." I nodded as she began, then my face dropped.

"I'm sorry, come again?" Grace and I had never been apart. Everywhere she went, I went, and vice versa. What would I do if she wasn't living with me? Who would be there to snap me into shape, keep me in check and give me harsh opinions when I really needed them? Who was I going to hug when I needed to, sing in the car with, dance around the lounge with? How was I going to cope living with Mum and Dad without her there to understand my frustration? Grace watched my eyes panic.

"It's only for about five months," she said.

"Half a year!" I said, a little too loudly.

"One month short of half a year, that's not that long," Grace said, trying her best to comfort me.

"Grace, I could have grown breasts by then! It is a long time," I said, still in shock. She chuckled and looked around to see if anyone heard. I breathed deeply, trying to accept it.

"So, when do you go?" I asked.

"About a week," she said. I spat out my champagne, and she smiled trying to ease the shock, giggling at my classy addition to the jacuzzi. "Anyway, so my New Year's resolution is to make sure I talk to you as much as I can while I'm away, if you ever need me, just call me." She stared at me like I was a lost puppy.

#

The next day we came home and I spent the rest of the day getting ready for a school reunion party, doing my hair and makeup and rocking out to some music, singing into my hairbrush (yes, that happens, not just in the movies and if you haven't rocked out with a hairbrush you're seriously missing out). Brad knocked for me at about eight-thirty. He often pops out of nowhere, invites himself in and chats whilst I do whatever I was already doing. I chucked him out when it was time for the girls gathering at Kirstein's for her seventeenth.

When I arrived, there were lots of girls from our secondary school. It was nice to catch up with them whilst I was sober enough. We all chatted, updating each other on that all-important gossip which was overdue as we hadn't seen each other for ages. The screams and screeches from updates of new relationships, boy dramas and other things was wild. I did more of the listening to everyone's new lives rather than talking because, well, I had no new friends in college and boys... let's not go there. I managed to keep quiet about my life for a while.

"What about Delphine's world, what's going on there?" Questions flew my way. I tried joking or changing the subject.

They all started chanting. "Dee's goss, Dee's goss, Dee's goss!"

"Okay, alright, alright. I'll let you all in on my secret in life," I shouted over them. They all huddled in close. I cleared my throat. "Life is about no regrets so, number one, seek all adventures and never look back. Number two, if the cliff is too high, don't be a wuss and go around it, just jump. And number three, the most important so pay attention girls - in most circumstances, boys are dicks and boyfriends are pricks so don't waste your time worrying about them, just have fun and do you. And with that knowledge with you all now, we will have a toast to not caring about what others think, to being us, and not following the rules." All the girls screamed and shot glasses swung in the air, clanging together.

"So, no boyfriend then?" a girl asked, the only taken one there.

"Babe, if you're happy then go you, you're one in a million, but for me no, I'm way too uncontrollable to be loved." I then mimicked being sick at the word love.

Obviously, Kirstein decided that the alcohol intake needed to increase, as she demanded everyone played *Never Have I Ever*. The secrets all came out then. Lola had had sex and she's the quietest one there. Ellie was a lesbian now and had a crush on Bonnie who was in the room. She was bisexual and those two got it off upstairs. I don't know how many drinks I had mixed by this point. I went outside for a chat with Jess, who is a goth kinda girl, where I had my first cigarette. I know. Shit.

Back inside, one girl was crying and being sick. She was definitely the worst and regrettably I was probably the second worst. I didn't even pull my jeans down to go to the toilet. Luckily, my girls helped me out. At about 1am, I had passed out on the sofa and Jess carried me onto Kirstein's brother's bed where I woke up about an hour later. Don't worry - the brother was out. So now that the alcohol was flowing through me, silly old Delphine decided she would ring Carl. What a brilliant idea. Not. I won't go into details but from two through to four in the morning I was disturbing his sleep. When he hung up the phone there was a banging on the front door. I left it as it wasn't my house. But the banging didn't stop. I got up still wobbly and walked towards the door. I redialled Carl.

"Someone is at the door, should I answer it?" I asked, waiting for the 'absolutely not, Dee go back to sleep.'

Instead he said, "Yes." I walked up to the door and twisted the handle, opening it. There was Carl, his phone to his ear still.

"It's a boy, should I let him in?" I said, not really knowing why I just said that.

"I think so," Carl said. I walked back to bed and lay down, letting him follow.

"I decided that as you weren't going to let me sleep, I may as well come and be with you," he said, kicking his shoes off, lying down beside me and making himself at home.

"Shhh," I said. I held my hand to his mouth because his voice was too loud for the state of my head.

"Oh, now she wants me to be quiet," he said, closing his eyes and shaking his head. I snuggled up to him, not sure as to why I did so - he seemed huggable and comforting. I didn't get much sleep at all, spending most of the night walking to the toilet, thinking I was going to be sick. I must have slept a little though, as I woke up, remembering walking down the road shouting, having to be mummied all night, stealing any kind of alcoholic beverage that was near me and almost throwing up. It was lucky that Nikos didn't pop into my head!

"Morning sleepy head, how are you feeling?" Carl's voice came from the bed. The bed, the one I was lying on. The one we were lying on, together. I looked at him and down at my body. I still had clothes on. So did he – that was good.

"Did I, did we," I said, stuttering.

"We didn't." I breathed out in relief and quickly jumped up, feeling odd being in a bed with him and confused as to why he was there. I pulled him up and put his shoes in front of him.

"Quickly" I said, gesturing at his shoes. He put them on and stood up, waiting for the next instructions. I looked at him wondering why he wasn't leaving.

"You can go now," I said, slowly nodding to the door. He laughed a little.

"Right, well okay." He started walking.

"It's just if the girls see, it will be weird," I said, confuzzled.

"I get it," he said, opening the front door and walking out. I leaned against the front door and breathed out, wiping that from my memory. Then Kirstein came sprinting down the stairs and tripped on the last step.

"Was that Carl!?" she yelled, her face hitting the floor. I helped her up and she examined my face.

"Did you sleep with Carl?!" Her voice stayed on the same high-pitched, shocked tone that went straight through me.

"Shh, no, of course I didn't sleep with Carl. He slept on the sofa." A total lie.

"Why, why was he even here?" she asked, lowering her voice.

"I really don't know," I said honestly, just as confused as she was.

As heart rates settled, mine stayed beating, thinking of waking up to Carl's face, his soft eyes gently staring at me - the warmth from his body close to mine. Was there something more to Carl that I hadn't seen before? Or was I stupid for leading him on? *This is Carl. Hello... nothing more.*

SEVEN

I was sitting by the window in the kitchen sketching when a crash of thunder made me jump and turn to look out the window. Rain was coming down like a waterfall. I was staring out the window when I felt a drop on my hand. I looked at the paper which was all smudged from several drops of water that had come through the roof. I looked up at the ceiling.

"Umm, Dad," I called, thinking that the roof leaking is probably not the best of things.

"Yeah?" he called back. He walked into the kitchen when a section of the roof collapsed in and a pool of water fell straight onto my head. I screeched, frozen in my chair. Dad ran towards me and pulled me up.

"GRACE TOWELS!!" Dad shouted. He grabbed the tea towel and threw it on the floor. Grace glanced in the kitchen. Her eyes widened, then she ran up the stairs and grabbed all our towels. Dad chucked them on the floor, and we all watched the water drown them.

"I think we need to do something about the roof," I said, trying to be funny.

"You don't say," Grace said, giggling.

"This isn't funny girls," Dad said. We all looked at each other and started laughing. Dad flicked the dropping water at us, and we all started splashing each other. Then lightning flashed and lit up the room. Grace and I very quickly ran.

I jumped in the shower and sang along to Rihanna at the top

of my lungs, trying to drown out the storm. I wrapped myself in a fluffy pink towel and wrapped my hair up in a matching head towel and brushed my teeth remembering I didn't brush them this morning. I was still humming along to the music trying to remain calm when the lightning flashed. Grace called me from downstairs.

"Dee, come here."

"I'm in my towel," I mumbled through my toothbrush.

"Now," she called. I rolled my eyes and went down the stairs where Grace was standing at the front door. I walked up to it as she walked away thinking it would be Kirstein or Brad.

But Carl was standing there in a suit. The dim light showed the raindrops bouncing off his umbrella. I stared at him confused, then remembered I was in my towel and looked around anxiously.

"Of course, your head towel matches your bath towel," he said, laughing. The thunder crashed, and I screwed my eyes up whilst holding my ears to leave my toothbrush hanging out my mouth. I looked at his umbrella and thought how dangerous it was to have one up in a storm. I grabbed it out of his hand and dragged him inside, leaving him dripping on the doormat. I went to the downstairs bathroom to spit out the toothpaste. As I turned around from the sink, he was behind me. Grace walked away smiling like a creep. She winked at me. I rolled my eyes. The thunder crashed again, and my body jumped, tensing up. Carl held me.

"I thought you weren't scared of anything." I squeaked until the thunder stopped.

"I'm not," I said, acting brave. Then I slowly backed away remembering I was naked under this towel.

"What are you doing here?" I asked, confused as he looked like he had come from a wedding or something.

"I'm taking you out," he said, smiling.

"What?" I said, looking out the window. Was he feeling okay?

"Come on, it will be worth it, I promise," he said, walking

upstairs and into my room. He opened my closet and grabbed a jumpsuit the same colour as his tie. I watched him, baffled by his confidence and dominant attitude.

"Grace," he called from my room. She entered.

"Could you work some magic?" he said, plonking me down on a seat next to my desk. He turned my lamp on and it shined in my face.

"Of course I can," she said smiling, sitting down opposite me on my bed and opening my makeup box. Carl went downstairs and I could hear him chatting to Jake and Dad. I stared at Grace as she brushed my face with powder and instructed me to suck in my cheeks, close my eyes and pout my lips.

"What's going on?" I asked, feeling like she knew.

"He's taking you out. You'll love it," she said, holding a pallet up to my face.

"Yeah, but why?" I asked.

"Well, duh," she said. Obviously I was 'duh' because I had no idea what was going on. The thunder crashed and she jumped, painting my cheek with eyeliner. I sighed at her but we both started laughing. Once my face had been painted, my hair had been bouncy blow-dried and I was glamourfied with sparkly jewelry, I was sent down the stairs. I walked into the lounge. Dad and Jake stared, raising their eyebrows. Carl smiled at me, his eyes twinkling.

"Ready?" he said, giving me his arm.

"Um, I guess."

"WAIT," Grace shouted, pulling us towards her and pointing her camera at us. She smiled and went all gooey.

"Oh stop!" I said. Everyone's soppiness and them all knowing what was going on except me was irritating.

Carl opened the car door for me, and we headed off. When we got onto the motorway, I figured we were going somewhere in London. My body was constantly tensed up, watching the sky. Carl glanced at me and turned the music up to drown out the storm. I relaxed slightly then jumped again as he bellowed out a note that shouldn't exist.

"Stop, stop, it's worse than the thunder," I said, crying with laughter. He held his heart, mock offended. "So where are we going?"

"It's a surprise," he said. I sighed.

"Okay, well why are we going then?"

"Because I want to take you out, take it as a Christmas present," he said. We got into the heart of London and he parked the car.

We got out and he led me to the Shard. I stopped outside, looking up.

"We're going in there?" I became self-conscious that I wasn't fancy enough.

"No, we're just going to look at it from here." I laughed, nudging his arm and took the lead walking in. He followed with a massive grin on his face. After going through the metal detectors, he watched me adjust myself in the mirror of the lift.

"Dee, you look beautiful," he said, meeting my eye in the mirror. I wanted to cringe, but I had never seen him so serious. I hesitated to get out the lift. He took my hand. "Come on, you're the most elegant girl I know, you'll fit right in."

We walked into the restaurant on the thirty-second floor still hand in hand. We were led to a table by the window. Music played, so I couldn't hear the thunder. I could just see extravagant bright bolts strike down from the sky over London. The lights lit up the city and reflected over the River Thames. I looked out the window as Carl ordered us drinks.

"So how are you so good at shooting?" he asked. My head flickered for a second then I remembered the paintballing. I shrugged my shoulders, not really knowing. He laughed. "You're very mysterious," he said.

"What, because I can shoot a gun?"

"No, just in general, I feel like you have lived a hundred lives and have many skills you don't even know you have," he said. I laughed a little, sipping my drink.

"It's my mission to find all these skills, I have decided," he said.

"Is that an excuse to take me on more dates?" I said.

"Maybe, so we are on a date?" he said. Luckily it was a rhetorical question, or so I hoped seeing as he looked out the window and not at me for a reply. I stared at him watching the lightning bolts through the reflection of his eyes. His perfectly chiselled jawline went well with the smartness of his suit. Why couldn't I like him? *Come on Dee. There's a good guy here, a kind-hearted guy, some may even say a perfect guy, and he wants you. Why don't you want him?* I sighed to myself, disappointed by my lack of feelings.

Being the gentleman, he insisted on paying and we went for a walk. I never really saw the hype of London. It's just a busy town with thousands of people who only care about work, or tourists who see only what they want to see and not everything that's wrong with London. Like the homeless on the street or the graffiti on the walls or the girl walking past who was leading this guy on. Was I? Well, I didn't think I was until we stopped on London Bridge.

The river was calm at night and the streets were not busy but oddly quiet. I was nattering on about how I wanted to travel the world and my hands were flying around a bit like Grace when she tells a story. I said I really wanted to go to the Bahamas to see the pig beach and Bali to visit the monkey forest and I knew it sounded silly, which is why we were both laughing. Laughing so much. We stopped walking and he kissed me.

I'm not sure if I kissed him back. I wondered if fireworks went off for him or if his sky was as dull as mine. I hoped the latter. At least then I wouldn't break his heart as much as the way mine was already shattered into a million pieces.

#

In the morning I jumped when I opened my eyes to see Grace's directly above me.

"So?" she said, excited.

"So, what?" I moaned, stretching out.

"How was last night?" she said, wriggling impatiently.

"It was fine, nice, it was nice," I said, knowing she expected more but there wasn't any more. Not really.

I had been dreading today because it was the day Grace was leaving for work as a chalet host. But I had also been in total denial and pretended she wasn't going until now. I was no longer going to have my sister around to turn to about this situation with Carl. And everything else.

We were all taking her to the airport before dinner. I sat on the floor of her bare bedroom where a lot of her stuff had been packed up. I helped her pack the last few bits when she got out the shower. Well, I say help, I was more trying to unpack to get her to stay. I watched her look around for anything missed and then her eyes trailed over to me. She walked towards me and gave me a cuddle and cried and I blinked hard trying *not* to cry. I didn't want her to feel guilty for leaving my sorry state to fend for myself at a time I probably needed her the most. I had to act strong for her at least. She sniffled on my shoulder, and held my shoulders, looking me in the eyes.

"Try be a good girl, yeah?" She smiled, kissing my cheek. There was a bulge in my neck and the tears were fighting to get out, but Mum came in and Grace let go. She gave Mum a hug who was also crying but trying not to show it.

Later, we had multiple hugs in the departure lounge. Dad picked her up and span her around.

"Good luck chicken," he said, placing her back down. Grace hugged us all one last time, then she disappeared around the corner. And just like that, she was gone. I sighed with a lump in my throat. Mum and Dad both looked at me like they didn't understand me. The concern on their faces was clear. They smiled a fake smile, and I started walking towards the exit.

EIGHT

Bad love brings bad habits and my bad decisions seemed to be increasing. I call this my experimental stage. I still went to college when necessary, but I avoided normal lessons. Chelsey didn't bother me anymore. If I wasn't there, I was with June or at the gym. I went out with the only people I could tolerate. Kirstein, Brad and Carl.

It was Friday and unfortunately, I had to go to hell, aka college. I only managed to come in five times for the whole of January. But Jolene decided to make it a rule that you can only submit assignments in person. She clearly had something against the existence of the ever so useful, timesaving, money-saving email method.

So, I went into college frustrated that I had to pay for the train to give in an assignment that could be done just as easily by a click of a button. Walking up to the building made me gag, watching all the grungy gangs outside, nerds walking a little too quickly past for their legs to keep up, goths doing whatever they do, and the Barbie's crying over broken nails. I didn't fit in anywhere. I ran straight up the stairs to the third floor into the staff room. I scanned the room for teachers who were likely to catch me, reel me in, shout and then send me to Butterfly World. Twelve o'clock was Albert. He was talking to another teacher, so he was well distracted. Nine o'clock - Jolene was tapping away at her keyboard looking flustered. Perfect. I walked in quickly and handed my assignment to one of the collectors. I tapped on the desk impatiently as I noticed Terry walking towards me. The collector grabbed a receipt and slowly started signing it and ticking boxes. I bit my lip impatiently and brushed my hair over my face hoping Terry hadn't noticed me. The collector handed me my receipt and I snatched it and walked away quickly.

"Dee," an irritating voice called from behind me. I tried to ignore it and carry on walking. I flinched as my name echoed around the room and each teacher I was avoiding spotted me. "You know you've missed like every mentoring session?" Morgan moaned.

Jolene rose from her seat and started walking my way. Terry also changed his path to me, and Albert stared. I turned around and marched up to Morgan realising it was too late to run now. I got close to him.

"You brat, why can't you keep your mouth shut? And it's Delphine to you." I glared at him.

"You can't just get away with not coming when everyone else has to," he said.

"No one is making you. You just have balls the size of peanuts." His face went red.

"Well, at least my small peanuts have kept me from the agro you're about to get. Remember when you snitched on me?" He smirked, nodding towards all three of the teachers waiting behind me. I opened my mouth and stepped forward to fire back at him, but Terry stepped in front of me.

"Not another outburst, thank you, young lady," he said calmly. I glared at him, remembering his dyslexic joke.

"Let's have a chat Dee. I'm disappointed I haven't seen you for so long," Jolene said.

"Not really in the mood for a chat Jolene. And why does everyone keep calling me Dee like we're the best of buds?" A little too sassy a comment, clearly, as Albert's voice pierced through me.

"Delphine." His voice bellowed around the corridor.

"That's more like it." I nodded at him.

117

"My office now," he said sternly.

"Already on my way," I called, walking out.

I stomped through the corridor, students going quiet and watching me as Albert followed, including Brad, Kirstein and Carl staring at me in shock. I didn't look at them. I couldn't deal with their disappointed faces. I rolled my eyes and huffed as I sat down opposite Albert at his desk. I've only been in here twice, once for the rumours that were going around and to see if I needed support. And the last time was for accidently pouring my cherry pop all over Chelsey's hair when she was making fun of a girl in the canteen.

"I'm waiting for an explanation," Albert asked.

"Explanation for?" I decided to drag this out.

"The absence, the poor behaviour."

"Oh that," I nodded.

"Well, for the absence, I detest Chelsey in my class and being in her presence makes me feel quite ill. Also, I can do all my assignments without the poor teaching that your teachers provide..." I paused for a breath to carry on my rant but was interrupted.

"Firstly, let's think about who you are talking to..." I interrupted him, annoyed.

"You're just a person, like me," I said, thinking he was no more important than me just because he was the Head of Year. He ignored me and sighed.

"Secondly, you have to put up with all kinds of people throughout life. And yes, your assignment levels are very good, I don't doubt that but, in your course programme you must have an attendance above ninety percent to pass and yours is currently forty-five percent. He frowned at me. *That's surely not a rule.*

"Bullshit," I blurted out. The second I said it my heart skipped a beat and I sucked in a gulp of air quickly trying to pluck the word back in me. His eyebrows raised and his face hardened.

"You're stepping on very thin ice, Delphine."

"Sorry, I just didn't realise that was a rule, and as for the behaviour, I assure you I am a pleasant human the majority of the time but when I come to college that goes out the window, because everything is just so annoying, I don't know why," I tried to explain politely.

"I'm at a different campus for a week but after that, for the next three weeks you will have full attendance and come to my office at the beginning and end of each day." I squirmed inside.

"But…"

"No buts Delphine, I've had enough, you can go now," he said, nodding at the door. I searched for something to say to get out of this, but he stood up and opened the door for me. I walked out slowly. "See you in a week on Monday morning," he called, and then shut the door. I rolled my eyes. I was slightly relieved because I wasn't going into college for a week, as I had signed up to a lifeguard training course.

As I walked out, it started raining. I fiddled about trying to find an umbrella, but I didn't have one. Then I spotted a coloured butterfly on the pavement with *Delphine* written on it. I bent down and picked it up. The colours were all faded, and the paper was soggy.

"That reminds me, I never got given my daisy chain," Carl's voice spoke softly from behind me. I turned to face him.

"I never got given my butterfly," I said.

"Yes, you did," he said, nodding at my hand.

"I found it, that's different to being given it."

"Where have you been?"

"Wonderland," I replied, unable to answer properly.

"You do know people say that when they're on drugs."

"I know." I blinked through the rain. He sighed and started walking away from me. I ran after him.

"Hey hold up, what's wrong?"

"Drugs, it's not funny."

"Wow, I was joking."

"Look I don't know what's happening to you, you are not the girl I met in the lift, I don't know who you are anymore." His voice trailed off.

"Carl, what are you on about, you never knew me, you just knew of me. I'm sorry I'm not what you expected but this is who I am."

"I didn't have to know you to know you were a good person. Your eyes said that. But now they're dull. Brad tells me how much you're changing." His voice became loud enough to attract a crowd.

"Well if you don't like it then why don't you just go away," I yelled at him.

"I can't!" he shouted at me.

"Why, I don't need you!"

"Because I love you," he shouted, "because I love you," he whispered, coming close and holding the side of my face. All I felt was anger. *What an idiot, why?*

"Are you that stupid to let yourself love someone you don't even know? You know how much love sucks, you don't love me, you don't want to. Seriously what goes through your head?" I shoved his hand off.

"You, you, all day, every day. Yes, I love you and I don't care, it's not like I 'let myself' you don't control it, it just happens and Delphine I..."

"NO, shut up, shut up," I shouted, holding my ears. I started running away.

"You got hurt, I get it. Nikos is a prick and he doesn't deserve you, but you don't have to shut everyone else out," he yelled after me. I stopped dead when he said his name, like my legs had turned to steel. My heart started beating heavy in my chest and like it was bursting up in flames of fire. I clenched my jaw.

"What did you say?" I whispered. He was close behind me now and his hand rested on my shoulder, turning me to face him.

"Brad told me," he whispered, pulling me into a hug, his arms wrapping around me and his head resting on mine. He was holding me like I was a delicate, fragile doll. My head started pulsing. *Brad told me, Brad told me, Nikos Nikos Nikos, I understand, I under-*

stand. I screamed louder than I ever had and pushed him hard away from me and kept pushing him again and again. My breathing was fast and out of control.

"You don't understand, how could you? Don't say you understand, you don't," I screamed after each push. He didn't push back. He didn't say stop; he just let me carry on. The next minute, Brad was holding my waist with my arms held against me.

"Count Delphine, come on, from one," he said, holding me tight as I struggled violently in his arms.

"You told him! I trusted you!" Kirstein was now in front of me counting. The crowd was staring, and my head was spinning. Then I saw black.

#

The hospital bed was hard, the air was warm and full of germs. It smelt like cleaning products and stale milk. A tube was coming out of my arm, a clear liquid running through it. My other arm had three needle pricks in it. It was pulsing. My phone was buzzing on the side, so I looked over at the screen which read, sexy sister would like to FaceTime, and a picture of her smiling face. I looked at myself lying in the hospital bed. I sighed as a numb feeling grew inside me, watching her face disappear from the screen.

"I would say it's nice to see you again, but maybe not in this state," the familiar looking nurse said from over me as she fiddled with tape and pads to cover the needle marks in my arm. "You passed out from hyperventilating, but you're alright, luckily your friend caught you, so you didn't bang your head."

"He didn't catch me, he was restraining me, probably why I panicked," I mumbled to myself. An alarm went off from someone else's bed and my nurse ran off to assist them. I noticed June sitting next to me.

"Why are you here?" I asked confused.

"Your mum asked me to come in, she was with a client," she said. I sighed thinking about how typical that was, but it was probably for the best anyway.

"How did it happen?" June asked. I paused thinking about it.

"Carl said he understands me, and he said he loves me," I said.

"Carl is one of your friends, isn't he?" she asked. I nodded. "Well, being told by a friend that they have deeper feelings for you can be a shock, but what's wrong with him understanding you?"

"He doesn't love me, and he doesn't understand," I told her.

"From what you have told me, Carl seems like a lovely guy, a kindhearted guy," she said. I wasn't sure where she was going with it.

"Well he is," I agreed.

"You've been on a date with him haven't you, maybe he is the one," she said. Was she my counsellor or my relationship adviser?

"Wait, what are you saying. The one? I don't feel anything for Carl, I don't feel anything for anyone, I never have, after Nikos it's like I can't feel anything, I'm just empty." She frowned at me and the nurse came back.

"I'll discharge you now, shall I call Mum or Dad to pick you up?" she asked.

"Neither, I'll walk," I responded.

When I got home, I wasn't questioned. Mum was at work and Dad was painting. I went into the kitchen looking at the full fridge, but I was unable to think out a combination of foods. I sat down on the sofa and FaceTimed Grace now that I looked slightly healthier.

"Ah hello, my little chickpea," she said through a scarf as she was walking up a mountain. Snow fell on her face.

"Hi!" I said, trying to act enthusiastic and not like one hundred thoughts were bursting inside of me. I wanted to tell her everything.

"I am just on my way to the chalet, how are you?" she asked, wiping the phone free from snowflakes. As I went to reply, my phone buzzed.

Kirstein - Are you coming? You're late for pres

Crap, the college party.

"Oh, I am meant to be going to a party. I totally forgot!" I said. She giggled.

"Better get up and choose what to wear then."

"How do I choose without you?"

"Go for something pink and sparkly, that always does the trick," she said, elongating the 'trick' as she slipped on some ice. I crumpled my face as she recovered without face-planting. We both giggled.

"Okay, pink and sparkly, got it. Thank you, love you," I said, getting up.

"Love you too, have fun," she said.

I grabbed a bottle of wine out of the fridge and a glass and ran upstairs to get ready. My phone rang as I was half in, half out of a dress. I ran to it and picked it up, tangled in my straps.

"The taxi is outside, where are you?" Kirstein shouted down the phone.

"I am lost in a sea of sequins; go without me, I'll meet you guys there," I said. My room was a sea of outfits which stressed me out more than deciding what to wear. Once I was finally saved from drowning by skinny jeans, and a pink sequined top with pink heels, I had to tidy up before I left for peace of mind. I rang a taxi and finished the bottle of rosé whilst waiting for it. It was rude to leave the quarter I hadn't drank, right?

When I stepped out the taxi, the hotel was booming with music. I gave the taxi driver some money and walked inside. As I entered Kirstein came charging at me with a shot and dragged me into a circle with Brad and Carl. It was useful having Carl because he could buy drinks. But when I reluctantly approached him, I could see the worry in his eyes. I didn't know how to be around him anymore. Brad also looked at me in an odd way.

We all had the shots and slammed them down on the table. No one said anything. There was an awkward tension like they all wanted to say something but didn't. I turned around, walking outside to the smoking area. Brad and Carl raised their eyebrows, watching me. It didn't take long standing out there before two guys came chatting to me. There was a cigarette in my mouth before I knew it and an angry Brad marching towards me. He shoved the two guys out the way, ripped the cigarette out my mouth and threw it on the floor.

"What the hell," one of the guys said, brushing off his shoulder where he had just been shoved. Brad turned to him.

"Exactly, what the hell. Why are you giving her that? She doesn't smoke!"

"Looks like she does mate, I didn't shove it down her throat, she took it," he said, squaring up to Brad who turned to me, wanting me to disagree with the guy. I breathed out turned around and walked back inside. I went to the toilets and stared into the mirror. I looked at my reflection wondering if I could ever go anywhere without causing problems within the first five minutes. *Maybe I should just go.* Kirstein popped up behind me.

"Let's dance," she said, holding my hand, wanting to distract me. We got to the middle of the dance floor and danced away the stress. I noticed a guy had been staring at me. He was tall and muscular; he was smiling as he watched me dance. Carl had noticed too. He was watching us make eye contact. Towards the end of the night I took my cocktail glass back to the bar where he was leaning. I stood directly in front of him and reached behind him to stand my glass down. I turned to walk back away but his hand caught mine and twisted me around.

"What's your name?" he whispered into my neck.

"Delphine."

"A name as pretty as she is, I'm Mateo." I giggled, thinking of course, Italian. I never fell for an English guy. We chatted for a while and danced. By the way, he had the best rhythm. At least I think he did. He bought me so many drinks I probably would have thought someone like Morgan had good rhythm. It was about an hour before the party would end and my feet were killing me from all the dancing and my head was spinning from the drink. So, when Mateo invited me to his room that was conveniently in the hotel and knowing it was only a few steps to a comfy bed, I couldn't refuse. We were walking out together as Carl caught my arm, pulling me towards him.

"What are you doing?" he asked. I raised my eyebrows knowing he knew what I was doing.

"Now I know you're going to be stubborn and disagree, but it really isn't a good idea, you're drunk, and you will regret it." He stared at me like his heart was aching to reach out and cuddle me in protection. I shook him off.

"It's fine."

"It's not Dee, not with him," he said, more concerned and desperate. I looked at him, confused. Brad appeared, taking in the situation.

"No, no, you're not taking her with you," Brad said directly to Mateo, noticing I was too drunk to reason with. Mateo stared at Carl. They knew each other. I could tell.

"Looks like you've got an army of protectors here," Mateo said to me.

"Best friends don't let someone get their best friend beyond drunk, then take advantage of them," Brad said, holding my hand. I could feel his hand shaking with anger. My face screwed up. I wasn't being taken advantage of. The thought of it made me sick. *No, it's my decision. I am in control.* I lied to myself, knowing I wasn't. I shook Brad's hand off and started walking with Mateo.

As he opened the hotel door, I walked in, my eyes drifting over the dark, dull room. Then my eyes stopped at the bed. I stood still not really knowing what to do. His hands wrapped around me from behind and his lips tickled my neck. I wasn't sure if it felt good. I had goosebumps running from my neck down to my toes. He kissed me gently for a while, and his hands began exploring under my top. In a split second, he turned me to face him and whipped my top off over my shoulders, throwing it on the floor. His eyes snaked down my body and he picked me up and laid me on the bed. And I felt almost paralysed.

I felt like I was ripping parts of Nikos away and replacing him with a stranger.

In the morning, I woke up, my head hurting. I rolled over to see this muscle of a man lying next to me. I stared at him, panicking slightly. *Why did I do that? Why am I still here?* I considered waking him, then decided this was one of those situations where I was meant to leave halfway through the night and forget his name. I got out of bed as quietly as I could, grabbing my clothes that were scattered across the floor. I slipped them on and scanned the room for anything else of mine. I noticed my phone under my pillow right where his face was. *Crap. Just leave it. No, you need that.* I leaned over the bed and slowly pulled up the pillow, his breath on my hand. Once I grabbed it, I quickly left and called a cab. In the taxi, my eyes flickered over the buildings out the window, feeling like each car passing was hitting me.

When the taxi pulled up outside my house, I decided what excuse I would be using when or if any of my family asked where I had stayed. As I walked in the door my phone started buzzing. I rustled around in my bag and answered a FaceTime from Grace after stroking down my hair. Grace's smile bubbled through the screen.

"Grace," I said, "how are you, how are the mountains, have you made friends?" I kept the focus on speaking only about her life.

"Were you with Carl last night?" she asked quickly, obviously noticing I was walking in the house still dressed early in the morning.

"What, no of course not, I was at Kirstein's." She sighed.

"Was the party you went to at that fancy hotel?" she asked, tilting her head.

"Yeah, why?" I said.

"There were a group of guys there that have a bad reputation, in a gang or something, the leader is called Dagga, did you see them?" she said, nibbling on some toast. I swallowed hard. Is that why Carl was being so funny about it? Did I just sleep with someone in a gang?

"Not that I know," I said, yawning down the phone.

"Girl, I don't want to see your tonsils. Right, follow my instructions. Boil the kettle and make green tea, put bread in the toaster and sit." It felt almost as if she was reaching through the phone and plonking me down at the kitchen table with them two things in front of me.

"Um thanks, but I don't really feel like..."

"No buts, it will help," she said, raising an eyebrow.

"Okay, okay." To be honest, all I wanted was my bed right now.

"So, tell me about everything then," I said, as I followed her instructions searching for a green tea bag.

"Well, my roommate Jane is really nice, and we work well together in the chalet, although I have the most awful guests at the moment." I nodded, munching on the toast that felt like sand in my throat. "But everything is so amazing, like waking up to snowy mountains every day and going out every night," she said, smiling happily. I smiled back at her; happy she was enjoying it. After we finished chatting, I went upstairs and took off my makeup. I jumped in the shower scrubbing harder than normal as I remembered last night.

I could still feel hands on me. I tried to remember everything - anything. But I couldn't. My mind was blank, but my body was sore. I had slept with him - that was obvious. But I couldn't remember. Why couldn't I remember? I felt sick - sick of the thought of him on top of me when I wasn't conscious of what was happening. But I was in control, wasn't I? If I didn't say stop, it's what I wanted, wasn't it? I tried to shut my mind up by scrubbing off a layer of my skin.

I stared at my body in the mirror and it stared back at me, and I saw black writing of the word 'used' appearing all over me. It grew all over me like a disease. I closed my eyes tight and counted. By the time I counted to ten over and over again, my body was almost dry. I put on a baggy tee and jumped into bed. I decided I wouldn't think about it. Wouldn't talk about it. I might remember things I didn't want to remember; I might remember things I was trying to forget. *He was fit, you had sex, you were in complete control, no big deal.* That is what I would believe. I spent Saturday recovering from the hangover and reading and ignoring texts.

Brad - I can't believe you.

Nothing new there.

Kirstein - SCORE!! Did you see his muscles? I'm jealous!

Well yes, I definitely did see his muscles. I cringed.

Carl - Are you okay!?
Dee??
Dee, Mateo isn't the kind of guy you want to be involved with. He will get you involved with things you shouldn't be.

I looked at Carl's text wondering how he knew Mateo and what he was on about.

Dee - I'm not going to get involved in anything. Stop worrying.

Saturday merged into Saturday night as I slept and woke repeatedly. On Sunday morning, I went to the gym to get myself back together. When I got back home, I got a text from Mateo, asking if I wanted to chill at his for the day. I didn't remember giving him my number but I was very drunk so I may have forgotten. I thought about Carl's text then thought, '*he was fit, you had sex, you were in complete control, no big deal*'. I also thought about Mateo's muscles. The muscles won.

I agreed to meet him because if he wanted to meet me again, that meant he wasn't using me. It wasn't forced. I could ask him what happened – see if there was a possible pregnancy. I got off the bus and followed Google maps to his house. As I approached, I saw the number ninety-five in gold on the side of the wall. I knocked, hoping he would be the one to open the door and not a relative. I saw a figure walking to the door through the glass. He opened it and gave me a hug.

"Hey, come in, I just found the best movie," he said, leading me into the lounge. Everything looked so small compared to him, like he was a giant living in a doll's house. It was odd. There were no photos, and all houses have photos.

I sat on the sofa whilst he fiddled with the remotes. Maybe he lived on his own. I never actually asked his age. I scanned the room for evidence of other people that could live here, but there was nothing - just boy stuff. It was like he could pack his things in a matter of hours and move out.

"I hope you're not squeamish, because it's about to get very scary," he said, grabbing my waist. I jumped for a second. I was in a mysteriously empty stranger's house, my friends told me not to get involved with him and no one knew where I was. He started tickling me. "I'm just kidding, it's a chick flick actually."

Oh, the movie. He was talking about the movie. I relaxed back into the sofa, but still thought I should find out about him.

"So, have you lived here long?" I asked, thinking that a normal enough question.

"Yeah, about seven years now," he said nodding. Why didn't it look homelier? Maybe that was a girl thing.

"Oh right, so did you move out of your parents when you turned eighteen?" I asked, tackling the age question.

"No, I moved out the orphanage when I was eighteen," he said quietly. Shit. Well done Dee. I didn't know what to say. He looked at me.

"It's okay, I've got all the family I need in friends," he said, putting his arm over my shoulder. I felt so stupid and bad for him. Imagine not having any relations! All of a sudden, I wanted to give him the love of a mother and I saw straight through his harsh exterior. I snuggled up to him as he played the movie. We watched about half of the movie. Well I did. He just seemed to watch me.

"Where were you Saturday?" he asked.

"At home." He reached forward, grabbing the remote, and paused it.

"You weren't there in the morning, where did you go?" He had re-worded his first question. I looked at him confused, like I was being questioned by my dad.

"Home, I just said that."

"So, you didn't rush off because of another guy?" he asked. His hand became a little tighter on my waist. I laughed, wondering where the chilled-out Mateo had gone.

"No," I said, baffled by the situation.

"Okay, good." He pressed play on the movie again, his hand stroking my arm. I looked back at the TV screen but couldn't stop replaying that conversation in my head. *Where did that come from? When did I become his belonging?* A guy I had only met once before. When the movie finished, he got a call. The screen said *Dagga calling*. What a weird caller ID. What a familiar name as well. Dagga. I had heard it. OH! Grace. She asked me if I had seen a gang at the party and said the main guy was called Dagga! I panicked slightly. But Mateo was a nice guy. Plus, what's the definition of a gang? It could be minor, right? I looked out the window where there was a car with a group of guys in it.

"I can't today, it wasn't meant to be today. I've got company... fine but behave," he said, looking out the window at the car too. He hung up and smiled at me.

"Come on, I want you to meet my boys," he said, getting me up. I walked reluctantly, still wanting to ask if he had used a condom, but how? How do you ask that? I should have used the morning after pill. I should have already gone to the clinic. But I was too scared to do either of those things. Walking out, a couple of wolf whistles came from the car and Mateo went to play-fight with them, reaching through the window. I approached nervously, not really knowing what to do. The guy in the front seat was smoking a joint. He had dreadlocks that hung down in front of his eyes, with tattoos all over his body. He reached his hand out of the window and took my hand, shaking it.

"Dagga, nice to meet you," he said. He smiled, showing a row of gold bottom teeth. I smiled back. Another boy leaned forward from the passenger seat.

"Aye, Delphine from the party, right?" he said. I recognised him and another guy from the party.

"Yeah," I said. He turned to Mateo who was beside me, before biting his lip, smiling and looking back at me. Mateo got in the car slapping the back of his head. It's like they communicated telepathically. Dagga blew out a puff of smoke, tapping his hand on the wheel, then bopped his head at me, gesturing for me to get in too. I hesitated considering he had a reaction time-minimising drug in his system. But everyone else in the car was still alive and young people did it all the time, so I'd survive. I wondered if all of them were from the orphanage. I thought about how likely it was that Carl could have been in this group.

They drove like lunatics, but it didn't scare me one bit, because what's the worst that could happen? The bass in the car ripped through my body, beating my heart for me. The car engine roared like a lion hunting its pray and it felt like I was finally wild, not caged. I bet from miles away you could hear the car's bass. That was us - the teenagers. I was in a car full of big guys I didn't t know but it was the best I had felt in a while, carefree, like I wasn't being judged. Like I could take this roll-up out of this guy's hand and place it between my lips without Brad staring me down, without feeling like I'd lead Kirstein astray. I coughed after puffing on it once.

"Ew, that's disgusting" I said, handing it back. He laughed.

"Yeah I know, cigarettes are better than roll-ups. Taste-wise not health-wise."

"Yeah I gathered that," I said. Being experimental is fun and exciting – a distraction from everything else. I spent the rest of the afternoon with the boys trying to achieve the ability to blow smoke rings - a respected skill I was yet to accomplish.

Whilst I was practising this with one of the guys who I didn't yet know the name of, Mateo and Dagga were talking.

"No not now, tomorrow," Mateo whispered. I didn't know what they were talking about, but Dagga was looking at me through the mirror. I pretended not to see or hear.

"Bring her," he said. Mateo looked at me, then back at Dagga.

"What? No! I'm not getting her involved, absolutely not." We drove through the night and I didn't get home till Monday morning. I decided I was too tired to hack college so I would skip that. When I got in, I ate a million mints and sanitised my hands, trying desperately to hide the fact I had been smoking. By the way, the smell stays forever if you don't sanitise. I mean, the amount of times I washed my hands and it didn't go...

As I walked passed the office, I could hear Mum on the phone.

"I think she's doing well. She goes out more with friends, she plans to go to uni after college, I think it's really helping," she said. I didn't know who she was talking to, but I gathered it was about me and the counselling. I instantly felt guilty. I didn't like lying to my family, but I couldn't tell them what I actually was doing and who I actually was with. I listened to the conversation, feeling sick with shame. I wasn't the girl she thought I was.

How did I solve the issue? I planned to go out with the boys again that night. I got through a day of nothing and went for a swim with Kirstein when she got back from college.

"Why weren't you in today?" she asked as we were doing some old lady breaststroke up and down the pool.

"I was out late," I said.

"With who?" she asked. I went underwater for a stroke to delay my response and consider what to tell her.

"With the guy from the party," I said.

"Oh, are you like dating?" I thought about it.

"Um, I don't really know," I said honestly. We spoke about it for a while then I tried out some lifeguarding stuff that I looked up online, practising for my course.

When I got home, I dried my hair and got ready to meet the

boys.

\#

It was late, and we were in a car park chilling. A car pulled up beside us. It was Carl. He stared at me like I was a lost puppy. The boys started shouting abuse at him. Carl ignored them and his eyes were stuck on me.

He gestured to the passenger seat. His look at me made me feel empty and weak. I hadn't spoken to him since I tried to push him off the face of the earth, yet he was still being nice to me. I debated it in my head then shook my head slowly, ignoring the boys shouting. His face screwed up. The boys shouting started to feel like I was drowning in their words. I felt like if I opened the door, I would tumble out with a wave of water releasing the pressure.

The boys grew louder and the engine kept revving. Mateo's eyes were locked on Carl, like he knew him. I said nothing. I was frozen in confusion. Carl slowly nodded, clenching his jaw and drove off. Then our car sped off, pushing me against the seat.

"Do you know him?" Mateo whispered into my ear over the base.

"Not really, do you?" I muttered back.

"I used to," he said. It wasn't Carl getting mad that was deflating - it was the constant feeling of disappointing loved ones. The car got slower and Snow (the guy in the passenger seat whose name I knew now) turned the music right down. My ears always buzzed when the music went.

They stopped the car on a back road where there were garages, empty buildings and little alleyways lit by the dim light of a single lamp post. Mateo stared at Dagga like they were arguing through eye contact.

"Dee," Dagga said, looking at me through the mirror. I looked at him, as did Mateo, but with a death stare. "Could you take this to that guy down there for me?" Dagga said, holding a small black bag out to me and nodding down the alleyway.

I swallowed and looked at Mateo, but he didn't say anything, like he was scared to object. I guessed I shouldn't ask what was in the bag. I heard myself saying, 'I won't get involved in anything' to Carl as I took the bag out of Dagga's hand. He nodded at me.

I opened the car door and as my feet hit the pavement, my legs felt like jelly. The cold air bit my skin and felt like ice in my lungs as I slowly walked down the alleyway. All the muscles in my body were fighting me, telling me to stop walking towards the hooded figure leaning against the wall. This is what we are warned about as kids. What not to do, was everything I was doing, but I couldn't stop. I walked up to him, holding my breath with fear.

There was a dripping noise coming from the walls, making mini puddles all around me. I got half a metre from him and slowly raised my hand with the bag. He didn't look up. He took it out of my hand and opened it slightly, looking in. Everything was slow until he moved like lightning and his hand shot up to my stomach, pushing something against it.

I heard our car door open and Mateo's voice shouting my name in the distance. Even though he got me into this, I wanted nothing more than to be back on the sofa with him under his protection. But the car door slammed shut as Dagga grabbed Mateo back in. He wasn't coming to help me. The guy holding me smiled and looked into my eyes. My breath was shaking, and my heart was racing. He leaned forward to whisper in my ear.

"It would be a shame to waste a pretty life like yours, lucky your boys brought the right stuff this time." His voice was deep and threatening. I swallowed, not moving an inch. He looked up at the boys in the car still smiling like he was playing a game, then he turned, releasing me and walking away. I looked down at my stomach, expecting to feel a warm trickle of blood run down my hand. But I wasn't injured. I was holding a wad of cash. So, what if the right stuff hadn't been in that bag? Which obviously had been done before to this guy. Would I still be here now? I couldn't believe I hadn't blacked out yet.

I turned back to the car and started walking towards it. Mateo opened my door from the inside. I watched them all, sitting in their box of shelter whilst I did their dirty work. They were using me. Mateo's eyes raced over me with worry, but Snow and Dagga sat calmly and quietly in the front. My body was on fire with rage as I marched up to the car and threw the cash inside. It hit Mateo. Snow quickly grabbed it, handing it to Dagga who looked down at it and nodded. I started storming off in the opposite direction. I wasn't getting in that car again. I wasn't going to be used. I wasn't going to be involved in any of this.

"Go get her," I heard Dagga say. After a couple of seconds, Mateo called.

"Dee, come back." I wasn't stopping for anyone.

"Fuck you!" I screamed back at the car. The car door slammed, and tattooed arms were wrapped around my waist. Within a couple of seconds, Dagga was carrying me back to the car.

"Get off!" I shouted, kicking Dagga. I carried on violently scratching and kicking until he put me down, but he pushed me against the car, bending my arm backwards behind me. I took a sharp breath in, not wanting to scream.

"Get in the car," Dagga said, twisting my arm more. I moaned slightly; the pain unbearable.

"No, I'm not coming with you."

"Well, you don't have a choice," he said, picking me up and practically throwing me in the car next to Mateo like a rag doll. Mateo held my wrists as Dagga got back in the car and locked the doors. Breathing heavily, and looking into Mateo's eyes, I had never been so angry – it clawed at my insides. I was clenching my jaw the whole ride back to Mateo's.

"Sort this out," Dagga said to Mateo as he unlocked the doors.

I opened the door aggressively and again started storming off but was very quickly dragged into Mateo's house. He locked the door behind him and turned back to look at me.

"Dee, please don't be difficult, can we talk calmly?" he said, moving his hands like you do when you're approaching a vicious dog.

"Open the door," I said, sternly, trying to remain calm. He sighed, shaking his head.

"Go and sit down."

"Open the door!" I yelled, marching up to him and trying to grab the key out of his hand. He held my wrists and led me into the lounge. I had no chance of getting out of his grip. So, I screamed - I screamed as loud as I could, praying someone would hear me. He pushed me against the wall.

"Shut up Delphine." I carried on until his hand covered my mouth. My small nostrils seemed unable to supply an adequate supply of oxygen. I panicked. I panicked more than I have before, and everything went fuzzy. But my brain switched. I was fighting it. My head wanted to shut down and my eyes wanted to go black, but I was fighting it. He was shouting but I couldn't hear the words. All I heard was noise. I had to be calm. I couldn't pass out. Not here. I counted in my head. I kept counting till my body stopped struggling and my head stopped spinning.

He released me and I was standing calmly. I controlled it! He wasn't going to let me out yet, so I walked passed him and sat on the sofa. He sat opposite me.

"Dee I'm sorry, I didn't want you to get involved. I tried to talk to Dagga, but he wouldn't listen. I told him, people with families are always more complicated, we need nobodies." I stared at him. So, I was in a gang without even knowing it. "You're in too deep Dee, I can't let you just walk away, Dagga needs you."

"You 'need' someone disposable, you need someone to do the bits where you're most likely to get killed. Well guess what? If I die there will be a big investigation that's gunna come back biting at you, because I'm not a nobody Mateo, I can't just disappear," I said firmly.

"I know, and I said this to him. Which is why you can't tell anyone about us, you don't know us. We do everything right now, we sell the right stuff, you won't have a reason to be killed," he said.

"Then why don't you do it yourself?" I asked.

"It's an unpredictable business," he said.

"Oh, like when you thought I got stabbed an hour ago? Yeah me too, I almost felt the sharp slice penetrate me before he had even touched me. So, actually, there is a reason for me to be killed because anything to do with you is dangerous. It's not a business Mateo, it's illegal," I shouted at him. His face screwed up because everything I was saying was right.

"Let me go and I won't tell anyone, don't and I'll tell the whole fricking world and I'm not kidding," I said as severely as I could.

"It's a bad idea to threaten us Dee," he said calmly. "Look, I don't have a choice, I'm protecting you."

"Protecting me?" I laughed. He punched the wall and my body tensed up. He relaxed and he wrapped his arms around me, like he was sorry.

"I care about you. Just don't do anything stupid, I'll text you," he said, getting up and opening the door.

I walked out and down the dark street feeling so confused. In the space of one night I had joined a gang, been manhandled way too many times and taken part in a deal. I couldn't stop asking myself questions - my head wouldn't shut up. I could tell the police, but I was involved. I chose to take the bag, to give it to the guy, to take the money... that was all me. I could block Mateo, avoid them and forget it ever happened. But they knew where I lived. They would find me. I could carry on doing what they needed me to do at the risk of my life or prison.

My body was shaking in confusion on the bus home and every guy that got on in a hoodie scared me. I wanted to curl up in a little ball and hide from everything.. And that's exactly what I did in the corner of my bed when I got home. I tossed and turned for half the night, the guy from the alleyway waking me up every hour with his touch and his smile haunting my dreams. I looked at my phone. 2am. I had a reminder on my phone calendar that popped up: Lifeguarding Course 5th march. Yikes - the lifeguarding course started tomorrow! I convinced myself that I had forgotten how to do a backstroke turn, even though I trained for years. Sleep was not happening. It was now 3am and I lay there researching backstroke turns on the internet. *God Delphine*. At about 4.30am, I finally fell asleep.

I woke up at 6am feeling sick with a banging headache - fabulous. I got all my stuff ready and forced a quick bite to eat, I then paced around the house for about an hour and did some housework to distract myself before leaving. Mum seemed to be okay with me going on the course during college time, even though she knew I was meant to be at college. She also knew I never really went into college, so this was a better thing to do with my time than nothing.

I felt a little more confident knowing the basics of the course from my research and from yesterday with Kirstein. Not to mention that I choked her twice and drowned her once, but I think I got the hang of it in the end. It was lucky I practised on her first and not someone from the course. Today we started with a water test to see if I was able to get on the course. I could do all the requirements, but the only downfall was not being able to wear goggles. It was like trying to drive blindfolded - I mean, I know I wasn't in control of a big vehicle, but I could have still crashed into the wall. Dad said I was being silly and that I should just open my eyes. But I was sure it wasn't that simple.

I was met at the reception desk by Steve, whose lips didn't even attempt a small stretch of a smile to greet me. He seemed very dull, which was a problem as I like to crack the jokes when I'm nervous. I get that from Dad. and the jokes too, which is even worse.

I had to wait for the schools to finish swimming. Jake, Grace's boyfriend, was teaching where I was waiting. All the kids got excited that Jake's almost sister was here, which was cute. They slowly filed out.

"You gotta do six lengths front, knock ya self out," Steve

said, unenthusiastically. I slipped into the pool and positioned myself along a black line printed on the bottom of the pool, so I would be able to follow a straight line. I took a deep breath, ducked under and pushed off. I squinted, opened my eyes and started swimming softly through the water - one length, two lengths, three, four, five and six. Done. It didn't sting too bad - a little prickly but not half as bad as I thought. Steve looked over.

"Ya done?" *Um hello. You're meant to be assessing me. Surely you should be paying attention.* Any ho.

"Yeah." Thank god he was passing over to Sam.

"You alright, ready for next part?" Sam said.

I finished swimming over and gripped the side.

"Yeah, sure."

"Okay, so you just need to, pick up the brick from the bottom, then get out and dive in collecting the other brick. Go whenever you're ready." I took a breath but not quite a big enough one as I ran out of air halfway down. It was too tempting to come back up, but I couldn't do that – I'd look stupid. I forced myself down, gagging for air, grabbing the brick and powerfully pushing off the bottom. I took a breath of sweet air and climbed out, acting as though it was easy peasy lemon squeezy, although I huffed a bit when talking.

"Well done, I hate going to the bottom of this pool," Sam said.

"Yeah. I know, the ears init." Then I positioned myself to dive in to get the next one, making sure I took a big gulp of air beforehand. I reluctantly opened my eyes in the water and picked up the brick, coming back up to the surface.

"Okay great, just the timed swim left now, have a little breather then dive in and swim fifty metres, aiming for under a minute, we'll go in forty-five seconds when the red hand gets to the top," he said, referring to the racing clock on the wall. I aligned myself above a black line again and got ready to dive. "Ready... go." I jumped, flying, pushing through the water and swimming to the end. I flip turned and swam back.

"Very good, thirty-five seconds, okay we're done, you've

passed." I was handed a pink slip that I needed to bring with me in the morning to start the intensive training. So not too hard after all, although my lungs were a bit confused as to what I had just done to them. When I got home, I got into my pyjamas and sipped on some tea, trying not to panic about tomorrow.

Mateo - I'm coming to pick you up, had hard day, need to relax.

I'm sorry - had he forgotten how our last meeting went? I didn't know whether to reply. I could just keep making excuses each time he texted. He would eventually give up.

Delphine<3 - I can't. I start my training early tomorrow.
Mateo - are you serious? Training for what!? Whatever, it doesn't matter, I'll go out with the boys, but we are meeting soon.

When I arrived for the course the next day, there was a group of boys about my age sat around a table in the cafeteria. I joined them, then a man named John came over.

"Hello everyone, I'm John and I'll be your trainer for the week. This is Jake who will be assisting me," he said, pointing to Grace's boyfriend. We made our way upstairs and thankfully there were two girls on the course who were sisters. I was relieved I wasn't the only girl, but they were always partnered up together and I went with one of the boys anyway. The theory part was boring, and the medical side was a lot to take in, but super interesting. The practical pool part was great. I really enjoyed it and was rather good, so that was a bonus. We learnt everything you could possibly think of to do with pool rescues and first aid.

After day one had finished, I felt exhausted. As I walked out of the centre, the cold air froze my wet hair to my neck. I pulled my hoodie sleeves over my fingers. A familiar car pulled up beside me.

"Hello babe, in you get," Mateo said as the window went down. My body tensed up as I looked at him. *Say something - play it cool.*

"Huh, I'm exhausted, I can't come out tonight, especially like this," I said, pointing to my face.

"No problem, you can sleep at mine, I live closer to here anyway, so I can drop you off tomorrow morning. You look perfect, you don't need to dress up for anyone," he said. I chewed my lip. Did I really want to stay with the guy who was so aggressive with me, or was he only doing that because he was forced to? He was perfect without the gang, wasn't he? *I could just stay at his. No gang business. It'll be okay, won't it?*

"Alright," I said, slipping into the car.

He cooked some pasta as I did my coursework, then we went up to bed. He gave me a T-shirt to wear which was literally a dress on me. I lay falling asleep as he hugged me from behind.

"Looked like there was a lot of guys on your course?" he said through my hair.

"Mhm," I agreed sleepily.

"Do you talk to them?" he asked. I yawned.

"I mean, obviously... they are on my course," I said with as much sass as possible. He sighed.

"Have any of them followed you on social media or anything?"

"One or two of them I think have, yeah," I said, still wanting to sleep. He pulled on my shoulder, so I was lying on my back and he leaned over me.

"Who? Show me."

"What? No, I'm tired." I tried to turn back over, but he picked up my phone from the side, still not letting me. I huffed.

"Who is Brad?" he asked, squinting at the phone.

"He's my best friend. Can I please go to sleep now?" I said, irritated. I snatched the phone from him. Brad should have known that I was still angry at him for telling Carl about Nikos.. His text was asking what I was doing.

Delphine<3 - can't talk, training as lifeguard. Stressed.
Brad - I don't know why you're so stressed, lifeguards don't even

do anything they just sit on poolside.

As you can guess, I got very angry. I probably blew off more than I should have as I was so stressed already.

Delphine<3 - What the hell Brad! You know this is really stressful, a bit of support rather than whatever shit that was would be a better idea. Wow some friend u are!

Brad - Wow, that was a joke. You are really aggie lately, chill. I don't know what you're hiding from me but whatever it is I'm gunna find out.

Delphine<3 - ha, go away. Stop pretending like u know everything.

Brad - you're impossible

Delphine<3 - give up then!

Brad - you know what, okay, I will speak to you when you've calmed down.

It annoyed me how much he could keep calm and not fight back. I hated people trying to dig around in my business even if he was my best mate. But right now, all I needed to focus on was this course. I groaned and slammed the phone down on the side. Mateo was still leaning over me. I raised my eyebrows at him, a hint for him to get off.

"Okay, okay," he said, raising his hand in a surrendering sign. He kissed my forehead and then settled beside me. I didn't know why he was getting so protective. I felt trapped and regretted going over.

When my alarm went off, I woke up with his heavy arm pinning me to the bed.

"Ugh, turn that off," he groaned.

"Well I would but I can't move." I wriggled under his arm. I turned it off and went to get up, until he pulled me back, hugging me. I laughed a little.

"Alright, get off, I need to get ready," I said, pushing him off.

"Well Miss Subtle, of course, I'll get off if you promise to meet me tonight."

"No, I can't, I have to focus on the exam."

"You aren't going to make it to the exam then because I'm not letting go," he said, hugging my waist and pulling me back, lying down next to him.

"Seriously, you're going to make me late," I moaned, trying to pull his arms apart.

"You can miss today."

"No, no I can't, this is important, I can't miss it." I was getting irritated now.

"Am I not important?"

"Mateo get off," I said, ignoring him. He climbed on top of me and his hand clasped my face to look at him. "Am I not important?" he repeated more sternly. I breathed indignantly. He sat up, his hands gripping my sides. It felt like my ribs were bruising. I moaned a little.

"Mateo, you're hurting me." His eyes were angry. My head started feeling pressure and I couldn't breathe properly as his grip tightened. My voice abandoned me. I could feel it happening and I started counting. Then he loosened his grip looking down at his hands as if realising he had lost control for a second and felt bad. I shoved him off. Neither of us said anything. I stormed out angry and confused.

After five full days of intense training and sneaking out the back exits in case Mateo was there, I only just survived the exam. We started off on the pool practical. Before it started, I stood nervously, staring at my soggy toes on the cold tiled floor. It went quite well.

We moved on to the CPR and medical section and that also went well. The theory part which I was most scared of was so much better than I thought. We just sat in a circle on the floor casually and discussed it. And ta da, I passed!

I text Kirstein straight away. About ten minutes after, Carl posted in the group chat to go to his for a celebratory drink. Although we were all on a rocky patch from the other night, I thought it would be good to start afresh. I was the first to arrive. After he had hugged me well done, he sat me down on the sofa and handed me a cider. He broke the silence after a couple of sips.

"Dee, we need to talk about Mateo," he said. I rolled my eyes. "Why?"

"Because he isn't a good person."

"You don't even know him," I said, thinking he was just jealous.

"Dee, trust me, I know him. He was involved with some bad stuff, and I'm worried about you," he said. I wanted to ignore it but wanted to know more at the same time.

"Well, I'm not going to get involved in any bad stuff, I told you."

"That's not what I'm afraid of." His face crumpled as he tried to figure out what he was going to say.

"It's his ex, he was on trial for assault Dee." My head flickered through the last couple of days with Mateo - the aggressiveness that morning, the questioning, the tight grip - Carl watched my body tense up. I didn't act shocked and that was the problem. I already knew and I chose not to pay attention to it.

"Has he hurt you?" Carl said. I was still stuck in a slideshow of all the times that weren't right with Mateo. "Dee." Carl shook my shoulders. I zoned back in, looking at Carl's worried eyes.

"No," I said quickly. I didn't want to look weak. I wasn't the kind of girl that would be controlled by someone. Carl went to say something, knowing I wasn't being truthful, but Kirstein arrived banging on the door whilst screaming. Carl let her in, and she charged at me and took me out on the sofa.

"CONGRATULATIONS! You can now perform mouth to mouth on super hot guys in swimming trunks!" She waved a bottle of bubbly, that she had obviously stolen from her house. I laughed.

"More like watch the elderly swim up and down a pool." Kirstein looked at me.

"That is not the spirit," she said disappointed, going to collect glasses from Carl's kitchen.

"Where's Brad? That boy should have been the quickest to

get ready," Kirstein shouted from the kitchen. Carl watched her march around, searching for glasses.

"Top left cupboard," he said. Kirstein grabbed the glasses and poured out four but very poorly as she had to wait two minutes for each glasses' bubbles to go down. Carl rang Brad on speaker phone.

"Hi mate, where are you?" he said.

"I don't know if Dee wants me there." Kirstein and Carl looked at me and I swallowed. I sighed.

"Don't be stupid Brad, it was a little tiff," I said, grabbing the phone.

"So, you won't bite my head off?" he asked, half-joking.

"Only if you don't make a joke about me passing an exam on being able to sit on a chair and watch a pool."

"I was joking. I know there's much more to it than that, I promise I'll be on my best behaviour, I'll be there in ten," he said, and he hung up. When he arrived, we had already had a glass of bubbly, and decided it was a good excuse to have two toasts. Kirstein was being overly excited, not due to the drink but just in general. She was trying to act happy for me, but it didn't seem right. She had been speaking like she had word diarrhoea for the last twenty minutes straight. I watched intrigued and concluded that she was hiding something.

"Kirstein," I interrupted. She paused and took a much-needed breath. "Spill," I said, clocking her. She squirmed a little and the boys looked at us confused.

"Well, remember in Year Eight... when I told you I would have to move back to Denmark..." she said.

"Yeah, we both cried for a day, but it's four years later and we're going strong."

"Yeah, well, we can't afford to stay here any longer. Mum wants to move back to where our family are." I stared at her.

"Wait, you really are going, when?" I choked, squinting and waiting for the answer.

"Two days." All energy flooded out of my body and my hand went weak. I dropped my glass which Carl caught. I stared at her and saw her getting smaller and smaller, flying miles and miles away. I couldn't say anything.

"Wait, is that why you wouldn't let me come over, because you were packing your house up?" Brad said in realisation. Kirstein nodded biting her lip and still looking at me.

"Why didn't you tell us?" Carl asked, placing my glass on the side.

"Because, Dee is doing an important course and has a lot going on. I didn't want to add anything to her plate," she said, breaking eye contact with me. The boys looked at me and I felt tears racing to my eyes. I wriggled across the sofa and snuggled up to her, letting her stroke my hair like a mother would.

"I'm sorry to put a downer on the day." She sighed. I was worried. I was so worried. What if she wasn't treated nicely there? What if it would be like going back to primary school for her when she had no one? I wouldn't be there to help. I looked up at her kind face and sobbed. She rubbed my back.

"Oh, Dee I'm sorry," she said, sobbing now too.

"How can you leave me with these two?" I tried to laugh at the same time as the boys rolled their eyes. I made sure I left before Kirstein and Brad so Carl couldn't catch me and question me again.

In the morning, I got a call from the sports complex that Grace worked at. They invited me in tonight for a shadow shift. I FaceTimed Grace as soon as I got off the phone. She picked up after the second ring. I spoke before she could say hello.

"I have a shadow shift tonight at the sports complex!" I squeaked, half excited and half nervous. She giggled.

"That's great! I wish I was still that excited to work there for when I come back."

"Don't put a downer on the situation."

"Sorry, sorry, that's really good though, well done, who is your manager tonight?" she asked.

"Um I'm not sure, I think the guy on the phone said his name was Jason."

"Okay, he's not as scary as he pretends to be. Also, if any staff ask you to stir the pool, add kettle water or count the steps in the building, they are playing a prank on you okay?" I nodded, taking in the information.

As I walked into the centre, my manager introduced himself and did a little induction presentation, then he handed me over to two lifeguards who would teach me the ropes. The two guys were massively flirtatious. As we were watering down poolside, they threw buckets of water at me.

"Oh my god, stop I'm going out after this," I said, screaming and running away, only to be cornered off by both of them. One and then two buckets of water were chucked at me. I squealed and stood still dripping for a second, then looked up and smiled, running towards one of the guys. I gave him a wet hug. He didn't squirm like I hoped. Instead, he engulfed me back in a bear hug.

"Awh here, I'll warm you up," he said, rubbing my back playfully. I giggled then jumped as the pool door slammed. Mateo stormed in. He had text me earlier saying he was at the gym and would wait for me to finish. Obviously, I had ignored it.

"What's going on here?" he shouted.

"Mateo, calm down," I said quickly, walking towards him, putting my hand on his arm. He shoved it off and carried on walking towards the boys.

"No, who are you? And what do you think you're playing at?" He pointed and waved his finger at the lifeguard who had been hugging me.

"Mate, chill," he said, lifting his hands up in the air. The other lifeguard stepped in too.

"Sorry, even if you know Delphine you can't be on poolside right now, so I think you should make your way outside," he said, gesturing to the door. Mateo's face switched to anger and his body tensed up.

"You what?" he threatened, stepping towards them. I ran in front of him.

"Mateo! What are you doing? Just leave."

"You're asking me to leave. Okay, fine you're coming with

me to get your stuff."

"No, I'm not coming with you," I said calmly.

"Yes, you are Delphine, now!" he said through clenched teeth, grabbing my arm and pulling me along.

"Mateo get off, let go!" I shouted. But then I couldn't breathe and couldn't think to count. My boss walked in, standing in the doorway with a look of concern on his face.

"Excuse me, you need to get off my staff," he said. Mateo was still breathing heavily as his hand gripped my arm tight.

"No, we are leaving."

"Look, I don't want to have to call the police on you," my boss said. Mateo's grip loosened at the word police. He looked at me, waiting for me to agree to go with him but I didn't react. He threw my arm down and stormed out.

Precious oxygen made its way back into my lungs and fed my body.

"I am so sorry," I whispered, looking at the lifeguards and my boss.

"That's not your fault Delphine. If you need help, you can talk to me. I have the right to protect you as my staff member."

As I was walking home, I was scared in case Mateo would be waiting. Walking through dark alleys made me all jumpy. So, when my phone pinged, my heart skipped a beat. I let out a sigh reading the screen.

Mateo - You've got one chance to solve this, meet me at the glen at midnight or ur never gunna see me again.

I replied, then blocked his number straight away.

Delphine<3 - That's fine by me, I don't want to see you again, you've known me for a couple of weeks, you can't come and try control me like that.

Pretty boys don't have pretty hearts; a lesson I kept being taught. The bad part was that I didn't care at all. I had zero feelings for him. He was just a distraction.

NINE

Dear Kirstein,
It always seems to amaze me, how quickly change occurs.
It seems like only yesterday, I met the blonde little girl from next door.
We grew up together hand in hand, we were hardly seen apart.
I want to thank you for being my second sister, and for remaining in my heart.
If it wasn't for you I wouldn't be the person I am today.
I see you in myself, in many different ways.
I enjoyed every moment we spent giggling the days away.
I loved every hour we spent playing games.
I will cherish every moment, we ever spent together
no matter if it was happy or sad. I'll remember it forever.
We knew this day was coming, when you would have to leave,
but that means nothing, because we're one, you and me.
I will always be here, no matter how far you go.
You could climb mountains and cross oceans and I would still follow.
I will be your shining star, not always seen but always there.
Kirstein, I am more than grateful to call you my best friend till the end.
Love Delphine. X

The bare, boxed up house made my heart sink as I walked into Kirstein's house. Her mum walked passed me carrying boxes, giving me a guilty, sad smile. I helped load up the car and lorry. After all the hard work was done, I took Kirstein upstairs and looked up.

"Surely you're not going to leave without ever entering the loft?" I dared her. She has a fear of lofts and heights, so she had never been up there. But I was determined to get her up there. "Come on, why not tackle your fear of heights?"

"Ah, why do you do this to me?" She reluctantly unlocked the loft and pulled down the ladder. I smiled and climbed up. It was cold and dark. Kirstein had a bit of a panic and then realised it wasn't too bad from my wonderful skills of encouragement. We sat cross-legged facing each other. She handed me a little gift with a half heart bracelet and was wearing an identical one on her wrist with the other half. I opened it and smiled and then we both, of course, sobbed a little and hugged. We nodded at each other meaning we were ready. I hid the letter I had written to her in her suitcase before she went. She waved out of the window as the car drove off for the last time.

I was left standing outside her empty house in the middle of the road, waving as her outline faded and the car disappeared. I whispered the numbers, "One, two, three, four, five, six, seven, eight, nine, ten." *It's okay.* I looked back at her house and stood up a flowerpot that had been knocked over by her suitcase. I kicked a pebble across the road back to my house.

I wanted so badly to run into Grace's room and have her cuddle me and tell me it was okay, but she wasn't there. No one was there. I wrote the poem out again for June to add to her collection in the expressive arts drawer for figuring out Delphine. So, we added "best friend moves away" to the ongoing list of why I felt so broken.

In the morning, I woke up to my alarm for college that I decided to set after the warning from Albert. I lay there contemplating the consequences of not going in. I didn't want to go in. Kirstein wasn't even there. But I forced myself to get up knowing she would kick my ass if she was here and knew about Albert's warning. I got to college and wanted to be sick at the sight of it as I arrived. I don't know why I detested it so. I ignored everything and everyone around me and headed straight to Albert's office. I walked in and huffed seeing that he wasn't even there. I went in and sat on the chair opposite his desk for about two minutes, tapping my fingers and watching the clock. Bored of waiting, I grabbed a pen and paper from his desk, then scribbled a note that said, I was here, but you weren't- Delphine. Then I walked out. I thought about leaving a note for the end of the day too so I could go home now, but I didn't.

I had to think very hard to remember what class I was meant to have on a Monday morning. Once I figured it out, I forced myself into class and everyone stared as I walked in.

"Are you new?" Chelsey asked sarcastically.

"No, I'm just your worst nightmare," and I smiled at her, "oh no, I forgot - that is cherry pop." She squinted at me and Jolene quickly butted in.

"Delphine, what a surprise, I'll chat to you about what you've missed in a while," she said, disappointed. What I have missed... probably nothing important and nothing worthwhile listening to.

"Right, everybody to the main hall, there's a presentation for your year in this period," Jolene said, rolling her eyes as presentations always seemed to be in her lesson times. I wished they could be in Terry's lessons.

Everyone stood up gathering their bits and made their way to the hall. Chelsey politely shoved passed me. I easily could have snapped and gone girl crazy at her, but I breathed and nodded. I couldn't be bothered.

As we entered the hall, I spotted Brad. I tried to sit next to him but was made to sit with my class. I sighed and sat down, looking to the front where there was a big man and a girl. The projector said, Gang Talk.

After everyone had filed in and the noise had quietened, the man began talking. He spoke about what a gang was, what they did and what they got other people to do. Then the girl stepped forward. She looked about nineteen and she had sad eyes hidden by a beautiful smile.

"I was seventeen when I joined a gang. I didn't intentionally join one, it just happened through making new friends. When I got into it, I didn't know how to get out, I was too scared to do anything about it. I was involved in an abusive relationship with one of the gang members. Before I knew it, I was carrying packages and collecting money for them. I was sent all over the country on different deals, my life was threatened many times. On the last deal I did, I got this..." She stopped talking and pulled her top down, showing a wound on her shoulder. Everyone gasped. "I was lucky, I ended up in hospital and that's when I got out of it all. But the other person that was doing the deal with me wasn't so lucky. He was stabbed three times in the stomach and died in my arms. He was only sixteen at the time."

A picture came up. I froze when eyes like Dagga's stared at me through the screen. He looked like him. The girl's voice faded as Dagga flicked through my head. I thought about him. I thought about his tattoos. He had one on his arm that said 'brother' and a date next to it. My brain was racing, making all the links. I looked at the girl.

It's his ex, he was on trial for assault Dee. She was Mateo's ex, and Dagga's brother died on a dodgy deal! Why weren't Mateo, Dagga and Snow in prison if she came clean? I didn't realise how fast I was breathing till I glanced at Brad who was watching me closely. He screwed up his eyebrows and tilted his head to say as if to say, are you okay?

I looked away from him and back at the girl. After another half-hour of the man speaking, it finished. Everyone stood up and exited but I was still sitting, watching her. I had to talk to her. But not here.

I went to the canteen facing the hall door deciding that I could catch her when she came out. I sat munching an apple feeling sorry for myself as Kirstein used to be my break buddy. Carl stopped a couple of metres from my table and walked towards me before stopping again.

"Don't worry I won't freak out," I reassured him, nodding to the chair in front of me. He sat down.

"Dee, I didn't mean to hit a nerve the other day, but everything I said..."

"Can we not talk about it?" I interrupted, still looking at the hall door.

"Not really, because I can't stop thinking about it." He sighed and I realised he was talking about us, not Mateo.

"Look, you took the pin out the hand grenade, it has happened, it doesn't matter." I shrugged.

"Not that, I mean that part was good because I finally got something out of you, I mean about loving you," he said. I peeled my eyes off the hall door and looked at him.

"Stop loving me."

"I can't," he said, searching my eyes.

"Then good luck," I said.

"What does that mean?" he asked. My thoughts were whirling. What it meant was good luck, because if he did 'love' me, then it was going to hurt, and he needed a lot of luck to get through it any better than I did. I saw the hall door open out of the corner of my eye. There she was. She started walking out to the front entrance of college. I sprang up, grabbing my bag and ran after her.

"Dee?" Carl called as he got up to follow me. I got a metre behind her and went to tap her but stopped. I went to say something but stopped. She was walking while texting and I was following closely behind. She stopped and turned, looking at me. I guessed she was good at knowing when someone was around her.

"Can I help you?" she asked.

"Um, I, I was just in your presentation and um..." She raised her eyebrows, wanting me to get on with it. "It's just the guy in the picture, he looks a lot like Dagga." Her hand shot up to my mouth when I said his name. Her eyes widened and she took my arm, walking me down an alley behind the college.

"Girl, are you stupid? Don't say his name out in public like that. That was his brother."

"He isn't bloody Voldemort," I said sarcastically. She glared at me.

"How do you know him?" she asked, looking around still.

"I, I dated his friend. Mateo." Her eyes flooded with pain and she looked deep into my eyes like she was trying to find pain in mine.

"It was him wasn't it, who abused you?" I asked. She looked flustered and she turned away from me, walking away.

"Wait!" I said, grabbing her wrist to come back.

"I can't talk to you!" she said.

"Why, I'm not involved with them anymore," I said, desperately trying to get her to stay.

"What do you mean, involved with them?" she said.

"I mean, I was but I didn't get in too deep, I stopped before it could get out of control." She shook her head.

"They wouldn't just forget you if you've been involved, you know their names which means you already know too much," she said anxiously.

"Well they have, why are they not in prison if you came clean?" I asked, curious. She looked flustered again. She was hiding something.

"I didn't tell the police everything. Snow threatened me, he told me what to say in court so that Mateo would be released," she said, bursting like she had never told anyone before, which I guessed she hadn't.

"You lied to the police, you let them get away with it," I said, shocked. She looked like me before a panic attack.

"Well you haven't told the police, have you?"

"But I wasn't stabbed." She breathed deeply.

"Look, I don't know how you got away so easy, but I have been fine for three years now, I'm not going to open that door again, we are done talking. I'm sorry." She walked off.

I sighed and started walking back into college where Carl was sitting on a bench outside.

"That looked intense," he said. I forgot he had followed me out and must have seen her taking my arm and dragging me into the alley.

"It's nothing," I shrugged, my brain failing me in thinking of a good enough excuse.

"Just Mateo's ex," he said. I stopped and looked at him confused.

"I know who she is," he said, noticing my confusion.

"Right, yeah."

"Why did you want to talk to her so badly?" I didn't think to answer. I wanted to do the questioning.

"How do you know so much about everything to do with them?" I asked. He had obviously figured I knew the whole loop.

"Russ was my best friend," he said. I guessed Russ was Dagga's brother.

"Were you ever involved?" I asked, forgetting to be sympathetic, seeing as he had just told me his best friend got stabbed to death.

"No, I never went there." I nodded, everything making more sense.

The rest of my lessons were long and boring. I couldn't concentrate at all with all this new information in my head. At the end of my last lesson I walked into Albert's office. He didn't look up - he just handed me a note reading, 'knock next time, see you tomorrow morning.' I nodded and walked back out again, liking this nonverbal communication method.

After a whole day of college, which I was not used to, I also had to endure a shift at work. When I finally finished, I flopped into bed. I poked my curtains up onto the windowsill to block out the streetlights. I closed my eyes and huffed out, as my phone lit up beside me on my desk, making a little Snapchat sound. I grunted and rolled over, reaching for my phone, squinting my eyes at the light.

Nikos Kyprios <3*gun* is typing...

I dropped the phone on my lap and pushed myself up, cramming myself into the corner of my bed up against the wall. I hugged my knees in close and stared at the phone screen with wide eyes as it rested on my blanket in front of me.

Nikos Kyprios<3*gun* has sent you a snap!

Fuck.

June had decided he was a bad person to be involved with and to solve the problem I had to break away from him. We planned that when I saw him in Greece, face to face, I would end us. I knew I wasn't strong enough to do it. I swallowed my heart into my stomach and breathed slowly, trying to control my breaths like the doctor had advised me to do when I felt panicked. I let the phone naturally turn off, letting darkness race round the walls.

I stared straight ahead in panic and confusion for about ten minutes, seeing him watching his phone, waiting. After about two attempts of trying to pick up the phone with tingling, shaking hands, I eventually snatched it right up and let it lie in my sweating palm. I clenched my teeth and tears pricked the back of my eyes. *Pull yourself together Delphine. Come on - you can do this.* I swiped the phone, punched in my passcode and selected Snapchat. My fingers twitched and lingered above his name. I took a moment to absorb the fact he had text me.

Nikos Kyprios<3*gun*- Hi.

That was it. but it was better than nothing. He had a second in his life where I, Delphine, crossed his mind and allowed his thoughts to instruct him to text me, unprompted. Keeping it simple and not too desperate sounding, I decided I would be stubborn.

Delphine<3 – hello.
Nikos - Are you coming to Poros this year?
Delphine<3 - yes
Nikos - oh kl, when are you coming?

Delphine<3 - 8th-31st

Nikos Kyprios<3 *gun* - okay, that's good I might be coming too

Delphine<3 - k

Well, that was that. Had I done that right? Should I have approached that differently? Now I sounded like I didn't care. It could discourage him from coming. Or if he had any intentions of trying with me, he may now just give up realising how unbothered I was about him, which obviously was absolutely wrong, but I didn't show how I felt at all. I should have opened up and told him that every bone in my body was dying to see him, that I couldn't stop thinking about him, that he was driving me crazy, that... *SHUT UP. Breathe Delphine. One, two, three, four, five, six, seven, eight, nine and ten.* I held my head tight, trying to squeeze my thoughts out and stop a brain-full of questions from bouncing around in my head.

I lay awake for four hours, the first hour punching my pillow, yelling at myself internally and hugging my Greek blanket. The second hour was spent constantly checking my phone, stalking his social media where I found nothing and flicking through photos of us. The third hour was down in the kitchen, drinking tea, then vodka. The fourth hour was spent lying completely still, staring at the ceiling of glowing stick-on stars and eventually my brain refused to think anymore. My eyelids dropped, blocking out my sight, forcing me to sleep.

Then morning came and my alarm dragged me out of sleep. I stretched as all of last night's issues flooded back into my brain as if someone had stuck the USB memory stick back in. Then I found one of those hidden files you forget about. My dream last night. Full of Nikos drama of course. Luckily dreams are those things you involuntarily forget.

I had no plans for the day and no college which was good, but also bad, as I had nothing to distract myself from those texts. Just me, my head, an empty house and a phone with the ability to ping all these questions straight over to Greece to one boy's phone. But I restrained myself from doing that, and instead, I turned off my phone. I didn't want to talk to anyone. I decided to take a stroll to the park and get some air, paying attention to how down I felt. I looked at the flowers in the park and thought about how they were going to die soon. I used to think how beautiful they were - how colourful they were.

But now all I could see was black and white. I felt like nothing could make me happy. I didn't care about anything. I had felt like this for ages and I didn't know how to feel normal again. I wanted to be able to feel happy and feel love without being afraid. I didn't want to distance myself from everyone, but I couldn't help it.

I went through about five minutes of overthinking before being disturbed. A black car pulled up beside the park and Carl came marching over. No matter how many times I pushed this guy away, he always came back. He plonked me down on a bench in the park next to him.

"Okay, what's up Miss No Makeup, Baggy Jumper Sad Inside Girl?" His blue eyes were fixed on me. "Hey, come on, you hardly ever used to shut up, over the past months you've changed, and now I don't know what's going on with you." His deep voice bounced through me, right to the emptiness inside. I couldn't find my voice. It was like it had abandoned me.

What was going on with me? I didn't want to talk about my heartbreak because it only made the problem more real. I didn't want to talk about the first time I had sex because I didn't want to believe it happened as it did. I didn't want to talk about my sister and my best friend leaving me. I didn't want to admit I was lonely and hurting and that I found it so hard to remember how to be happy. Carl grew impatient and started talking with an assertive voice.

"What can be so bad to screw with you so much, to change who you are. I miss the old Delphine, I can't bear not being able to help, but I need you to talk to me." Even though he was just trying to care about me, I grew angry. It was my life, my hurt and I didn't need to share it. I couldn't have someone judging my decisions and telling me what to do next. I didn't need that. It was difficult enough dealing with my own head telling me what was right and wrong. "Delphine."

My brain and mouth were battling inside; a tug of war was happening. *Do I say, do I, do I not?*

"What messed you up so much, both emotionally and mentally, to make you push everyone away, to cut off everyone who tries to help you? You're letting negative people in, making shit decisions with the smoking and drinking out late, not eating. What happened?" His words made me notice the reality of how bad I was getting. How out of control I was. I wanted to run away from the whole thing. I pulled away from Carl, flung the park gate open and stormed off, ignoring his voice.

"Come back," he shouted, "talk to me Delphine, if you're not careful you're going to lose everyone who cares about you." His words raced after me like knives through the air. I wondered how much longer I could keep running for. And I was scared of what would happen if I ever stopped.

TEN

Albert and I carried on our notes each morning and each afternoon for the three weeks without fail. I had also forgotten how his voice sounded until the last day when there was no note, just an empty chair he gestured to.

"I understand you have finished all your coursework and had 100% attendance for the three weeks like I asked. I hope you will keep this up after the holidays. Is there anything you want to talk about before college break up?"

"No, thank you."

"Okay, have a nice break." I finished the first year of college with distinctions, and my results came back with distinction star which is the highest grade you could achieve. See - even though I was in my experimental stage, I was still doing well with 'important' things.

Going home, I felt happy that college was done for a while. I got my key out of my bag and went to stick it in the door, but it flung open before I could. Grace's big green eyes danced over me. I stared at her for a second then leapt at her, knocking her to the floor. I smiled, hugged her tightly and buried my face into her, taking in that familiar sister scent. She was still wearing a bobble hat and clothes from her season, her luggage dumped in the lounge. We both giggled and cuddled on the floor for a good ten minutes.

"You may as well be conjoined twins," Mum said, appearing from around the corner. We smiled up at her, then Dad jumped on top of us, bundling Grace. We moaned until he rolled off.

#

Night came and so did a storm. I sat in bed not knowing how to lie down and go to sleep. It's a strange thing us humans do. We lie down, we close our eyes and our brain shuts down. We are not conscious of anything going on in the whole world for a few hours.

It was midnight and the storm had stopped. I stared out the window at the puddles reflecting the streetlamp lights. The lights were fuzzy, and the world was dark.

Grace coming home had filled me with so much joy and happiness. I was feeling pretty reflective and had a spontaneous urge to write in my blank journal I never wrote in, so I grabbed a pen and let the words appear on the page.

As you grow up you realise all the little things happening and changing. Everything seems to go so fast. I know I'm only young but I'm never going to be a little girl again. I'm always going to have no responsibilities to worry about. I'm no longer the little girl with bunches holding daddy's hand, running to the park with a smile on her face. I'm almost an adult and all of sudden the whole world changes, you understand that being a teenage girl makes you vulnerable to men who lurk in the shadows and a target to teenage boys who just want to get in your pants. A girl needs to be strong, confident and independent. You have taken your first steps alone without your parents holding your hand or ready to catch you when you fall. You're ready now. Ready to face this world alone. I guess I can tick the independence part, as I'm working. I would like to think that I'm strong, physically. But mentally I'm not sure. Everyone has insecurities and everyone has dark times so it's only normal, but not everyone has someone who can drain you of all your strength, make you feel so small, worthless and broken. If he is in my head, I am weak. It's funny how a person can do that to you. You can hate them so much but at the same time you would do anything to be with them, for them to re-

ciprocate the same feelings.

I was in a full state of flow when I heard that sound to let me know someone was typing on Snapchat.

Nikos Kyprios <3*gun* is typing...
Nikos Kyprios<3*gun* sent you a snap!
Nikos Kyprios <3*gun* sorry

I was so tired and drained of this feeling. But I texted back. I thought that finally, maybe, I might get answers.

Delphine<3 for?
Nikos Kyprios<3*gun* being a dick. Ignoring you for a year. Literally I'm the worst person.
Delphine<3 yep.
Nikos Kyprios<3*gun*you don't have to say anything; I know I treated you like shit.
Delphine<3 why'd you do it?"
Nikos Kyprios<3*gun* I don't know, I had a hard year, I was scared. My mum and stepdad got divorced, my real dad has done some shit I can't talk about, I've changed.
Delphine<3 changed?
Nikos Kyprios<3*gun* I've done stupid things, I'm not gunna lie to you. I started smoking and drinking.
Delphine<3 same
Nikos Kyprios<3*gun* look, I thought about you a lot the past year, but I fucked up. Do you want to see me?
Delphine<3 well I waited a fricking year, so I guess yeah.
Nikos Kyprios<3*gun* I'm saving up to come. All I thought about was when we were together, how you feel, if you found someone new.
Delphine<3 ha, I can't go anywhere near anyone. I'm too scared of getting hurt again.
Nikos Kyprios<3*gun*- I had my chances, but I always backed off.
Delphine<3 why?
Nikos Kyprios<3*gun*- you know why.
Delphine<3- do I? from what I'm getting I didn't think you cared

about me at all.

Nikos Kyprios<3*gun*even though I was a dick it doesn't mean I didn't think of you. I don't deserve you.

Delphine<3 I know

Nikos Kyprios<3*gun* I wanna see you now.

Delphine<3 well you can't.

Nikos Kyprios<3*gun* I need you now

Delphine<3 I waited a year, I'm sure you can wait a couple weeks. Plus, it wouldn't be a good idea to see me rn.

Nikos Kyprios<3*gun* I fucking like you, y?

Delphine<3 I'd probably beat you up.

Delphine<3 but then it's okay I would kiss it better.

Nikos Kyprios<3*gun* UGH! I need you now.

Delphine<3 in fact no, you can wait the whole time till the last day for a kiss on the cheek then that's it.

Not really but I thought that scaring him a little wouldn't hurt. I had a cheeky smile typing, and I got all the feelings that rushed around me when I was with him.

Nikos Kyprios<3*gun* no please.

Delphine<3- you made me wait, u can wait 2.

Nikos Kyprios<3*gun* I promise I'll be there to see you.

Delphine<3 don't make me promises you broke them before

Nikos Kyprios<3*gun* fuck you <3

Delphine<3 go to bed

Nikos Kyprios<3*gun* no

Delphine<3 fine I'll go to bed, you stay up all night.

Nikos Kyprios<3*gun* night *middle finger*<3

Delphine<3 night prick

So, in the space of a year we had gone from, night Omorfos and Omorfi, to, 'night prick' and *middle fingers*, but there was something about that that made me feel better, like it wasn't just a young summer love. It was real. We were young adults with genuine feelings. Well, on my behalf anyway. I still didn't know if I could fully trust him.

I woke up excited as Kirstein was coming back to do a beauty course in London for a few months, but she was going camping for a week with me first. Brad said one of his friends could take us to the airport to pick her up. I was at Brad's waiting for his friend, but he called to say something had come up.

"What?! We need to get to the airport!"

"Calm down, I'll ask Carl," Brad said, scrolling through his contacts. I refused because of the last chat Carl and I had, but he was our last option. When Carl arrived, we ran straight into the car so that we wouldn't be late.

"Go, go, go!" Brad shouted, tapping the glove box. Carl; looked through his mirror at me in the back.

"Can we forget about it?" I said before he had a chance to talk. He nodded. When we got to the airport I ran through the crowd and stood at the front. Carl watched me as I got a pink banner out of my backpack and held it up next to all the taxi drivers. It was a beautifully painted, sparkled and sequinned sign saying, 'MY BITCH' in bold. An old lady looked at the sign smiling at the effort I put in but quickly scurried away when she read the words. Brad and Carl shook their heads in embarrassment.. I watched the gates, barely containing my excitement.

When the first crowd of people started filing through, I started jumping up and down and my eyes flew passed each one until I saw Kirstein dragging two suitcases along. She glanced up and saw me, then dropped her suitcases in the middle of the crowd (which Brad and Carl kindly collected). She sprinted towards me. We collided, screaming and hugging on the floor for about five minutes. She hadn't even been gone that long but in best friend life, it felt like years. The boys came up to us with the cases.

"Jesus Kirstein, you're here for a couple months - what the hell have you brought with you?" Brad complained.

"Brad I am a girl." Brad nodded, that being enough explanation.

"But it's so heavy!" Carl added.

"Oh, that's her big knickers." I giggled and Kirstein whacked me on the arm.

"Can you manage, or would you like some help Carlos?" I said in a baby voice. He squinted at me. The car journey back was a karaoke spectacular, and I think Carl questioned how he ever got involved with us three weirdos.

Camping was different to other years. Apart from the fact that there was no one else there other than my family and a lady named Doris, it was different for other reasons. We had lovely weather, including the hottest day of the year, so we did a bit of sunbathing under the burning sun and I got a little tan - great before Greece. Kirstein and I also swam in the lake. Yes, the dirty muddy lake, but there was no stopping us. We were like little girls together, clasping on to our childlike personalities. We had a mud fight with the tons of clay mud at the bottom of the lake. We gulped massive breaths of air and shoved it down into our lungs, diving down through the murky water and grabbing handfuls of mud, coming up to the surface and launching at each other.

We played some catch and racing to the Coke bottle (we didn't have a ball, so the Coke bottle seemed like a suitable replacement after I downed the fizzy liquid). After that, we lay like stars in the water making gentle ripples that travelled out to the edges of the lake and brushed the sides. We gazed up at the blue sky, pointing to the fluffy white candy floss clouds that floated above us. The sun sunk down behind the trees surrounding the lake and we became dark dots floating in the water.

Eventually we decided to jump out and take a shower in the cold, dirty shower room. Yeah - nice I know - but it was good to get the lake stench off us. Each evening we would take a shower and go back to have dinner, which was always a basic one, and then after, maybe one of nanny's oat cookies. Then we were on washing up duty. I was the master drier and put awayer and Kirstein was the professional washer upper. The evenings were spent sitting around the campfire roasting marshmallows making s'mores. Yum. Then off to bed - very cosy in the tent. It was like our own little nest.

We talked and walked in the woods and built a den over two days. After we finished the den, we sat inside, us both looking like wild jungle people, with mud on our faces and frizzy hair. Kirstein burst out laughing.

"So how is everything?" she asked. We talked every day on the phone but in person she could see right through me.

"Everything is okay, I went college for three weeks straight and finished the year with really good grades."

"Alright smart ass, and the counselling?"

"Uh, yeah, actually, it's going quite well. I actually do talk to her about everything."

"That's good. What about Greece, you go soon, how are you feeling about him?" she asked, getting to the point. I took a deep breath in.

"Well, it still hurts, and I don't know what is going to happen when I see him but I'm not going to plan it, I'm just going to see when I'm there." She looked at me, then back down at a flower she was playing with.

"If he hurts you again, I will personally execute him." She smiled sadly. It was cute, but I wasn't scared of that. I didn't think I could get any more hurt. I had hit the limit.

On the fourth night, I opened the message Nikos sent a day ago. I had to leave it for as much time as he always left mine.

Nikos Kyprios<3*gun* how's life?

Delphine<3- existing in a tent at the moment hbu?

Nikos Kyprios<3*gun* idfk

Delphine<3- well hello Mr. Positive

Nikos Kyprios<3*gun* I don't know if I'm coming this year

I stared at the message and the words flew right out the screen and stabbed me right in the heart.

Delphine<3- what

Nikos Kyprios<3*gun*- I don't know if I can come

Delphine<3- no you don't get to just say that, I need more than that. Why?

Nikos Kyprios<3*gun* I'm sorry I can't give you more than that

*Nikos Kyprios<3*gun* look bby girl, I'm sorry I don't think I'm gunna make it*

The thought of not seeing him for another year dragged me under; a billion thoughts were suffocating me. I grabbed my phone and my Greek blanket, wrapping it round me and ran out to the forest. My legs kept walking and walking. I had no idea where I was going or where I wanted to be. My feet stung from the twigs and forest floor. Plants scratched my legs and snagged at my pjs as I ran through the trees. Mosquitos buzzed around me like I was a midnight feast. I could feel them biting my skin, but I didn't stop.

*Nikos Kyprios<3*gun* talk to me*
*Nikos Kyprios<3*gun* Delphine?*
*Nikos Kyprios<3*gun*...*

I ran quicker and quicker till my foot became entwined with a tree and sent me flying flat on the floor. It wasn't till a couple of seconds later when I realised the plant was sharp, and thorns were piercing through my leg. I used my phone light to untangle myself and limped over to a fallen down tree. I climbed up it and lay in the dark.

*Nikos Kyprios<3*gun* fine, read my messages and don't say shit.*
*Nikos Kyprios<3*gun* say something*

I punched some words into the phone.

Delphine<3 what do you want me to say Nikos. Every fricking day ur in my head. I hate that u control my emotions, I hate that I can't forget u. Every single day all I want is to see u and it's killing me. I'm not stable because of you.

One, two, three, four, five, six, seven, eight, nine, ten. How could I not panic?

Nikos Kyprios<3*gun* I'll try. It's fucking me up.

One second he was promising to come, and I was full of hope and the next he couldn't come, and my whole world turned dark. I lay on the tree and looked up between the branches above, watching the distant stars. He could be looking at the very same star right now. We used to do that a lot. We even saw a shooting star together. As I rested, a drop of water fell on my legs and trickled down my thigh, absorbing into my pjs. I watched drops hit the leaves above and drip off. *Shit, it's 4am, my pjs and hair are wet, I'm dirty and scratched and my phone is about to die.* I jumped down and ran through the trees in the direction I thought I came from, anxiously glaring at my battery percentage on one percent. Any minute it was going to die, and I would be in the dark forest without any light.

My shadow chased me all the way through to the lake entrance and then disappeared as the phone died and darkened my surroundings. The sky above the lake was like the northern lights blocked by a total eclipse. Once so bright, now dull and empty like the feeling inside my chest. Luckily being at the lake, I could just about find my way to the tent, after tripping over a couple of times and walking into a tree. I reached my campsite and as quietly as possible, grabbed my shower bag and a torch from the tent. I walked back along the lake (not into any trees this time) to the shower room. I took a cold shower, spending most of it standing like a drowned rat that had just got caught in a storm. Standing with crossed arms, I allowed the water to transfer the blood from my legs to the shower floor and run around my toes down the plughole. Eventually, I turned the tap off and took my hair out from its messy bun, trying to dry off the rain, then shoved it back up again. I wrapped the towel around me and sat on the sinks outside for a while, the water dripping to a puddle on the floor where my feet hung down. Somehow my body was doing all this but, in my head, I was still sitting on the tree blank-minded, my brain shutting down.

I woke up tangled in my dirty Greek blanket which I refused to rinse out when showering, as it was all I had that had a little bit of him on. My body had no urge whatsoever to get up. Kirstein must have climbed over me and was outside with everyone as I could hear them chatting away. I pulled the blanket over my head and pretended I wasn't alive. Until Nan came marching in.

"Delphine, it's about time you got up, do you want porridge or a bacon sandwich?" I took my time to let the words struggle through all my tangled thoughts - to be processed through my brain before composing a muffled reply into the pillow.

"No thanks."

"That wasn't a yes or no question, it was a choice. I'll do you a bit of both, up you get." I flopped out of bed and pulled on my leggings. Although it was shorts weather, I couldn't reveal my scratched legs and deal with all the questions flying at me. I tugged my jumper over my head and slowly swallowed a couple of mouthfuls of porridge, leaving the sandwich. Luckily, being on washing up duty you can cover that up without anyone realising.

After a few days of intense thinking, sitting at the lake, strolling through the woods, beating up a couple of trees, shedding tears to water the plants and long restless nights, camping was over.

I really needed to get my head straight. When I went into work, I was standing on poolside staring at one couple in the water getting quite touchy feely. Seeing them happy just made me grumpy.

"Excuse me, there's no petting in the pool, it says right there on the pool rules list," I called, pointing at the wall. They slightly separated and looked round embarrassed. Kie, the other lifeguard came over, pushing my hand down and tried to lighten the atmosphere which I had filled with awkwardness.

"But there is a good spot in the health suite, if you're feeling it." He winked, then glared at me. That look was all I needed to back off and go back to my guarding point. Well it was a rule, but maybe I was a little snappy. I tried to engage myself by counting how many people had swimming hats, then goggles, then the number of girls to boys, and then how many guys had tanned skin, brown hair and eyes and a decent body so I could imagine they were Nikos. Shit.

The next morning, my phone bleeped.

Kirstein<3<3 is typing...

Kirstein<3<3 sent you a snap!

Kirstein<3<3 wanna go on a walk with me and Brad?

Delphine<3 nah

I ignored the next text and grabbed an apple and a banana deciding that would be my lunch. I knew I had to eat but I never felt like it. I also made a quick cup of tea in my new pink tea set with little butterflies on. Sitting at the kitchen table with an empty cup and an apple core, there was a knock at the door. I could see Kirstein and Brad's silhouettes through the window. They rang the bell. Kirstein's figure reached out for the letterbox and shouted through.

"Open the door girl, we ain't leaving." I reluctantly opened it, putting my hand over my face as the sun shot through the door. I could see Brad's slight frown and his eyes examining my dark eyes and scruffy jumper hanging down my thighs.

"Thank you, come on then, let's go," Kirstein said. I struggled to search for an excuse.

"But I..." Brad pushed through and marched up to my room. I followed quickly.

"Um, dude?" I saw him roll his eyes at all the empty mugs and he nodded to the apple core.

"Well, that's a start I guess." He threw my leggings and a vest top at me from my drawer and picked a pair of trainers from my cupboard, putting them on the floor in front of me before walking back downstairs. I huffed as I put on the leggings and trainers, leaving the jumper on.

We walked to the park with Kirstein nattering on and me silent. We sat on some swings and Kirstein walked off.

Brad dropped in a word to fill the silence. The classic, "So."

"Sew? I have no thread or anything to sew for that matter."

The corner of his lip raised up in a half-smile.

"Funny." But he came back with a smarter comment than mine. "Well, metaphorically we can start sewing up your life and you don't need a needle and thread for that."

"My life is fine, thank you."

"Clearly."

"I'm a big girl, I can handle myself."

"Clearly." I mean I wasn't handling it too well, but I didn't want his help or sympathy.

"Just stop looking at me like you can put your hand straight through the empty black hole in my chest you *think* is there."

"Think? Is."

"You ever gunna give up?" I asked rhetorically. I got up off the swing and walked away.

And here came the speech.

"Dee, he doesn't deserve you, no one should ever make you feel like this. He's ruining you." I stopped and turned back to him.

He got off the swing and punched the frame. I flinched at the bang, watching his jaw clench.

"Why are you letting him do it? You were strong, independent, you didn't let anyone..."

"Okay, okay. I don't need another lecture."

"Is that it?" He looked at me with disappointment. "So, you're just gunna let him..."

I started getting angry and started yelling.

"Yeah, that's exactly what I'm gunna do Brad. Because I'm purposely letting him hurt me, of course. Because it's so easy just to forget him, cut him off, but why not carry on the fucking fun for a little longer?" My voice stretched. I sucked in some air, feeling like all the oxygen had abandoned my body. My breath ran a race and my eyes filled with panic. Brad ran towards me, holding me as my legs went weak. He allowed us both to lower to the floor and then he started counting.

"One, two, three, four, five, six, seven, eight, nine, ten." His counting faded into a whisper as he pushed my hair out of my face and the panic drained out of me into a puddle below us.

By this time, Kirstein was on top of me.

"Move bitches, I know CPR, my friend is a lifeguard!" She placed her hands over my chest, fake pumping. I giggled and shoved her off. We all smiled at each other.

"Let us be here for you, you don't need to do everything on your own," Kirstein said gently. I nodded and smiled a half-smile.

ELEVEN

It was August 5 and we were leaving on the eighth. Three days. The excitement was sort of there but knowing Nikos wasn't going to be there killed me. The wait had been long. Every day I was waiting - hoping for a text that wasn't going to come. Until it did.

Nikos Kyprios<3*gun* is typing...
Nikos Kyprios<3*gun* has sent you a Snap!
Nikos Kyprios<3*gun* three days till you come
Delphine<3 that means nothing to you
Nikos Kyprios<3*gun* add three more days onto that count-down.

Delphine<3 why what's so special about the 11th
Nikos Kyprios<3*gun* me.

It felt like a fairy had raced to my bed and poured glitter into my heart. The word me flew through my tingling body and jumped around in my brain. I sat up and smiled, showing all my teeth to Angel who was curled up at my feet.

Delphine<3 you?
Nikos Kyprios <3*gun* I'll see you there bby girl <3
Delphine<3 r u kidding?

Nikos Kyprios <3*gun* nope ☺
Delphine<3- OMG! omg ahhh

After my first excited panic attack counting to ten technique, I proceeded to bombard him with a trillion questions. We spoke till 3 am and then I fell asleep.

Waking up in the morning, I felt the happiest I had all year, smiling on automatic. I skipped downstairs, bidding a cheerful good morning to everyone. I made tea and had some cereal.

I was seeing June the day before I left, and I knew what was coming. The talk of when I saw him. If I saw him, I was to stop whatever it was that we were. June spoke about this for ages and I was silent. We had gone back to square one. I thought I could do what she said, and we were getting somewhere but since he came back into my life, I was against June again. She kept asking how I felt and tried giving me a paper and a pen, but I was uncooperative.

#

4am. The alarm went off, and I whacked it quicker than I ever had before, throwing off my covers and practically jumping into my travel outfit. I took my hair out of the plaits I did the night before, letting the curls fall to my waist. I put on a little makeup. Shoving the makeup bag into my suitcase, zipping it up and lugging it downstairs, I grabbed the sarong off my bed and stuffed it into my travel bag. I had a quick Weetabix cereal, brushed my teeth and waited for Dad to load up the car with suitcases, then jumped in.

Hours later, we were pulling in to Poros with the Collins family, and not to the blue sky I expected. No, it was stormy. I had never been in Greece when it had rained like this before, so it was an odd experience.

We walked into the new apartment for the first time, which was even closer to the beach this year. The apartment was beautifully unique. It was painted white inside and out like all Greek buildings because of the heat. As you walked in, there was a lounge area with two big sofas around a fluffy carpet placed upon the tiled floor. Small, square paintings hung from the walls and the dining area had an eight-person large, brown table. Visible from there was the open kitchen.

There was a little walkway to two separate king and queen bedrooms for the parents, both fitted with giant double beds, bathrooms and dressing tables. Each had a back balcony overlooking a garden of trees and pink flowers. In the lounge was a spiral staircase, where there were two more bedrooms, both identical, except one was with green fittings and the other baby pink. This was where us 'kids' would be staying, the only issue being that the roof was one half of my height, clearly designed for dwarfs, so it looked like backache and bumped heads for us tall lot. Not even little Lucy would avoid this one. I had already managed to bang my head twice from putting my suitcase in my room.

After we had all explored inside, we gathered onto the balcony which was big enough to throw a party on. The parents had gone to the shop downstairs to stock up, but it was more so for Dad to stock up on his special cookies and hide them in the kitchen. I was first there and stood watching the waves being hit by lightning. The water absorbed the bolt and made the depths of the sea glow bright for a mini-second. Will then stepped through the soft cream curtain, joining me on the balcony, also mesmerised by Mother Nature's work of art. Grace and Lucy soon followed and joined us, leaning on the side rail.

"Would it be crazy to suggest we went in now," Will asked. I couldn't quite tell if it was rhetorical, but his slight smile suggested otherwise.

"I like crazy," I said in an excited whisper. We peeled our eyes from the stormy sea to each other and I could sense the race before he opened his mouth.

"I'll race you."

"And I'll beat you," I shouted, already running halfway up the stairs.

"Not if I get there first," Grace said, pushing passed Will on the stairs. Lucy giggled, legging it up to her room too.

Grace and I started our dream team methods and set to work, flinging open suitcases and throwing each other towels and costumes. Grace tied up my hair as I stretched on a costume. Will was already flying passed having changed into his shorts and was straight down the stairs, forgetting his towel, sparking the perfect opportunity for sabotage. I ran into his room and hid his towel under his bed and came out to meet him on the stairs.

"Forgotten a certain type of water absorbing material that may have gone mysteriously missing and is extremely hard to find, by any chance?" I spoke softly, making my way down as he frantically marched up on the search.

"Your ninja skilled tactics are respected but terribly poor and in need of practice," he said, grabbing the towel from the first place he looked and joining me on the outdoor steps which led to the beach. Cheeky Lucy was already feet in the sand, making her way onto the pier for the sea jump as Will and I sprinted past her, dropping our towels. With Grace a few steps behind, we all ran and leapt into the dark water with an impressive super-sized splash.

We swam over to Passage where Bob, the main ski instructor, was fixing a boat part under some cover.

"Good weather for skiing, aye Bob," Grace called over.

"Would you like some help controlling the customers?" Will joked, as the platform was normally heaving with skiers. Bob smiled when he heard our voices, dropping his equipment and stepping down into a speed boat we were clinging on to. He peered over the boat down at us sea creatures.

"Ugh, why are you here, you horrible lot?" he groaned, ruffling Will's hair and giving us the 'I'm a scary mean guy' look.

"Only the English are crazy enough to be in the water now, you mad kids."

"Better jump in then hadn't you, stay true to your roots and all that," I said, referring to him not actually being Greek but an English guy who lived here. He pulled a face.

"No chance. Right climb out and make yourself useful instead of risking being hit by lightning. Lightning, kids and sea. Bad combination," Bob said, trying to keep his mean man act on but actually concerned. We all giggled. "OUT, if you're going to irritate me by being here, you may as well irritate me while helping."

"Yes sir!" Lucy said, climbing up onto the boat and taking Bob's hand to step onto the platform. Each of us followed, then stood straight, saluting like soldiers in a line.

Bob broke the act and gave us all a hug. For two hours, we helped Bob carry all the life jackets, skis and wakeboards from the garage onto the platform for safety checks and counts. Grace oversaw the clipboard, ticking the tables and notetaking etc. Will did the carrying and lifting as well as repairing what he could on skis and boards. Lucy and I tested the life jackets by popping them on, jumping in and climbing out, which proved a good workout. By the time we had done that and reloaded them back into the garage, the storm had calmed, and the rain had slowed down into a gentle spit spot and the wind had stopped ripping through trees. The sun was trying to push through the clouds, revealing the blue sea every so often when it managed to beam down.

As we made our way back to the apartment, we were spotted by Vasilis Restaurant waiters who knew us well. They called us in and fetched us a welcome smoothie drink. The restaurant was outdoor and empty at this point, so all the waiters huddled around the table with us, chatting away. Blaming us for bringing the storm with us from England. We finished our drinks and set off back up to the apartment. We all unpacked, and the kids played cards until we went down to Vasilis for dinner. After the long day, we all fell asleep quite quickly that night.

I woke up refreshed at 11am which at home is 9am, so not bad. I stretched out and popped myself up, soon remembering that the ceiling would be my worst enemy this holiday.

"AH crap ouch, for fu..."

"Ah language."

"Sorry Mike it's just the roof," and my voice trailed off, realising he wasn't there anymore but out on the balcony. I slipped out of bed, glaring at the ceiling.

"Now listen here you, I am not having you hurting my head anymore, I'll be nice to you if you be nice to me, so please."

"You're talking to the ceiling Delphine," Grace groaned, putting the pillow over her head.

"I'm talking to a celling, yep okay, I think I need tea." I slipped on a bikini and put an oversized white shirt over the top and allowed my bare feet to guide me to the kitchen. A shirtless Will was standing by the frying pan, making what looked like a cheese toasty.

"Morning grumpy," he said, chuckling and watching me yawn. I plonked myself on a chair opposite and scratched my head, leaning on the kitchen surface.

"Who eats cheese in the morning?" I said, ignoring his observation of my morning attitude.

"Nice people who make tea for their crazy ceiling talking friends." He smiled and handed me a cup of tea.

"Hmm," I replied, slurping the tea. After three sips, I was ready and awake. I danced around the kitchen, leaning over Will who manages to take up great amounts of space. Once I'd completed the Olympic sport of finding the kitchen equipment and avoiding Will, I successfully made myself cereal and ate it out on the balcony. There were two tables and the parents sat at one drinking coffee. Dad had his special cookies on his lap. Both Nina and Mum already had their laptops out, 'quickly' checking work emails. I rolled my eyes at their work bubble and sat at the other table with Lucy.

"Delphine," Dad said, watching my eyes roll. He hated Mum working just as much as me but wasn't keen on the attitude teenager act either.

"Dad, cookies are not for talking with whilst in your mouth," I said, grinning and watching the crumbs roll down his shirt. He raised his eyebrow but laughed, brushing them off.

We spent the day on the beach sunbathing and reading. We

had lunch up at the apartment and then we swam to our cave around the island, playing on our rubber rings, teaching each other tricks. After a day of relaxation and fun, we all had a shower and joined for a game of cards out on the balcony. Lucy went for a nap leaving me, Grace and Will playing a competitive card tournament with added hilarious aggressiveness from not being able to open the wine bottle. Eventually Will managed to pop the cork and all was good. I won that night and the scores were to be carried over to the next evening.

We decided to go out for dinner at Pedros that night. We were greeted with open arms and a smiling Sofia and her daughter Maria who led us to a table many smiles and hugs later.

Sofia spoke quickly, wanting to be updated with our lives and then she took our order, fetched drinks for us and sat back down to join us.

We ate and drank sharing stories with cries and laughs and we ended up on the beach opposite toasting to a good holiday and looking up at the stars. One by one the group left the beach and I stayed watching the stars shimmer, reminding me of him. Was he looking at the stars now? Would he be by my side the day after tomorrow?

I sat on the sand with my knees tight up on my chest. I watched the reflections of the town's lights from across the water dance along the waves. A tear rolled down my cheek, thinking that I could leave this year just as hurt as before. Will came down and sat beside me, letting me rest on his shoulder. We walked back to the apartment and chilled on the balcony for a while.

In the morning, I woke up on the sunbed on the balcony with a cover over me.

"You looked so peaceful there last night. I thought I would bring the bed to you," Lucy said, sipping a glass of milk.

"Why were you awake that late hun?" I asked her, remembering that Will and I got back at about half eleven..

"Will woke me up banging his head coming out from the bathroom at like twelve, and I saw you when I was getting some water."

"Thank you, sweetie," I said, smiling at her and stroking her hair as I passed.

Will was making his daily toasty and handed me tea.

"Want me to have a word with your ceiling too?" I mocked. He just laughed. Dad came bursting in, announcing that his cookies had reduced in numbers since he last put them back. Everyone denied having any. Although his hiding place was rather obvious, I didn't think anyone had eaten any.

The Collins were going to Petros that night and we decided to go into town. We caught the water taxi across to Poros Town and went to Safranos for a drink first. Here, a lot of free drinks flowed. We decided to go to The Snail for dinner - yes, they served snails and no, I would not be having any. After a lovely meal, we headed back to Safranos for refreshing mojitos and a couple of free shots from the owner and waitress. We took a quick trip to the cake shop and got our favourite almond cake, cookies and treats to take back to the apartment. The owner gave Grace and I two free cookies.

"Good to see you back," he said with a glowing smile.

"It's good to be back," Grace said, nibbling her cookie.

No doubt we would be back for more in a few days. We caught a taxi back home.

#

I woke up nervous and excited all at the same time, knowing he was arriving today. It was early and Will was the only one who had been up, but Dad's cookies were open on the side. I gathered Will was the cookie thief and had forgotten to put them away, so I did it for him. Will wasn't in the kitchen, but he left a note on the kettle.

Sorry I'm skiing, come watch?

I ran out to the balcony and saw Will about to start.

"WAIT!" I yelled over to Bob in the boat. I pulled off my shirt as I ran down the steps revealing my bikini and dived into the water. I swam over and climbed up onto the boat smiling.

"Thank you, you may continue," I said, nodding at Bob.

"Oh, may I?" He raised his eyebrows. I smiled.

"Ready Will?" Bob called to Will, who was chilling in the water at the end of the rope.

"Yeah," Will shouted back. And he was off. Will is an amazing skier, nearly as good as Nikos actually. As a ferry passed the bay, I wondered if Nikos was on it. I knew he was arriving today, but I didn't know when, or even if he would come see me today. I watched Will fly across the course and booked a slot with Bob at the end of Will's ski for twelve o'clock. Will and I went back and ate breakfast, then joined Grace and Lucy swimming and collecting shells.

It was time for my ski. I had a nervous feeling in my belly. What if he arrived whilst I was skiing? Mum and Grace were in the boat watching.

"Right trouble, you ready?" Bob shouted from the boat.

"Yes Bob," I shouted back, trying to override my nerves with confidence.

"You can do it, take the pull, let the knees come into the chest, stay down," Bob said rhythmically as the engine started and pulled me up. When I was little, I always had bad starts and it took me like, five attempts, so I got into the habit of repeating those three steps. I got up on the first time today and it felt good. Bob whistled, signalling it was okay for me to start skiing from side to side. I did a couple freestyle, then went onto the course. I always got four buoys rather than six. But this year I would do it - I could feel it. After six passes my arms ached and I managed five buoys. Bob was proud and surprised. I surprised myself to be honest. I had more fight this year. Back on the platform, I was rinsing my gear.

"Well done Delphine, you are going to do it this year girl, what's happened?" he said, high fiving me.

"Aha, thank you and I don't know, but you're the teacher, must be your magic Bob," I said giggling.

"Well, I mean, I am the best."

All day I was constantly watching the road to see if a white mini would pass, and constantly checking the water taxi passengers in case he came that way. Every hour of the day I went up to my room and checked my hair, re-curled my eyelashes or sprayed perfume.

I typed a text.

Hey slow coach, where r u? *delete* No, too weird.
Hey you, how's it going? *delete* No, too casual.
*Are you here? *delete** No, too pushy.
Are you gunna come down today? *delete* No too... just no.

Maybe he would find me annoying. But no - he wanted to see me. Why hadn't he text me though?

So, after a long day of waiting, he didn't come but that was okay. He was probably on the island at his aunt's house or arriving late.

Tonight was girl's cocktail night anyway. Grace, Mum and I went to town and spent the night at Safranos. Mum rarely drinks so when she does, she gets tipsy quite quick. In fact, her nickname is TA2 standing for, 'tipsy after two'.

It was nice to spend time with Mum rather than my instructor mum. We laughed all night and enjoyed many different colourful, sparkling cocktails which helped the disappointment of not seeing Nikos fade a bit. At the end of the evening we decided to walk home. Why? I do not know. I swapped shoes with Mum as she didn't want to walk back in heels. Luckily, we have the same size feet.

Walking back meant I would pass all the hotels and Nikos' aunt's house to look out for the white mini. We walked through town passing the shops then reached the end where there was a big car park. I scanned it and found one white mini and squinted at it. Nope - that was cream to white, plus, it didn't have the black line across it.

We carried on walking passed the boats, then down a long road. There was a white mini parked on the side of the road, but it had an English number plate, so I gathered it wasn't the one. At this point, Mum had caught on to what I was looking for.

"WHITE MINI there!" she called out like a child playing who could spot the object first on a car journey.

"Yes, thank you Mum, I saw it," I said, quickly trying to hush her. She giggled, then her face screwed up a little.

"Oh, so it wasn't the one?" I shook my head. We turned into the next road where the aunt's house was. I slowly walked passed it. Outside was a small car, covered with a sheet so I couldn't make out what it was. I peered in the windows and saw figures at a table but couldn't work out who. Trying not to annoy Grace more, I decided to keep going till I noticed Mum was over at the car peeking under the car cover.

"MUM! What are you...? Leave it," I hissed in a whisper, running over to her.

"I can't see, it's too dark," she said, still rustling at the cover.

"It's fine, you don't need to. Mum move away from the car." She did, so we walked ahead linking arms with Grace. Back at the bay there was a party at Vasilis. Hundreds of people and one white mini with a black stripe. Grace and Mum were already upstairs, and I was left staring at the car, peering into the restaurant and looking through the crowds. I couldn't see much but then it occurred to me that maybe I couldn't see him in the crowd, but he might be able to see me out in the open. I quickly ran upstairs and checked my phone for any messages. Nothing.

The next day, I ran out to the balcony, looking down at Passage at his chair but it was empty. Just Bob sipping a coffee. He caught me peering down.

"Look Delphine I know I'm an attractive man but if you really want to see me more why not come ski?" he shouted up to the balcony. I smiled and giggled, noticing that my voice was not going to be loud enough to reach over to him. As I turned around to go back outside, there was Will directly in front of me, rather close.

"OH my god, William, don't do that," I said, jumping.

"William?" He chuckled, handing me a cup of tea.

"Yeah that's what your dad calls you when you're being, well you." He grinned, nodding towards Passage.

"Still not arrived then?" I looked up at him.

"I don't know what you're talking about," I said, half sarcastically and half seriously. He drummed the side of the balcony with his fingers and awkwardly swivelled round, swinging his arms back inside. He walked backwards with his hand to his lip.

"I've been watching you young one, I know a girl in love when I see one. Our secret aye," he whispered, just before tripping over the doorstep and gritting his teeth in pain. I walked past him as he was hopping and holding his ankle.

"I've been watching you annoying one. I know a cookie stealer when I see one, shh our little secret. If you're nice." I winked and ran upstairs.

I went down for a ski with Bob and I got five buoys, missing the last one each time which sucked. I had an iced coffee with Bob on the decking before joining Lucy on the beach to gather shells for her collection.

In the afternoon all the 'kids' went into town. It took a little convincing as I didn't want to leave the bay in case Nikos arrived. But eventually we all hopped on the water taxi heading into town. We visited the biggest ice cream shop on the island which had, like, sixty flavours. I had one scoop of Blood Orange. Will and Lucy both had White Chocolate which they always had, and Grace had Poros Special which was vanilla and fruity bits. We ate them on a bench by the seafront and we all grinned as the flavours went off like fireworks in our mouths. We each dug our spoons into each other's, trying each flavour, giving our taste buds a party. We concluded that mine was best.

After licking the pots clean, we walked along where all the boats were moored and chose which boat we would have if we were multimillionaires. Will picked the biggest one he could see. Grace picked a medium-sized pure black one. Lucy picked one with a hot tub and I picked the white and gold one with a chandelier hanging inside. Will being the idiot he is, walked up the stairs onto the boat and got carried off by crew. Lucy cried hysterically. Grace walked off pretending she wasn't with us and I panicked. As we walked on, a ferry pulled in. I tugged my messy bun out and brushed my hands through my hair just in case he was on it. Will was watching and stopped in front of the ferry.

"Nikos where are you my love?" Will called in a high-pitched voice (well as high as his voice could go). Luckily, Grace and Lucy were a few passes ahead.

"For god sake Will shut up," I whispered, holding my hand over his mouth, as if Nikos was only a metre away from us. Will shrugged me off and I shoved him forward, catching up with the girls.

We then visited the bakery and bought a couple of cakes to take home. I nodded at the cookies, winking at Will. We both laughed. We strolled around the shops for a while, met some Greek friends in the town centre and caught a taxi back.

An agonising week and a couple more days passed with an empty chair and a constantly on edge Delphine. I didn't text him, but he did text me, on the eighth day which was five days after he was supposedly coming. He said the money he was earning on the boat wasn't going to be enough to come so he

wouldn't make it. On the tenth he said he might have enough as he had done more hours. That same night, he went out as I saw from his Snapchat and alcohol isn't normally free, so surprise surprise, the next day was the I can't come text. At first, my replies were sad and upset, but once he kept changing his mind, I stopped replying.

On the twentieth day I had given up hope. It was a week till my birthday, and I wasn't that excited. I felt like he had ruined the whole holiday. All I'd been doing was waiting for him and he wasn't even coming.

Although Will was annoying about the whole thing, secretly he cared, and it was good having him around. One night I went to Love Bay a little distressed and Will followed, stopping me from punching the tree and I brought him up to date on everything. After he was filled in about the whole story, he decided that he didn't deserve me, and I needed cheering up. That was the night I got thrown into the sea fully clothed. At first, I tried drowning Will, but as he is almost twice my size, I gave up. We lay in the sea floating about. The stars must have been looking down on us thinking, what are these two objects in the night sea? A blue marshmallow (Will's shirt blew up in the water) and a yellow sunflower tree (I had a sunflower dress on). You would think that when the sea is a dark black and you can't see through it, it would be scary, but I found it more exciting than frightening. It was peaceful, calm and the cold was almost comforting. It wasn't freezing (obviously - we were in Greece), but it sent little tingles around my body. It felt like hundreds of water fairies' fingertips were holding me afloat.

From the cliff above, was a scream

"AHHHHHHHHH, AHHHH OH MY GOD, DELPHINE! WILL!" An extremely shocked and loud Grace came running down to the beach as she saw Will and I floating. Grace's screech shot straight through us and we both splashed about, almost drowning in shock. As soon as Grace saw us move, she dropped to the floor a few metres away in the sand hill, holding her chest and breathing deeply. I thought she was having a heart attack or something, so I sprang into action, running out of the water.

"GRACE, ARE YOU OKAY? Sit back, I got you," I said, trying to put her into the recovery position. She shoved me down onto the sand, which my wet dress clung to.

"You two are total lunatics, what the hell! Why would you lie in the sea in your clothes and not blinking or moving an inch?" I then realised that from the top of a cliff, that could have looked slightly odd.

"Oh." I started to giggle. Grace's shocked breathing slowed, and she started laughing too.

"You thought that we, because we and..." I starting crying laughing into the sand.

Whilst this was happening, Will was standing in the sea, still frozen from Grace's scream. When walking out, he stepped on a sea urchin and yelled. Grace and I ran to him and examined his foot in the dim light. Grace pulled the sting out and we helped him back, his arms slung over our shoulders.

The next morning, I woke up to everyone surrounding my bed. Will placed a cup of tea beside me. Lucy placed a tray with a croissant on it on my lap and they all sang Happy Birthday. We were informing Lucy of the events of last night.

"So ultimately Lucy, lessons to know are one, do not swim in the sea with your clothes on if you plan not to move much. Two, always be wary that cliffs are a place where people's minds make them believe the worst has happened. Three, when you're shocked don't hold your chest because it looks like you're having a heart attack. Four, don't be an idiot and step on sea urchins," Grace informed her.

"I'm sorry, unfortunately I can't see in the dark and therefore avoiding stupid sea urchin is a difficult task," Will said.

After I opened some presents, we went to Passage where Bob took us on his boat to the most stunning hotel. It looked like a cruise ship. The sea was crystal clear and so beautiful. We jumped off the pier and swam for ages. We had a divine lunch and cocktails and then went to the slide pool on the top floor.

Later that afternoon we all got ready for town, of course, with blaring music and complaining parents. Grace and I had the same long lacey dresses on with a slit down the leg, mine white and hers black. We went into town and had drinks and a meal. We were sat opposite a table full of Greek guys who were about twenty and they wouldn't stop looking over. I went outside to the toilet where one of the guys followed. He stopped in front of me but didn't say anything.

"Um, hi," I murmured, raising an eyebrow.

"Hi, me?" he said, pointing at himself smiling.

"Well, you are the person blocking my way so, yes, hi you." He chuckled.

"I'm sorry, I'll get out the way if you come to our boat party after dinner?" he said, smiling down at me and holding out a piece of paper that said Flying Ocean, which I guessed was the name of the boat. I snatched the paper out if his hand, pushing him aside.

"I'll think about it," I called back, waving the paper in the air. As I got back to the table, Will, Lucy and Grace were all staring at me waiting. I looked at them all with a, 'what're you waiting for?' look. Will rolled his eyes.

"Well..."

"He invited us to his boat party," I said, brushing it off.

"And we are going," Grace said. The parents and Lucy went home. Grace, Will and I went to a club to get in the mood.

We were found by the group of guys before we even walked in. The guy who asked me to come came over.

"Hey, this is not the boat," Will said, disappointed.

"Correct, it's a club, well spotted," I said sassily. Will raised his eyebrows at me, and Grace interrupted, introducing us all. As we walked into the club, Will pulled me aside.

"Why you being all snappy with Alex?" he asked.

"Alex?" I repeated.

"The guy, the guy that invited you to his boat party like two minutes ago, the one you're being defensive with?"

"Okay, got it, thank you. I dunno. I just guess I can see through him and what he wants, plus he's too demanding, like when I say he invited us, he basically told us." Will smiled.

"Dominance is attractive to girls," he said, pinching me.

"Ouch, shut up Will," I said, pushing him, us both laughing. I ended up spending most of the night with Alex. He had super long eyelashes so I decided I would call him Lashes. We danced the whole night, Grace and I stealing the dancefloor and spotlight from every other girl in the club, as well as their men's attention. Will acted as our bodyguard for most of the night. Once we had danced enough to make us incredibly hot, we walked back to the guys' boat. We all sat on the front drinking beer, until Alex took me inside for a 'tour'.

We ended up in his room. Nikos's face pierced the back of my brain and this rush to get it out came over me. Alex's body was close against mine within a matter of seconds. He pinned me against a wall and his kisses were hard. His hands were rough, but it felt good, like I wasn't seen as weak for once. He ripped his shirt off and carried me to the bed and he lay on top of me, his breath heavy and hot. I could still see Nikos watching me which made me want to go all the way with Alex. My body was on fire and everything was tingling, but my hands started shaking and my mind started screaming when all I could see was Nikos on me. I pushed Alex off, and lay breathing.

"What's wrong?" he said.

"Nothing's wrong," I said.

"Then why have you stopped?" he asked.

"Because that's it, that's all your getting," I said, sitting up.

"What? Well can I at least see you again," he said, confused.

"No," I said quickly, walking towards the door. Alex reached for the door from above me and slammed it shut, twisting my body round to face him.

"You can't do that, you can't make me fall for you like that and then leave me with nothing," he said angry.

"Fall for me?" I said laughing, "If you fall that quickly your life is destined to fail," I snapped at him.

"What the hell is wrong with you?" he shouted, and then held my arm, dragging me away from the door. "I want you to stay, I like you," he pleaded with me.

"I don't care," I shouted, shoving him off. The door opened behind us and Will walked in. He stared at Alex and I walked out. Luckily, Grace was drunk enough to need to go home and Will was fine with that too.

We jumped in the sea when we got back, and all slept on the beach.

TWELVE

I was so done with this guy, playing around with me way too much. It was a never-ending rollercoaster of emotional states and questions. He was coming, then he wasn't. I couldn't t cope with another decision change. I should have listened to June. I should have never met him - I hated him. As I got into bed, I decided in the morning that I was going to block him off everything: Snapchat, Instagram, Facebook - my life.

It was seven-thirty and I was woken up by Grace rushing around finding her ski gear.

"YOU'RE SKIING NEXT DELPHINE." I rubbed my eyes and stretched out yawning. I lay there staring at the ceiling, contemplating when to reach for my phone and hit that big bold block button, because I knew - I knew he wasn't coming. I felt like I had known this since I left last year. Somehow I felt like I wouldn't be seeing him for a long time. But I always hoped, clinging on to the small possibility of being near him again. Inside, deep down, I knew I had to let go. I forced my hand over to the phone and pressed the middle button, allowing the notifications to pop up on the front screen, and there at the bottom, of course, was a message from him. Perfect.

Nikos Kyprios <3 *gun*… I'm coming today.

I stared at the message. Went to type - didn't type. I threw the phone to the bottom of the bed, jumped up, grabbed my ski gear from the side, yanked on my costume and went to ski. It was a great ski actually, I had this urge like when you're angry and go to workout at the gym. *That* feeling. I pushed myself more than I thought I could, slicing through the wakes, turning sharply and creating a mighty wall of water behind me. I did the mini course for the first time and after that, I completed it almost effortlessly.

On the last pass, Bob put me on the short rope, so that I was closer to the boat wake and it was basically unavoidable. But I flew over it, flicking each buoy with my ski on the turns. At the end of the pass, I pulled over to one side of the boat, releasing the handle, gliding along the water for about five seconds when I looked up... and there he was, sitting right there, on the chair he always sat on. It felt more like five minutes as we stared dead at each other. As my ski became submerged in water, I sunk down slowly. My eyes were fixed on him, my mouth slightly parted and my chest began to feel crushed by my life jacket. I felt a tightening in my throat like seaweed from the depths of the water had tangled and wrapped tightly around my body. I lay flat on the water, kicking off the ski and clutching my neck. Bob's boat came up beside me. He cheered.

"Well done angel, you did it, you..." I clenched my teeth, trying to suck in some air. Bob's voice suddenly turned to a worried, panicked tone.

"Delphine, DELPHINE?" His eyes moved frantically on me and he jumped out of his seat, leaning over the side of the boat and reaching down to me. I wanted to reply but I ended up just squeaking desperately. I didn't notice I was kicking my legs around in the water. My head felt compressed as though the water had turned into a magnetic metal contracted to my brain. Bob pulled my body out of the water, my head hanging down. He placed me on the boat floor and ripped open my life jacket. I gasped in the air, rolling onto my front, coughing. I breathed slowly as Bob's voice became clearer after the head compressing faded.

"Are you okay, what happened?" I blinked and gradually

pushed myself up against the side of the boat, leaning back. I rested my head on the edge. Bob held my shoulder. I could see Nikos out the side of my eye, half out of his seat and looking worried. The seaweed untangled from my body and fell over the sides back down to the sea floor and the last of the metal liquidised, dripping off my head. I looked at Bob's concerned face and spoke quietly.

"I'm okay... I just forgot to count to ten." His facial expression didn't change. "I just got too excited about completing the course." I laughed halfheartedly, trying to convince Bob I was alright and peel that memory out of his head. He sighed and tapped my shoulder, sliding back into his chair to head back to Passage.

How am I going to do this then? I knew I had to get out of the boat but doing that meant no avoiding Nikos. I thought quickly and asked Bob for some water. Luckily, he didn't want to leave me unattended so called to Nikos to grab some from the garage across the road. I watched him stand up and peel his eyes away from me to make his way to the garage. I forced myself up and stepped out of the boat.

I quickly rushed away while calling to Bob, "I'm feeling better now, don't mention this to Mum... please." As I passed the garage, Nikos emerged out of the door with a bottle of water in his right hand. He stopped in the entrance. I carried on walking.

Delphine! What the hell are you doing. One year you've waited to see him. Don't just walk away you absolute idiot of a girl, turn around right now. I gave into my conscience, annoyed at it being right.

I turned back and walked over to him. I got about half a metre away and reached for the bottle. He looked confused but released the bottle a little. Our hands touched, both wrapped around the water. I drop-rolled from his finger to mine. I stared at him. He stared at me. His eyes seemed brighter and looking in them made me feel like I was falling in mid-air at one thousand feet. His chest and arms were bigger, allowing his T-shirt to cling on to his smooth skin and stretch across his abs. I felt completely stuck, like someone had pressed pause. I noticed I hadn't taken a breath for a good twenty seconds. I blinked and breathed deeply.

I was in my ski gear with soaking wet hair in a messy plait, and I hadn't even brushed my teeth, curled my eyelashes or anything! I was standing there absorbing his fricking gorgeousness and perfection when I looked like a below average possessed weirdo! *Oh my god. How embarrassing. One. Two. Three. Four. Five. Six. Seven.*

"Eight, nine and ten." He squinted, watching me. Shit - I said that out loud.

"Thanks." I shifted on my feet awkwardly. "For the water," I croaked. I turned quickly and scurried back to the apartment.

I got in, shut the door behind and leaned against it, banging my head on the door.

"Idiot, absolute and utter retarded weirdo, why do you have to be so..."

"Most probably because you haven't had tea." Will popped round from the balcony, into the kitchen, flicking the kettle on and sitting next to me where I'd sunk into the floor by the door. I groaned, flopping my head on his shoulder.

"I'm such an idiot, I just stood there like a guppy."

"No, you're not, because he did exactly the same thing and he didn't do that because you're an idiot or an absolute utterly retarded weirdo. I think that's how you worded it anyway. No, because you're beautiful Dee... because to even have a chance with you he's lucky, and if he doesn't know that he sure as hell doesn't deserve you. Now, stop doubting yourself, go make yourself pretty, however you do every morning, and sort it out." Will normally took the piss or was joking around, so him saying whatever that was and wherever it came from was either going to make me laugh hysterically or cry, and seeing as I was on my period, the emotional cry ruled. He pushed himself up off the floor, reaching out his hand and yanking me up to standing. He wiped my tear.

"None of that, off you go," he said, pushing me up the stairs.

I got dressed in my best bikini and lacey pink throw-over. I curled my eyelashes and unplaited my hair, leaving it down in the beach waves wet look.

"Tell me you're not going to let him hurt you again that easy," Grace said from the bathroom. I ignored it, knowing it would lead to an argument. I went down to Mum in her room. She knew I was saving this bikini for a 'special day' so she clocked straight away.

"No regrets." She smiled calmly. That's all she needed to say. I walked out to the kitchen and sipped the tea Will had left on the side, then poked my head round the balcony. Nikos was sitting on the chair. I spent five minutes watching him, not believing he was only thirty metres away from me. Then I spent five minutes walking out the door and walking back in, contemplating what to say. Eventually Will called up from the beach.

"If you open that door one more time Dee."

"Jesus Will, he can hear you, don't make it obvious that I'm..." I struggled for a word.

"Chicken?"

"No, I am not chicken."

"Prove it, go on Delphine, stop flapping about."

I pulled myself together and breathed.

I went back downstairs after getting dressed and sun creamed and made my way over to Passage. I paused a couple of steps behind him, studying his broad shoulders. I swallowed hard, glancing over to the other beach where Will was signalling, 'go on' with his arms.

All year I had wanted to be next to him in person: to talk to him and not to a phone that didn't reply. Now I was here, and I had so many things I could say but couldn't pick which one to say. Instead, I allowed myself to examine his body and to note the differences from last year. A haircut - slightly shorter. Slight facial hair. Enough to need to shave but not enough to be able to grow a full-on beard or moustache. Muscles. Bigger arms, larger chest and distinct back muscle. Less defined face - jaw line was more soft than sharp. Abdominal muscles about the same.

Skin the same, hands the same and eyes the same. Eyes - he was looking at me, looking at him. Or maybe it was the other way around. Maybe he was looking at me not realising I was looking at him and he thought I caught him looking at me, like I thought he's caught me looking at him. *One. Two. Three. No, you're fine. God, Delphine. What does it matter?*

Eventually we spoke, and the light-hearted banter and sparks were as strong as ever. But after an hour or two, I noticed how happy I was with him, which only reminded me of how sad I was without him. I knew we kind of had the conversation about why he did it on the phone, but it wasn't clear enough. I didn't understand how you could ignore someone you apparently missed. I needed answers from him the person, not him the screen.

"How can you ignore someone you miss?" I interrupted him mid-sentence, while he was searching his phone for a picture. He looked up at me and locked his phone, putting it beside him on the sunbed.

"I told you," he replied.

"The WiFi, right?" He nodded. "It doesn't make sense. You haven't gone a year without one second of WiFi."

He pushed himself up on the chair.

"You're right, I haven't..."

"So why didn't you..."

"Let me finish. None of the times were right."

"Right? What do you mean the times weren't right? You couldn't find one right time to... even when I broke down in December and you sat there reading my messages, when I was clearly hurt. You didn't think the time was right then?" I raised my voice, angry at how he was making such pathetic excuses.

"Okay, can we go for a walk, if you feel the need to shout?" he said, picking up his phone.

I grabbed my flip flops and kicked them on my feet, stomping down the road to where we always walked.

Once we reached our bench next to Love Bay, I sat down, crossing my arms like a toddler having a strop. He watched and sat down next to me. I waited for him to explain instead of exploding. But he walked down to some rocks which hung over a ten metre drop to the sea and lit up a cigarette. I rolled my eyes and followed him down, thinking maybe I'd get a better conversation when he was feeding his need for nicotine.

"I'm not very good at phones," he said eventually, after puffing out a rather long drag.

"Bullshit. And I'm not very good at identifying shitty excuses."

He sat down on a rock, taking one last puff and throwing it off the drop's edge below us to the beach. He rested his head in his hands. Why was I doing this to myself? Why was I allowing myself to be hurt by this lying prick? *How can you hate someone and love them at the same time?* I calmed down, realising that this conversation wasn't going to get any better, and it would end up with me jumping off that edge or pushing him off. I lay down beside where he was sitting on the prickliest floor. Okay, he was a prick and we both knew that, but for some reason, I was attracted to this lying asshole and he did something to me that I couldn't explain. I knew I was leaving tomorrow, and he'd probably ignore me all over again, but I'd waited all year to be with him and I didn't want to fight, even though there were so many unanswered questions. I knew that letting him back in was like walking into my own hell, but it was a bit like A *Bug's Life*, you know... 'the light, I can't help it. It's so beautiful.' Buzz, bang.

"You should quit," I said. He looked at me confused, and then noticed his cigarette pack was in my hand. "In fact, I'll help you." I jumped up with hundreds of prickles in my hair and dress and skipped down around the rocks to the small bit of sand under where we were.

"Um, Dee what are you doing?" he called down from above me, leaning over the small cliff.

"Helping you quit," I called back, flinging off my dress and walking into the sea.

"Delphine, come back. I can't get cigarettes on the island, that's my only pack." He started running, constantly checking through the trees on me. I turned around, my belly button now in the water, holding the packet above my head.

"Come and get them then," I teased, walking backwards slowly.

"You wouldn't."

"Try me."

"You haven't got the balls."

I opened my mouth, acting surprised at how chicken he thought I was.

"Oh really?" I smiled, dropping the cigarettes in front of me. He jerked and reached out, but I caught them inches above the water with the other hand.

"Last chance Mr."

He tugged off his shirt, throwing it down beside him on the small stretch of sand and stepped out of his flip flops. He walked towards me, smiling, and I held the packet behind my back. He tugged my waist into him and wrapped his arms around my back, holding his hand over mine which were clawed over the packet. His lips somehow were on mine and we shared a kiss.

"The only thing I need to quit is you," he whispered into my ear.

"But the only thing is, quitting is harder than it seems, and addiction is a powerful thing." His left hand reached up to my face and stroked my cheek.

"How can so much beauty be in one girl, and how did I ever get lucky enough to meet her?" I released my hand, allowing his right hand to hold the packet. He stepped back and lobbed them far into the sea.

"They never really helped my craving for you." I giggled and pulled him close and he rested his chin on my head.

We spent the day curled up on that prickly floor talking for hours. He picked a pink flower from beside him and poked it in my hair. We went for a walk hand in hand, laughing and joking. We reached another beach that was empty. And we went in for a swim with the sun resting behind the trees, slowly sinking behind the caved walls surrounding the beach. The last of the sun dipped away and the sky's deep orange faded into a deep red, then black. I had my legs wrapped round his waist and his hands supported my body. Smiling in a kiss is a beautiful thing. I was the happiest girl on earth. Until tomorrow.

He watched my eyes sadden. I stood up, my feet sinking into the sand and the water surrounding my ribs. I looked up at him, thinking soon this would just be a memory and he wouldn't be a metre away but a million miles. I blinked slowly and allowed him to rest his chin on my head.

"I don't want to hurt anymore," I mumbled. His jaw clenched and he looked as distressed as me.

"I'm so sorry," he whispered.

It was already late, and I had to get ready to go to a party which was only down the road from our apartment. It was a surprise party, so everyone gathered around the restaurant with balloons and shouted surprise as the birthday girl came in. We sat down to eat but it was a buffet and I wasn't too hungry or in the mood for eating. As we sat, there was some tension between my family and honestly, I felt like I was wasting time. I was on an island with Nikos, yet I was here at a party without him. I texted him under the table.

Delphine<3 meet me?
Nikos Kyprios<3*gun* where?
Delphine<3 anywhere
Nikos Kyprios<3*gun* walk towards my aunt's and I'll walk towards you.
Delphine<3 K.

I went to the toilet and then went back to the table.

"May I be excused?" I asked, looking directly at Mum as I knew she wanted me to see him.

"You may, but please have a serious chat with him about..." She started ranting on and I rolled my eyes and huffed out. She gave me a look; you know those mum looks that say, 'Come on now, it's for your benefit, only because I love you bla bla bla.'

That kind of look. She continued as her eyes beckoned me to stay and listen.

"Just ask him if he really cares and if so, he needs to tell his mum, so that you can plan to meet sometime in the year and..." She was stopped by Grace.

"Right, can I just come and have a word with him because you need..." I exploded with anger as everyone was always trying to butt in and know my business.. There was a continuous questioning and telling me what to do and how to do it.

"No, you know what, you don't understand what I need. None of you do. So, I'm going to do what I need to do without all your opinions, on my own. Okay?" I flew out of the restaurant before an argument started. I heard Dad mumbling as I walked away.

"You need to let her do her thing, stop bugging her." Mum fired something back and Grace backed her up, but I couldn't make out the words, only the tone of their voices.

But I didn't care. I didn't want to care about anything but Nikos right now. I walked down the seafront and tried to stomp out the anger up the hill. About ten minutes later, I saw him walking towards me. I tried to look normal but as soon as we got close, he clocked.

"What's up?" he asked. I searched for a reply, not wanting to have a negative night.

"The sky," I whispered, with a slight smile. He half smiled back and walked down some steps to a beach. After dragging two sunbeds together, he sat on one and I on the other, and he put out an arm, gesturing at me to come closer. I shimmied over and snuggled into his arms. He stroked my arm with his fingers and played with my hair. I could have fallen asleep on his chest with the Poros Town lights reflecting on the sea in front of us, the stars floating in the sky and the sound of his heart beating. I could have stayed like that forever.

He stroked my cheek and tilted my chin up to look at him.

"So, what's really wrong?" I noticed the change in wording of the same question. I took a breath and moved my eyes back to the sea.

"I just don't like being the centre of attention so much, I want to be able to do things without having to think about what others think or the feeling that I'm being watched." He nodded slightly.

"Your family?" This was a rhetorical question as he knew straight away.

"I just want them to stop looking at me like I'm hurting." He stared at me and stopped playing with my hair.

"I'm bad for you," he said with slight anger or disappointment.

"I know." Well I wasn't going to lie.

"And you're bad for me," he added. I looked confused and looked back at him, screwing my eyebrows up and moving away from him a little.

"How am I bad for you?" I asked.

"I started smoking because of you." I didn't know whether to be angry or guilty.

"Because of me? What did I do to you? If anyone should have started smoking because of us it should be me, I'm the one who got hurt, not you," I shot back at him, pushing myself further away.

"You fuck me up." His hand clenched into a fist on his knee. Ok; I'm feeling angry, not guilty!

"No, no, you don't get to say that. You had the power in this whole situation, you could have changed it, but you didn't. No, you ignored me for a year, a whole fucking year Nikos." My voice cracked. "I was the weak one, you control me." I sat up hugging my legs at the end of the bed, wishing I could choose not to like him.

He sat there for a while breathing deeply, pushing his head against the sunbed. I could feel his eyes on me. I ran my hands through my hair, gripping my head, trying to squeeze out feelings for him. I thought about what June said. I whispered to myself a little too loud.

"He doesn't care about you." I closed my eyes, screwing

them up and held my hands up to my face. His eyes shot through me. He gripped my wrist and pulled me back, one hand still tight around my wrist, the other clasping the side of my face.

"Don't you dare think I don't care, I care more than you know." His finger traced my lips. This should have really been the only thing I wanted to hear, but I still didn't believe him. He saw the doubt in my eyes and wrapped his hand around my throat as a joke.

"Sometimes I want to strangle you." I looked straight at him.

"Go ahead."

He moved his hand around to the back of my head, tugging slightly on my hair, the other pulling my waist closer. He kissed my neck and gently moved his hand down my back. I hated myself for letting him back in - for proving Mum right that I'd fall right back into him. I sighed.

"I hate you," I said, half trying to push him away and half trying to get closer.

"I know," he mumbled into my neck. I scratched my nails along his back, trying to inflict all the emotional pain he caused me, physically onto him. He pushed his lips against mine stealing too many kisses, his hands travelling around my body and mine on his. I lay back down on his chest, telling myself to calm down a little and get in control. He tried to kiss me, but I bit my lips in, nuzzling my head back into him. He moaned, trying again.

I squeaked a, "Mm mmh," pushing him away and still sucking in my lips. He gave up. Still stroking my arm, he smiled down at me softly.

Hours passed lying there, talking and watching the stars and sea. He had to go at one-thirty to try get back before his aunt arrived home. It was one-twenty-five., He frowned at his phone clock.

"I have to go in five, so come here you, I'm not wasting one second," he said. I refused to kiss him for about two minutes, just to irritate him, pushing his head away. He got all grumpy again and let his head turn away, waiting for me to show interest. I pulled his face back and kissed his cheek.

"You have to go." He turned back, biting his lip with a big grin on his face.

"No," he said. I giggled, trying to sit up.

"You have to." I swung my legs around, sitting at the edge of the bed but he pulled me back, laying my head onto his lap and pushing my shoulders down to stop me from getting up. He kissed me and I spoke through his kisses.

"Come on, your aunty." He spoke a few words after each kiss.

"No... I don't want... to let you go." I wriggled about, realising I wasn't strong enough to get up without his permission.

"Well you're going to have to, you will see me tomorrow morning before I go." He stopped kissing me.

"Don't go."

I bit my lip, gazing up at him. Tingles were sent all through my body. I wanted more than anything to be able to see him every day, to have his hands on my skin, his voice in my ear, his arms around me and his everything. I couldn't believe I was leaving again when I had only just got him back. Thinking about another year without him snapped something inside me. I was so wrapped up in my thoughts that I only just pushed through them to hear him whisper.

"I love you." I jerked up.

"Wow, what?" The powerfulness of that word was way too much to hear from him, even though I knew full well I loved him but him 'loving' me seemed impossible. I didn't believe him - not really.

"Okay, okay, too far," he said, as he watched my face. Eventually he let go and unwillingly allowed me to get up. He kissed me one last time and I began to walk away.

"I'm sorry," he called. I turned around.

"For what?" I asked.

"Everything," he said. I nodded slightly, knowing a sorry wouldn't be anywhere near enough to patch up my heart. Then I carried on walking away.

I wanted to turn around, run back up to him, hug him and

never let him go. Was that it? Was that all I got after waiting so long - through all the heartache - was that it?

In the morning, I went straight down in case he was already there, not that he would be at 8:30am but at least I was there waiting. I was leaving at 2:30 and the four hours and a half I spent waiting felt like an eternity. He eventually tuned up at one - the time I was meant to go pack, eat lunch and shower. But of course, I left all that to the very last minute, so I could spend every possible second with him.

We didn't even have to be talking - sitting next to him made me the most content I had ever felt. We sat with our feet resting on some stacked-up sunbeds, our backs to Passage, facing the sea. His hand rested gently on mine and we spoke softly every so often. We went for a swim, but nothing was the same knowing I had to go. As I went up to get ready, he picked a small pink flower and placed it in my hair, brushing the side of my cheek again.

At the very last minute, I went up and rushed myself ready. I yanked my suitcase down to the water taxi and stopped at the end of the peer. He was in the water at the back of the boat, ready to ski. Wow. I laughed to myself a little, thinking how typical of him to avoid a goodbye. He raised his glove out the water and waved me a goodbye. I nodded slowly, clenching my jaw, feeling hurt already.

The taxi boat driver came up to me.

"Excuse me, we are ready to go, yes?" I turned around in a daze, trying to compute this may be the last time I saw him.

"Yes, sorry, ready," I whispered, forcing a smile. As we were going alongside the ski path, the boat driver turned around to me, then to the ski boat and smiled. I was staring lifelessly at a zip on Mum's suitcase, not noticing that we were taking a slight diversion to the normal path, towards the ski lane. I heard Bob's boat and whistle which drew my attention to the window behind me. We were about five metres away from where Bob's boat stopped, and Nikos was dropped. I jumped up to the boat's entrance and leant out.

We stared at each other, and everyone in the boat stared at

us. The boat got closer and closer to him until he could grip on to the side. I leant over the side and he kissed my hand, his wet glove on the side of my face. A tear rolled down my cheek as I stared into his eyes trying to understand his thoughts. Everyone on the boat was smiling, and Grace rolled her eyes. No words were said. I turned away, nodded slightly to the driver and he drove on.

I watched the island blur through a million unshed tears, and in my mind, my footprints faded from the sand and the curtains closed, casting shadows on the bed. Flowers dropped and cakes were left. I already missed the small, elegant white houses, the pink waterfalls of flowers winding around balconies and the golden morning sun illuminating the white sheets that held me. Damn. I already missed the man from the bakery offering me freshly baked cakes, the elegant women wandering by in detailed summer dresses and sunsets splashed with shades of orange and red. I missed him. But, there and then, I made a promise to myself that I wasn't going to let it control or change me, no matter how many waves of heartbreak would come and go over the next few days, weeks or months. He would do his thing and I would do mine. I knew it wasn't going to be easy, but if there was one thing that this island had taught me, beautiful things don't come easy. And the most beautiful thing I could do now was find myself.

THIRTEEN

I was sitting in a coffee shop on a Saturday afternoon on January 2, 2017, accompanied by Carl. Hours before, I had decided I would walk and keep walking. I walked out of my street and tried to walk as straight as I could. In the mindset of a child, I would soon reach the edge of the world and find the drop off. Even though I knew this to be physically impossible, I went along with the idea of being able to see the end of something beautiful and dangerously destructive all at the same time.

I must have walked for hours before I stopped and noticed what a stupid idea this was. I ended up ringing Brad because what are big brothers for? The only problem - he was on holiday, but he told me to wait where I was. After what seemed like hours, Carl turned up. After Brad told him, he had tracked my phone all the way to the seaside at Canvey Island where I had ended up.

The coffee shop was elegant and petite, hidden away from reality. In the corner was a soft pink sofa, a small coffee table and a comfy brown chair. I sat with my legs curled up, playing with the frothed milk floating on top of the coffee. Pushing the chocolate sprinkles around with my little finger, I made patterns and then licked my finger, rubbing it on my jeans. It was dark outside by the time I'd finished my coffee. Carl and I were the only customers left.

Through the window to my right, I could see outside. I stared at the once red rose bush slowly turning black in the shadows of nightfall. Carl was sitting opposite in the brown chair watching me. He sighed, breaking the silence.

"Delphine, no matter how stubborn you act or how much you convince yourself you're okay, I see underneath. I know that the real you is inside and you're hiding her because you think she's vulnerable and weak. Look, I get that you've been hurt, so wrongly because, out of all people in the world you are most definitely not the one who deserved this. But please don't let it ruin you." I still stared out the window and clenched my jaw, and Carl watched waiting for me to start defending myself and arguing. But, for the first time, I listened. Me being me, I would normally have lashed out by now and I guess Carl was half expecting me to. Tension in his body made him grip the side of his chair. But I listened and this time I heard. I cleared my throat.

"I didn't think she existed anymore, I lost me in this whirl-wind of whatever this is. But I want to find her, and I know how. I, I have to let him go." A tear rolled down my cheek. Carl leant forward and held my phone up to me, indicating for me to tap in the passcode. I did so and flipped through my apps, finding Snap-chat. He flipped the phone to face me, holding it on his lap. On the screen facing me was a video call to Nikos Kyprios. I stared at it in panic, then up at Carl. He looked as nervous as me wait-ing for an answer. *Now? We're doing this now? Okay.*

The phone rang for the fourth time. I knew it would cut off on the fifth ring. I breathed out in relief knowing he wouldn't pick up.

"Hello?" a deep accent spoke from the phone. A boy stared back at me from inside the screen. I swallowed, his presence shocking my system and making me want to shrivel like the cold rosebush outside. "Delphine?" The thorns from the bush grew at extreme speeds in time with my count to ten, shat-tering the window and stopping before the ten pierced right through my chest. I struggled for another couple of seconds to form a sentence.

"I…" Honestly had no idea where to start. Carl watched me

squinting, seeing my brain fighting to string some words together. He nodded, reassuring me.

"I miss you," I said. Carl stared in shock, his fingers tightening around the phone, almost accepting the fact that I would
never get over it and this wasn't going to work. Nikos went to
say something. "The old you," I finished. Nikos tilted his head
inside the screen, confused. "The Nikos Kyprios I used to know,
the one who made me laugh and smile and look forward to that
one time a year that I would see him. The one that I fell in love
with. The thing is that, for two years, I've been holding on to
that memory - hope and love of that guy I thought I knew. But
now I get it. He doesn't exist. He's what I wanted to remember
and what I wanted to be real. But really this Nikos I'm looking at
now, isn't that guy at all. I don't know if you meant to hurt me,
or if you didn't realise or whatever, but you did and that sucked
real bad for me."

He tilted the phone back at the word 'you', his hand hesitat-
ing towards the screen, ready to hang up.

"Nikos, touch that button and this will never be solved. I
need to tell you this and you need to hear it so do me a favour,
don't be a coward and for once just listen." His hand lowered.
"Maybe now that I've given up on us, just maybe you will realise
what you've lost. I'm not saying I'm perfect, not at all. I'm saying you've lost someone who adored everything about you, all
your imperfections and self-doubts I learnt to love. Every time
you knocked me down, I covered up the scars from everyone
else to protect you. And what an absolute idiot I was." I laughed
inside, noticing the pain flow out of me. I looked at the thorns
outside, bleak and sharp and now in the dark. But their roses
would bloom again, and so would I.

"I'm not going to be controlled by you anymore. I'm not
going to wait for you, make excuses for you, and I most definitely am not going to love you anymore. Yeah it won't be easy
but it's sure as hell going to be the best decision I've made for a
while." His whole body looked deflated and his eyes angry but
wet. "I don't wish bad on you, in fact, by some miracle, I wish

good things for you. I hope you find a girl who will love just as much as I did, because I know she will never leave or hurt you. But, if you're not able to love her back just as much as she cares for you then stay the hell away from her. Because, I know for a fact that her flower might not survive the storm and even though my rose was almost certainly dead, I think now, I can grow again." Carl hung up on him.

My body collapsed into his arms as he ran over and sat beside me. He cradled me. It was like he had reached into the devil's dark, dangerous hell and pulled me out right before it was too late.

"Well you are sure the hardest person I have ever attempted to get through to, but Delphine, I'm so proud of you." I hugged him, muffling a thank you into his hoodie.

FOURTEEN

I never thought that it would come to a point where I physically and mentally couldn't think about him. Although it has only been a matter of months in the real world, in heartbreak world, that's a matter of years. I have poured so much emotion out on this one person that I have nothing left.

When your heart is broken, it feels like the internal aching and pain will never ever go away, and thinking about it slices through my chest, snaps my ribs and breaks my poorly stitched heart all over again. And you reach a point where there's nothing, like Carl said, you don't feel. You can't even cry because there's nothing left in you.

By no means am I an expert in love, and many choices I made in dealing with this are the absolute opposite of what should have been done. But maybe from my mistakes and my heartbreak, others will know that they are not alone in theirs.

I was so wrapped up in this hurricane of anger and pain that I flipped at everything and everyone. Being alone is the worst feeling. Pushing people away is definitely not the answer because you need them more than you know. Holding it in is so hard - you end up bursting in the end anyway.

Me being me didn't want to go near anyone who wanted to help me. I didn't want my parents to pay for counselling, where I sat and told someone about my hurt and everything wrong in my life. I didn't want to be a burden to family. I didn't want to be that person. That, I guess, was what scared me the most. Getting help meant I accepted there was something wrong with me. No, I had to try and solve it myself. So, don't follow in my footsteps. After accepting I needed help, June was surprisingly good, and I didn't always have to sit and talk like I feared. I expressed my emotions in my own way.

The thing with being a teenager in today's world is that we are pressured into making important life choices at such a young age. Many of us end up making the wrong choice. I don't want to have this set plan of uni and then work. It seems restricting. I don't want to go into the world of work with a massive debt. All my family seem to have such high expectations of what I am meant to become. But here's the thing - you're not meant to become anything. You're not born programmed to do one thing. You decide what you do with your life and don't let anyone pressure you to go down a different path from the one you want to follow.

My advice - seek adventure and happiness, live with no regrets, don't stress and be you. And if you don't know who 'you' is, find it.

Here's what I'm going to do. I'm going to go with the flow. I'm going to cut off all the bad things in my life like the bad people I hung around with. I will keep the people I love and care about and who are amazing enough not to have given up on me. I don't plan to do my second year of college. I spoke with Albert and he knows I'm not enjoying my course, so he told me to leave with the qualification I have and to go and do something I want to do.

So, I have a job in France as a chalet host, like Grace did. I am going to travel the world and work my way around it, finding myself and what I really want. Who knows? This gap year might last a lifetime.

I'm not ready for someone new. Once you've experienced something like I have, you will want to avoid being hurt again. But don't shut off the idea of love, because that's not what's risky. It's the person you fall in love with, and the right one is out there somewhere.

To stop loving him sure isn't going to be that simple, but it's possible.

If you only ever focus on the darkness, that's all you'll ever know. But if you let in the light, your flower will grow.

I've been losing myself for a while now and I don't really know who I am anymore, so I'm going to find me.

My once a year was once my love.

My once a year was once my hate.

My once a year got me here, and now I need to find myself.

It doesn't last forever.

After two years, his name doesn't make me feel weak. His face doesn't make me feel empty. My memory of us doesn't make me cry. My thoughts of him are not felt with pain. They have been replaced with strength, and my heart isn't broken.

It doesn't last forever.

Printed in Poland
by Amazon Fulfillment
Poland Sp. z o.o., Wrocław